DEDICATION

To my parents, who are my heroes.

Caped

The Omega Superhero

Book One

DARIUS BRASHER

ISBN: 1539418510
ISBN-13: 978-1539418511

ACKNOWLEDGMENTS

Scripture quotations are taken from *The Holy Bible*, New Living Translation, copyright ©1996, 2004, 2007, 2013, 2015 by Tyndale House Foundation. Used by permission of Tyndale House Publishers, Inc., Carol Stream, Illinois 60188. All rights reserved.

CHAPTER ONE

I never wanted to be a superhero.

I admired them, sure. I followed their adventures, absolutely. But be one? No thanks. Superheroes got punched, tortured, shot at, cut up, plotted against, and had buildings and other insanely heavy things dropped on them. And that was if you were lucky. If you were unlucky, you were killed like Avatar was. If it could happen to Avatar, the world's greatest and most powerful Metahuman and licensed Hero, it could happen to anyone. I had no interest in being one of those anyones. If it was up to me, I would have stayed a nobody and a no one. Being a nobody was no fun and God knew it would not get you laid, but at least it gave you the chance to die at home in bed instead of at the hands of some bloodthirsty supervillain. Being a licensed Hero was super dangerous, not to mention super scary.

Uh, no pun intended, I guess.

So no, I never wanted to be a superhero. But, like Dad always said, you had to play the cards you were dealt. I found out what kind of cards fate had in store for me the day I got into a fight in the men's bathroom at my college.

If I had known about all the crazy and deadly stuff that

encounter would lead to, I never would have gone to the bathroom that day. I would have just held it. Or, peed my pants. Gross and unsanitary, maybe.

Safer though.

***

I washed my hands after using the urinal. I was in the bathroom of the Student Activities Center at my school, the University of South Carolina at Aiken. My hands still were hot, as if they were being held too close to a fire. I held them under the faucet's stream of cold water for a while. The water felt great, but did not solve the problem. My hands still felt hot.

I was starting to get worried. Maybe I needed to go to the doctor, or at least to USCA's health clinic. Though I had been inside of air-conditioned classrooms most of today, I had spent a lot of time earlier this week working outside on my dad's farm. Maybe what I was experiencing was heat stroke. It was very hot outside. It was August in South Carolina, after all. It was supposed to be hot out. I had never heard of heat stroke affecting just one part of your body, though. Nor had I ever heard of it setting in long after someone had gotten out of the heat.

My hands had felt weird the past several days. The feeling had started as a tingle, as if my hands had fallen asleep and circulation was being restored to them. A couple of days later the tingling had become pins and needles. The pins and needles had then transformed into a dull ache, like the ache of underused muscles that had been worked out hard at the gym. Now my hands were hot, like they were in an oven set on low. They were not in pain, but if whatever was going on with them got worse, I could see them getting painful. They had been distracting me in class all day, like an annoying itch you could not quite reach to scratch.

I pulled my hands from under the stream of cold water.

I examined them carefully. Other than them being wet, they looked perfectly normal, like they always did. I held them up to my cheeks, like I was checking for a fever. They did not feel hot against my cheeks. Maybe the heat was entirely in my head. Maybe what I needed was a shrink, not a doctor.

I grimaced in distaste at the idea of going to a shrink again. I had been to one when my mother had died from brain cancer five years ago. My school counselor had recommended to Dad that I go, so go I did despite the fact I didn't want to. Even at the age of twelve, going to that shrink to talk about my feelings had seemed like a huge waste of time. My mother was dead, and no amount of talking was going to change that fact. When that knuckleheaded shrink had suggested I was secretly glad Mom was dead because I was tired of dealing with her lingering illness, I had gotten up and taken a swing at that know-nothing dummy. Dad had been mad at me until I had told him what the shrink had suggested. Dad never made me go back. I had thought at the time he kind of wanted to take a swing at the shrink too.

I grimaced yet again when I looked up to see myself in the mirror. I did not think I was ugly, so that was not the reason for the grimace. Brown hair, brown eyes, average height, average-looking face. If you did a Google search for "average white guy," I would not be the top result—I was too much of a nobody to turn up in an Internet search—but I felt like the poster boy for "nothing special." I had grimaced at myself because I was struck again by how skinny I was. Though it seemed like my stomach was a bottomless pit, I never could gain weight.

Whenever I said that to a girl, she always said she wished she was like me. Not being able to put on weight might be awesome if you were a girl, but it sucked when you were a seventeen-year-old college freshman who was trying to attract girls. Girls went for big dudes who were athletic, dressed well, drove nice cars, and were into sports,

3

not a skinny farmer's son who read all the time, wore clothes from Walmart, drove a hand-me-down powder blue Chevy Cavalier the inside of which leaked like a colander when it rained hard, and who knew more about actual falcons than he did about the Atlanta Falcons. It was probably why I was a virgin. I desperately did not want to be. I had never heard of someone dying from lack of sex, but it often felt like I would be the first to pull it off. What a way to make it into the history books. If my name were Mary instead of Theodore Conley, at least then I could put "The Virgin Mary" on my tombstone. On second thought, I would be a boy named Mary. I doubted that would help my virginity problem.

My hot hands forgotten for the moment, I rolled up the right sleeve of my Avatar tee shirt a bit and flexed. My bicep barely moved. Ugh. I really needed to go to the gym more. The problem was, every time I went, I felt like a weak baby in comparison to the meatheads who seemed to live there. It was demoralizing. I was only seventeen, though. I prayed I was not finished growing yet. Thanks to my bookworm tendencies, I had graduated high school early and was a year or two younger than most of my classmates here at USCA. I had always been scrawny compared to other guys my age, and being around older guys here at college made the size difference worse. Maybe I would have another growth spurt and catch up to my larger classmates. And, maybe pigs would sprout wings and start calling themselves pigeons. I was not optimistic about either prospect occurring.

The bathroom door swung open. Startled, I jumped a little. I pretended like I was scratching my arm instead of feeling myself up. Too many of my fellow students thought I was a weirdo as it was.

John Shockey slowly entered. His left foot dragged a little on the floor as he came in. He was blonde, and shorter than I with a slightly hunched back and severely bowed legs. His right hand was twisted around at a weird

4

angle, and the fingers on that hand pointed out in several different directions. He had a big overbite, so much so his mouth was never completely closed. His upper front teeth, yellow and angled like collapsing tombstones, were exposed a little. He always looked like he was grimacing, even when he was not.

"Hey Theo," John said to me. His voice was slow and nasal. It sounded like he was mentally challenged. I knew he was not. I had a couple of classes with him and had been in study groups with him. Whatever was wrong with him physically did not affect him mentally. Because of his appearance, most people treated John like he had leprosy or something. Not me. I knew what it was like to be different than the people around you. I made it a point to be nice to him. John and I weren't exactly friends, but we were friendly. I figured that those of us who lived on the Island of Misfit Toys had to stick together.

"Hey John." I glanced down at his shirt. It was identical to mine, grey with a big stylized red A on the front—the colors of Avatar's costume and the A that he had on his chest. I grinned. "Nice shirt," I said.

John's mouth widened into what was supposed to be a smile. It looked more like he was in pain. "Thanks. You too," he said in his slow, slightly slurred voice. "Shame what happened to him. I still can't believe it."

I nodded my head in agreement. "I know, right? The world's greatest Hero, shot and killed. I never thought the day would come Avatar would be killed, and certainly not killed by a bullet. I always heard he was invulnerable." Avatar had been murdered a couple of months ago. The world still mourned for him. I had seen more Avatar shirts in the past two months than I had seen before in my whole life. I thought of most of those shirt-wearers as Johnny-come-latelies. I had been a fan of Heroes like Avatar and Amazing Man and of licensed superheroes in general for as long as I could remember. They were everything I was not—beloved, strong, confident, and fearless.

"I met him once," John said. "He shook my hand. Greatest moment of my life." He shook his head at the thought, though it looked like more of a muscle spasm than anything else. John shuffled slowly off. He went to stand in front of one of the urinals.

My hands were still hot. I turned on the cold water again and put my hands under the stream. Though running water over my hands had not made the burning feeling go away, it did make me feel a little better.

The bathroom door opened again. Three guys walked in, laughing and talking loudly. I glanced at them. I immediately looked away. I willed myself to be invisible. I wondered if this was how a deer who had spotted three approaching lions felt. Guys like me were the natural prey of the guys who had come in. They were Donovan Byrd, Marcus Leverette, and a guy I only knew as Bubba. They were upperclassmen, star football players, very popular, strong as bulls, and not shy about reminding you of all of the above. They hung out together all the time; you rarely saw one without the other two. They called themselves the Three Horsemen. The Three Jackasses was more like it. I knew better than to say that aloud. I did not have a death wish. If you were a pretty girl, the Three Horsemen tried to sleep with you; if you were an ugly girl they made fun of you; and if you were a guy who was not an athlete like them, they pushed you around. They were bullies. I did not like them. The fact I did not like them did not mean I was dismissive of them. I respected them the way a mouse must respect a snake.

The Three Horsemen ignored me like a king ignores a peasant. They strode past me and the sinks to the urinals behind me. I sighed slightly in relief. Though my hands still hurt, I pulled them out of the water and shut the faucet off. This was no longer a good place to linger. The Three Horsemen might suddenly decide my mere presence somehow offended them. I got the sudden mental image of them pounding me into the floor of the bathroom like I was a nail. I suppressed a shudder at the thought. I hastily pulled out paper towels from the dispenser and started to dry my hands.

From the mirror in front of me, I could see that Marcus and Bubba went to stand in front of two empty urinals. Donovan stood in front of John's back. Donovan was a tall, good-looking, light-skinned black guy with a shaved head. He was the football team's star running back. He did not walk so much as he flowed, like a big cat. Bubba and Marcus were defensive linemen. Bubba was white, Marcus was black. Bubba had a head like a doorknob, a brain that was probably the size of a walnut, and a body like a side of beef. Marcus was equally imposing, though his head was more proportionate to the rest of his body than Bubba's was. They were a bit shorter than Donovan, but much bulkier.

"Move out of the way, gimp," Donovan said to John. "I gotta take a piss." There was a fourth empty urinal he could have used, not to mention three empty stalls. Donovan was being an ass again. Big shock.

John looked over his shoulder at Donovan. "I-I-I'm not finished," he said, stuttering a bit. He was obviously intimidated by Donovan and his friends. I was too. "That one is open," John said, nodding his head to the available urinal next to him. John was being bolder than I would have been.

"I don't wanna use that one, retard," Donovan said. "The one you're at is my favorite." He unzipped his pants. "Now move out of the way before I piss all over you." Bubba and Marcus laughed.

I hated bullies. I myself had been bullied more times than I wanted to remember, so I knew how it felt. And, John was not even able-bodied, making picking on him even more despicable. I wanted to say something. *You keep your big mouth shut,* my mind said firmly. *Who do you think you are, Avatar? The fact you're wearing a Hero's tee shirt doesn't make you one. Mind your own business, pick up your bookbag, and leave.*

"Why don't you leave him alone, Donovan?" my mouth said before my brain could stop it. "Why do you always have to be such an ass?"

My brain and my mouth needed to have a serious talk later about getting on the same page. Assuming there was a later.

As I watched through the mirror, Donovan turned to me. He looked stunned. "What did you just say to me?" he demanded.

I turned to face him. I had already put my big fat foot in my mouth. Might as well try to swallow the whole leg.

"I said leave him alone. He's not bothering you." I said it more firmly than I felt. Inside, I was quaking. At least I had the good sense to not call Donovan an ass again. What in the world had come over me? Maybe my hands were hot because I had a fever and was delirious.

Donovan strode over to me. He loomed over me like a mountain. He was trying to intimidate me. He was succeeding. "Why don't you mind your own business?" he said. "Or maybe the retard is your business. Maybe he's your boyfriend. I see you are wearing the same stupid shirt he is. You two are the retard twins. Is your retard twin also your boyfriend, faggot?"

"No," I said. Words flashed through my mind. I knew it was stupid to voice them. But, in for a penny, in for a pound. "Just because you walk around with your boyfriends all the time, that doesn't mean everyone else does. How does your threesome work, anyway? Are you always the bottom, or do you guys alternate? Maybe you draw straws. Does the short straw get the," I paused, moving my index finger back and forth suggestively, "long straw?" It felt good to talk back to a bully for once.

That good feeling only lasted an instant. Donovan grabbed me by the front of my shirt. With a single arm, he pulled me up, almost off my feet. My tiptoes dangled on the linoleum. Donovan leaned down and put his face right into mine.

"I don't know who the fuck you think you're talking to," he snarled. His breath was hot against my face. "I'm going to punch your loser faggot ass into next month." His free arm reared back. I pulled at his arm holding me up. It was like trying to uproot a tree. I turned my head away in fear. I was about to get my stupid head knocked off my stupid body. I did not want to watch the blow land. Feeling it land would be bad enough.

Suddenly Bubba and Marcus were standing on either side of me.

"Don't hit him," Bubba said, grabbing Donovan's arm. I could have kissed him. "The coach said the next time you got into a fight, he'd have to bench you. We've got some big games coming up. We need you on the field."

From behind the Three Horsemen, I saw John creeping up. Though I did not know how much help he would be, it was good to see I was not in this pickle alone.

John continued right past where the Three Horsemen were clustered around me. Moving as quickly as his legs would let him, he opened the door. John fled the bathroom without so much as a backwards glance at me.

Huh. I guess what they said was true—no good deed went unpunished. So much for the idea of all for one and one for all. Maybe that was only true in books.

Nobody other than me seemed to notice John was gone. The Three Horsemen were too focused on me. Lucky me.

"You're right Bubba," Donovan said after a long hesitation during which I anxiously visualized my head being knocked off my body like a golf ball driven off a tee. Donovan lowered his clenched fist reluctantly. He still held me up by my shirt. "I'm not going to risk getting benched over this loser. Can't let him get away with talking to me like that, though. Tell you what, faggot," he said to me, "since you're so concerned about where I pee at, how about I pee on you?"

"No thanks. I've been peed on twice today already. I've had my fill." I was trying to joke my way out of this. No one laughed.

"Hold him down," Donovan said to Bubba and Marcus.

Oh my God, he was serious! I started to kick and struggle. It was already too late. Bubba had me by my legs; Marcus had me by my arms. Donovan let go of my shirt. Grinning like kids on Christmas Day, Bubba and Marcus separated until I stretched out lengthwise between the two of them.

Looking up at the tiled bathroom ceiling, I twisted and bucked, trying to free myself. If the viselike grips of the two loosened even slightly, it was not enough to notice. They put me down on the cold floor. Already much taller than I, Donovan now stood over me like a giant. I continued to struggle, succeeding only in banging the back of my head against the hard floor. I saw stars.

"Get me go!" I shouted.

Donovan reached into the fly of his pants. "As soon as my bladder is empty, we'll let you go," he said. He laughed a short sadistic bark that made me want to punch his lights out. He aimed. A stream of wetness hit my face. I turned my face away from it.

"Let me go, let me go, let me go!" I screamed over and over. I tasted urine in my mouth. Some of it got into my eyes. I tried to blink it away. I snorted as some of the urine went up my nose. I bucked violently, still trying to free myself. Marcus and Bubba held me down as easily as holding down a child. I felt a combination of anger, impotence, and humiliation. Especially humiliation. I started to cry tears of frustration. Crying made me feel even worse about myself. I was nothing but a big baby who could not even defend himself. And, like a wet baby, I stank of urine. What if Mom was looking down at me and saw me like this? I was filled with shame at the thought.

The sounds of the Three Horsemen's laughter and the

splashing of liquid against my face and neck filled my ears. I bucked even harder in Bubba's and Marcus' grasp. My heart pounded, harder and harder, until it seemed it would explode right out of my chest. My hands now felt even hotter than before, as if they had been thrust into the hot coals of a fireplace.

I had the sudden mental image of being strong enough to pull Bubba and Marcus off of me and flinging them against the wall. Donovan I would shove backwards into the stall behind us, stuffing him into the toilet. I saw it clearly in my mind's eye like I was looking at a vivid photograph.

"GET OFF OF ME!" I shouted yet again. The words felt like they came from the depths of my soul. The burning sensation of my hands, already intense, moved up to a whole new level of pain, as if they had been left in the hot coals long enough to catch fire themselves.

Suddenly, all hell broke loose. Both Bubba's and Marcus' hands were pulled off of me. They both launched into the air, as if they had been picked up by an invisible giant and thrown. They cried out in surprise and confusion. They sailed through the air. They slammed into opposite walls of the bathroom with a loud crash. Bubba bounced off the wall a bit, landing face-first on the tile floor. The tile cracked where Bubba's face slammed into it. He did not move. As for Marcus, he slid like a wet towel down the wall he had been thrown into. He slid until he landed hard on his butt, with his legs splayed out in front of him. His head lolled a little from side to side.

Donovan was not immune from whatever was happening. He flew back into the partially closed door of the stall behind him like he was a cannonball shot out of a cannon. The stall door flew all the way open, crashing into the stall wall. The crash sounded like a shotgun blast. Donovan landed butt-first in the open toilet. He went down deep into the bowl, like a dunked basketball. His legs dangled from the toilet, with his feet barely touching the floor.

There was dead silence for a moment, as if the entire world was stunned by what had just happened. The silence was then broken by the sound of the automatic toilet flushing. Water sprayed up, hitting Donovan in the face.

I might have laughed at the sudden turnabout had I not been so astonished.

I sat up. I turned my head repeatedly from side to side like a crazy person, frantically looking to see who had done whatever had just happened. I saw no one. Other than the groans of Marcus and Donovan, I heard no one. The Three Horsemen and I were still alone in the bathroom.

I lifted my hands up. They still felt like they were on fire. They also looked different than they normally did. As I looked at them, twisting them from side to side, waves of energy radiated from them, like waves of heat coming off a hot highway. I tore my eyes off of them and looked down at my wet Avatar tee shirt.

I could scarcely believe it, though it was as obvious as the big A that was on my chest and the stench of urine that filled my nostrils.

I had superpowers. Like Avatar, I was a Metahuman.

Holy crap!

CHAPTER TWO

I held my hands up in front of me as my father, James Conley, drove our truck down the interstate. The faint waves of energy coming from my hands made the road look like it was rippled.

"Are you sure you can't see anything?" I asked Dad while I stared at my hands. Dad quickly glanced at my outstretched hands before returning his attention to the interstate.

"For the thousandth time, no," he said. He looked like me, only much bigger and stronger. "Your hands look the same to me as they always did."

I shook my head in wonder. Apparently, no one but I could see the energy that rippled from my hands like ocean waves. If it had not been for the incident with the Three Horsemen four days before, I would have thought the waves were just my imagination. Frankly, I wished they were. Being a Metahuman was proving to be a huge pain in the butt. At least the pain that had first accompanied the waves coming from my hands had gone away. That was cold comfort in light of everything else that had happened and was happening.

Dad was driving us to Columbia so I could register with the government as a Meta. I had an eleven a.m. appointment at the U.S. Metahuman Registration Center. Under the Hero Act of 1945, anyone who manifested Metahuman abilities was required to register them with the federal government. The closest registration center to where Dad and I lived on our farm in Aiken County was in Columbia. Columbia was South Carolina's capital city and located in the middle of the state. It was a little under an hour from our farm. Dad and I were over halfway there, traveling northeast on Interstate 20.

I would have been thrilled if we just turned around and went home. I had no interest in registering. As far as I was concerned, the government could mind its own business and I would mind mine. Besides, I had zero interest in using my powers in the future. My unintentional use of them on the Three Horsemen had not worked out so well for me. But unfortunately, if I did not want to register, I never should have let Dad know what had happened in the bathroom. As he had said to me so often I could have mouthed the words along with him, "A man—if he is any kind of a man—works hard, plays by the rules, and obeys the law." I had hoped he would make an exception to being so law-abiding this one time. I really should have known better. Once he learned I was a Metahuman, Dad had insisted I call the Columbia Registration Center and make an appointment.

Then again, I really did not have much of a choice about telling Dad what had happened with the Three Horsemen. Even if I had not told him, the college would have. I was still technically a minor, and both Donovan and Bubba had broken bones thanks to their run-in with me. Donovan would probably have to miss this year's football season. He was going around school telling everyone he would sue me. Since I was a minor and had no assets, really who he would be suing would be my Dad.

I felt guilty about that. Dad was a struggling small-scale farmer. He could ill afford a lawsuit.

"I can't believe USCA suspended me for two weeks," I said. I was still both pissed off and indignant. "They acted like I was the one who started the trouble."

"Well, it is your word against that of the other boys. They all say you were the one who started the fight."

"Oh sure, I was the one who went out of his way to start something with three gorillas who look like they popped steroids instead of Flintstone vitamins when they were kids," I said sarcastically. "Maybe because I wanted to commit suicide. Death by football player. I must have figured finding a noose or a gun was too much trouble."

Dad smiled grimly.

"You don't have to convince me, Theo. I believe you. It's not like you to go around picking fights for no reason. Honestly, I'm proud of you for standing up for that John kid."

"And how does John thank me? By telling the school that the Three Horsemen were telling the truth about me having started the fight." I shook my head, still in disbelief about John's lie.

"Try to look at it from his perspective," Dad said. "John's probably afraid of what those three guys would do to him if he did not agree with their version of the story."

I frowned. Dad was way too nice of a guy sometimes. He was a devout Catholic. Unlike a lot of other so-called religious people I had seen, Dad actually practiced what he preached. Dad always tried to see things from the other guy's perspective. "Before you judge a man, walk a mile in his shoes," he often said. That was a quote from the James Conley book of clichés I had heard far too often. I secretly called Dad's clichés Jamesisms. "If someone slaps you on one cheek, offer the other cheek also." Another Jamesism, that one cribbed from the Bible's New Testament. Thanks to me going to church so much with Dad, I knew the Old Testament said "You must show no pity for the guilty.

Your rule should be life for life, eye for eye, tooth for tooth, hand for hand, foot for foot." The lies John and the Three Horsemen had told about me made me want to forget about turning the other cheek and instead be an exclusively Old Testament Christian.

I folded my arms across my chest in frustration and annoyance. I should have been in class right now, not on my way to share all my personal business with the government.

"It's not fair," I said stubbornly.

"Life rarely is. You might as well get used to it," Dad said. I just knew he would say that. I had heard that line from him before too. The fact I suspected he was right did not mean I had to like it.

We completed the rest of the ride to Columbia in silence. Soon the tall buildings of downtown Columbia came into sight. I had been here several times before, mainly to go to the big farmer's market here with Dad to sell stuff we had raised on the farm. Columbia was not a big city in the grand scheme of things. It had less than a quarter of a million people. A place like New York City, by contrast, had over eight million people. I only knew that from reading, not because I had been there. I had not been much of anywhere. I was born about ten minutes from where Dad and I now lived, and I had lived my whole life in Aiken County. I had told Dad I wanted to go to college in Aiken because I did not want to leave him in the lurch and force him to run the farm by himself. Deep down in my heart, I knew that was not entirely true. The truth of the matter was I was afraid to leave Aiken. Places bigger than Aiken confused and scared me. Even a small city like Columbia felt overwhelming. I was glad Dad was driving instead of me.

The Columbia Metahuman Registration Center was near the center of the city, in a glass building that was taller by far than any building we had in Aiken. Dad parked the truck in the building's underground parking garage. We got into the elevator, pushing the button for the ninth floor.

While we rode up, I looked at the two of us in the polished brass interior of the elevator car. I was struck anew by how much Dad looked like me. Well, I looked like him, I guess. He had gotten to the planet before me, after all. The problem was he was about three inches taller and far heavier than I. Heavier as in more muscular, not fatter. Dad's parents had been farmers too, so Dad had been doing heavy manual labor all his life. He had the well-developed muscles to show for it. What in the world had happened to me? Had I not been fed enough as a child? I looked like a deflated tire next to Dad, like I was him with the air let out. If I was going to have another growth spurt, my body was taking its own sweet time about it.

We got off on ninth floor, and then walked down the hall to the registration center's suite number. There was no sign nor any other indication that the suite contained the Metahuman Registration Center. We opened the door and walked inside.

Honestly, I thought we were in the wrong place. I did not know what I had expected. Something out of a science fiction movie, maybe. I certainly was not expecting this. We were inside a small waiting room containing maybe half a dozen empty chairs. The walls were beige and undecorated. Old magazines were fanned out on a beat-up coffee table. A small receptionist's window was cut into the far wall, with a closed wooden door on the same wall. The place reminded me of the waiting room for a not particularly successful dentist or doctor, not where you went to register your Metahuman powers with the government.

We saw a woman's head in the receptionist's window. Dad and I walked up to her.

"Is this the Metahuman Registration Center?" Dad asked. His tone was doubtful. He must have been as dubious as I was.

"Yes sir, it sure is," the woman said. She had a very pronounced Southern accent. I had been told by the handful of people I knew who did not grow up in the South that I had a heavy accent too, but I did not hear it when I spoke. As far as I was concerned, I just spoke normally. "You gentleman have an appointment?"

"Yes, at 11 a.m. I'm James Conley. This is my son Theodore." The woman's eyes flicked over to me. She smiled at me. She was young, probably not too terribly much older than I was. Early twenties, maybe. And, she was cute. Long brown hair, big dark brown eyes, long eyelashes, even white teeth, and full pouty lips painted red. I found myself wondering what it would feel like to kiss her.

I opened my mouth to say hello, but nothing came out. I was suddenly struck dumb by shyness. I lifted my hand instead, intending to give her a cool guy wave. Instead I flashed her something that was half a finger point, and half a gang sign. Well, what I imagined a gang sign looked like. I had aimed for cool, but had hit doofus instead.

I felt my face getting red with embarrassment. I could not even greet a cute girl without getting flustered. It was no wonder I was a virgin. Some Metahuman I was turning out to be. Maybe I should go by the alias Kid Klutz, the Sexless Wonder.

The woman's smile faltered slightly, as if she did not know what to make of me and my twitching hand. *Join the club sister*, I thought. She looked down at the appointment book in front of her, and then back up.

"Oh yes, Theodore Conley. And right on time I see. I'm Jackie. I'll be getting you all started with the registration process." The woman was as cheerful as a dog being let out to play. I bet she had been a cheerleader when she was in school. "Just come right through the door over there."

Dad and I did as Jackie told us. We entered the area she sat in. She stood, and directed us to have a seat in a couple of chairs against the wall. Jackie had on a solid-colored top and matching pants that screamed "I'm a nurse." She walked down the hall a bit and disappeared into an open door. We heard water running. I looked around. No other employees seemed to be around, though there were a few closed office doors down the hall Jackie had walked down.

In a minute or so, Jackie returned. She stood in front of me. She started putting on a pair of thin latex gloves.

"Where's everyone else at?" I asked her. Curiosity had finally conquered my shyness. "I was expecting to see a lot more people."

"It turns out you're the only appointment we have today," she said. "That's not terribly unusual. Metahumans make up far less than one percent of the population, so sometimes we go days and days without registering a single person. Even when we have multiple appointments in a day, we spread them out so people won't run into one another. A lot of people want to keep the fact they are Metas private, and we want to respect people's privacy. That's the reason why we don't have any signage outside the office announcing what we do here. Our name is not even on the directory downstairs."

"Since we're your only appointment, are you the only employee here today?" Dad asked. Jackie shook her head.

"No. There's a technician in the back. Plus, Mr. Priebus is here. He's in charge of this center. He talks to every newly registered Meta. You'll be meeting with him later." She pulled a hypodermic needle out of a sealed plastic package. I shifted uncomfortably in my seat at the sight of it. "But first, we need to draw some of Theodore's blood and test it."

"What for?" I asked. The question came out high-pitched. I cleared my throat, pretending I had a frog in it. The truth of the matter was I did not like needles. It did not rise to the level of trypanophobia, but I still did not like them. Yeah, I know—trypanophobia. What can I say?

I read a lot. Not being good with girls freed up a lot of time.

"We'll test your blood for traces of the Metahuman gene," Jackie said. "We have equipment that can detect it once your powers manifest for the first time. We make sure you are in fact a Metahuman before we proceed further. You'll be surprised by the number of people who come in here, pretending to have powers. I guess some people will do anything to feel important." She must have seen the look on my face because she hastened to add, "Not that we think that is the case with you. We test everyone who comes in." She clearly had mistaken my anxiety about the needle for me being insulted at the suggestion that I could be faking being a Metahuman. I glanced down at the waves of energy still coming off my hands that apparently no one else could see. I was most definitely not faking them.

Jackie came over, bending over me with the needle in her hand. I flinched. Jackie paused, looking up at me.

"Surely a big strong guy like you is not afraid of a little old needle," she said. Even though I knew she was buttering me up, I felt myself flush with pleasure. Her face was inches from mine. Her eyes were pools of dark caramel, chocolatey and sweet. She smelled of antiseptic, shampoo, and girl. Heavenly.

"Of course not," I said. "I was afraid you were coming in for a kiss, is all. I never kiss on a first meeting." Or much at all, really, but Jackie did not need to know that. I was pleased with myself for coming up with that line. I felt a little like James Bond. I felt vindicated from that weird hand twitching thing earlier. Maybe I was not completely hopeless.

Jackie's eyes danced with amusement. She grinned at me. Her lips were blood red and glossed. If she had asked me to jump out the window at that moment, I would have done it gladly and with a song in my heart.

"Not kissing someone upon your first meeting is a good policy to have," she said. "I'll try to control myself. Now make a fist."

I did as she told me. Even with my forearm flexed, it still looked like a big piece of overcooked spaghetti. I really needed to hit the gym more often. Jackie wiped at my forearm with a cotton ball that reeked of alcohol. I looked away right before she jabbed me with the needle. I had fainted once years before when I had made the mistake of watching a doctor give me a shot. I would not make the same mistake again, especially not in front of a hot girl like Jackie. I did not want to ruin my smooth as James Bond moment. I did not remember James Bond ever once fainting, much less fainting in front of his love interest.

Jackie looked up at me. She saw that I was not looking at the needle sticking out of my arm. "Another reason why we draw blood is to determine what your powers are. We are required by law to keep a record of the powers of each registered Metahuman. We also use your blood to determine what level of Meta you are." I had the feeling she was talking to help distract me from the needle. She was not only pretty, she was a good nurse. Pretty and capable? A dream come true. Mrs. Jackie Conley had such a nice ring to it. "There are three Metahuman levels, from least powerful to most: Alpha, Beta, and Omega. The vast majority of Metas are Betas. Only a tiny sliver of the Metahuman population is Alpha or Omega. Unless you are exceptionally unusual, you are almost certainly a Beta." Outside of the context of Metahumans, a beta was someone who was unremarkable and all but invisible, the opposite of an alpha male. Though of course Jackie did not mean it that way, being a beta was the story of my life.

"There. All done," Jackie said. She pulled the needle out of my arm. I ventured a peek at it now that it was no longer sucking me dry like a vampire. Okay, a slight exaggeration. So sue me. A fat bulb filled with my precious red blood was at the end of the hypodermic.

Jackie straightened up. She smiled down at me in approval, as if mine was the best batch of blood she had ever seen in her life. She turned, put a cap on the needle and put it down, and turned back around with a small bandage in her hands. I was hyper-aware of her touch as she applied the bandage to where she had jabbed me. Did her hands linger for a bit longer than necessary on my arm? Probably wishful thinking. I wondered if she was into dating younger men who drove powder blue vehicles that were half-car and half-aquarium, at least when it rained.

"I'm going to go back to the lab and run your blood sample through our computer," Jackie said as she peeled off her gloves. "It will be just a few minutes. Now you make yourself at home until I get back." She walked back down the hallway. I followed her with my eyes until she disappeared from view through another door. She did not walk so much as she sashayed. It was mesmerizing.

"I never kiss on a first meeting?" Dad said, repeating my words from earlier. I jumped, startled. I had been so taken with Jackie I had forgotten Dad was sitting merely feet away. I shifted in my seat, embarrassed.

"Don't be jealous of my silver tongue," I finally managed.

"I'm not jealous of it. I'm admiring it. I should be writing this stuff down for later use," he teased. The fact of the matter was that Dad had not gone out with any women since Mom had died. A couple of years ago, I had asked Dad why he never dated or remarried after Mom passed away.

"I have yet to meet a woman who even begins to hold a candle to your mother," he had said. "If I ever do, maybe I'll go out with her. Until then—" he had trailed off with a shrug. I often wondered if he was lonely. All he did was work, work, work. Mom's prolonged illness had blown through the family's savings, plus some. Dad was still digging his way out of debt. After Mom died, Dad's lawyer had suggested that he declare bankruptcy to get from under the crushing load of debt. Dad had ignored his advice. He simply worked even harder than before on the farm. He had worked plenty hard before Mom died—he was almost always in the fields before dawn and did not return until nightfall—so I would not have thought him working even harder was possible had I not witnessed it with my own two eyes. "Even mountains can be moved if you chip away at them long enough and don't quit," Dad always said. Another Jamesism.

About ten minutes or so passed before we saw Jackie again. She opened the door of the room she had gone into. She stared at me with an odd look on her face. She then hurried deeper down the hall and knocked on and opened a different door. She entered the room, closing the door behind herself.

After a minute or so Jackie came out again. She was followed by a tall, very heavy man wearing grey dress pants, suspenders that swelled out over his big belly, and a white dress shirt and black tie. He looked at me from down the hall with interest and barely concealed excitement. They both went into the room Jackie had taken my blood into. Despite the fact they closed the door behind themselves, I heard voices raised in excitement.

I looked at Dad. He appeared as puzzled as I felt.

"What do you suppose that's all about?" I asked. Dad shrugged.

After a few more minutes, Jackie and the heavyset man came out again, this time followed by a thin older man in khakis and a polo shirt. The older man had a long white goatee. It made me think of a billy goat. The three of them came towards us.

"Gentlemen," Jackie said to me and Dad, "this is Lance Priebus, the director of the center I told you about before." The heavyset man in the suspenders nodded his head at us. His brown hair was closely cropped on the sides of his head, and longer on the top. "And this is Floyd, our office technician," Jackie said, referring to the older man with the goatee. Floyd was staring at me behind his thin glasses, like I was an elephant and he had never seen one before. His stare made me uncomfortable.

Jackie wore gloves again. She pulled a fresh needle out of a package. "We need to take a second blood sample," she said. Ugh. Despite the fact a second blood sample would mean Jackie would have to touch me again, one needle in my arm had been too many as far as I was concerned.

"Why?" I asked, already dreading the thought of being poked again. "Is there some kind of problem?"

"Not at all," Mr. Priebus said, speaking for the first time. His voice was deep, rumbly, and matched his size. "We just got some unusual results with the first sample and we need to get a second sample to confirm them."

"Can't I just pee in a cup or something instead?" I asked hopefully.

"Afraid not," Mr. Priebus said. "It has to be your blood."

I wanted to tell them I would not give them any more of my blood. I really did not like needles. What did they think I was, a blood bank? Dad must have read what I was thinking on my face.

"Give them your arm again Theo," he said firmly. I sighed. Dad did not give orders very often, but when he did, he expected results.

I stretched out my arm again, making a fist. After cleaning my forearm with alcohol again, Jackie stuck the fresh needle in my arm, not too far from where she had put the other needle in. I turned my head away again. I felt vaguely faint. Maybe this place did not register Metahumans at all. Maybe it was a front for vampires. Maybe Jackie and her friends planned to drain me dry, one needle at a time. Or, maybe I read too many urban fantasy novels.

Mr. Priebus and Floyd looked at me carefully as Jackie finished drawing my blood, like they were examining me under a microscope. Now I knew how amebas felt. Jackie pulled the needle out, capped it, and applied another bandage to my arm. The three of them then went back down the hallway. Floyd kept glancing at me over his shoulder. The urge to stick my tongue out at him was almost more than I could resist. The three went back into the room where Jackie had first disappeared with my blood. They closed the door behind them.

A happy thought occurred to me. I looked at Dad, excitement rising in me.

"Do you suppose I'm not a Meta after all?" I asked him eagerly. "Maybe that's why they need to retest me."

"Explain what happened in the USCA bathroom, then," Dad said. "And, what about the waves you see coming off of your hands?"

I looked down at my hands again. The waves were still very much there. Then again, I was the only one who could see them. Maybe they were just a figment of my imagination. And, maybe I had thrown the Three Horsemen around not with superpowers, but with mere muscle power. Mothers were known to lift cars off of their trapped children thanks to surges of adrenaline. Maybe I was just crazy and imagined seeing the waves emanating from my hands; maybe I had gotten crazy strong in the USCA bathroom due to a rush of adrenaline. Honestly, I almost would have preferred being crazy over being a Metahuman. Less dangerous. I never heard of an insane asylum patient being murdered the way Avatar had been.

I was about to find out it was not I, but my situation, that was crazy.

CHAPTER THREE

"Theodore, you are an Omega-level telekinetic," Mr. Priebus said. Dad and I sat across from him at his desk in his office in the back of the Metahuman Registration Center. He had summoned my Dad and I back here once they had finished testing my blood for the second time.

My mouth was open. I closed it, realizing I must have looked like a fool with my mouth hanging open. I had heard of people's jaws dropping before, but never had I heard something so impossible to believe that my own jaw had done it.

"B-b-b-but that impossible," I sputtered. "Avatar was an Omega-level Metahuman. He was invulnerable, he could fly, he had super speed and strength, and each of his senses operated on a superhuman level. It's said he could move the Moon out of its orbit if he had wanted to, and that he could hear a feather hit the ground from miles away. All I did was toss three football players around. There must be some kind of mistake."

Mr. Priebus shook his head firmly.

"There is no mistake," he said definitively. "Our equipment does not lie. That's why I wanted your blood tested for a second time to be absolutely sure. You are an Omega-level Metahuman. Your power is to move things with your mind. From what you have told me, you apparently channel that power through your hands."

Dad looked confused. "I'm sorry, but what does being an Omega-level Metahuman even mean?" he asked. Dad was not a fanboy of licensed Heroes like I was, so he did not understand the Metahuman lingo like I did. I was still too dumbstruck to explain it to him. "The nurse told us there are three kinds of Metahumans. Alphas, Betas, and Omegas. Each one more powerful than the last. But what exactly does it mean that my son is an Omega-level Metahuman?"

"It means Theodore is one of the most powerful Metahumans alive. Or at least he has the potential to be," Mr. Priebus said. He picked up a pen with his big beefy hand and made some quick scribbles on a pad of paper. "Think of Metahuman abilities as being distributed on a bell curve. They usually manifest for the first time when someone is in their teens. Like Theodore." He lifted the pad and turned it around so we could see it. On the paper he had sketched what looked like a large mountain with a tall peak, the sides of which tapered away at each end. Mr. Priebus pointed to the left side of the drawing. "On the left side of the bell curve are the least powerful of the Metahumans. These are the Alphas. They possess abilities that normal humans do not, but those abilities are very weak. A young lady I know who is an Alpha-level Meta has the ability to turn her eyes' irises any color she wishes. That is something a normal person obviously can't do, but it is hardly a world-changing power. Only a handful of Metahumans are Alphas."

Mr. Priebus' finger crept up the slope of the curve he had drawn. "The vast majority of Metahumans fall into the middle of this bell curve. These are the Betas. Almost all licensed Heroes and Rogues—that's the technical term for supervillains—are Betas. Betas have the ability to do things normal humans can only dream of. Fly, control animals with their mind, transform into metal, lift thousands of pounds, that sort of thing." Mr. Priebus's finger continued moving over the hump of the bell curve and down its slope until it got to the right edge of the drawing.

"And here is where the most powerful of all the Metahumans are," he said, visibly excited. I was not excited. If anything, I felt sick. "The Omegas. Omegas possess the kind of power that can literally destroy the world."

"Destroy the world?" I interjected. I was still in disbelief. I could not even get laid, much less destroy the world. "All I did was toss some football players around," I said again. I did not want to be a Metahuman, Omega-level or otherwise. I looked down at my hands again. The waves coming from them almost seemed to be mocking me.

"Yes, but what will you be capable of when your powers further develop and mature?" Mr. Priebus said. "What if you decide to shift some tectonic plates under the world's oceans and cause worldwide tidal waves? What if you decided to move the Earth closer to the sun and kill all life as we know it?" His eyes shined with excitement. He looked like he hoped I would do it, and he would grab a tub of popcorn and watch.

"I can't move the Earth closer to the sun. All I did was toss some football players around." I sounded like a broken record. I did not care. There had to be some sort of mistake. Dad reached over and put his hand on my shoulder. He was trying to reassure me. It was not working.

"You say there are only a handful of Omega-level Metahumans. How many others are there?" Dad asked Mr. Priebus.

"Well, Avatar was Omega-level, but he died a few months ago. Theodore here is the first Omega-level Metahuman I personally have discovered." Mr. Priebus made it sound like he personally gave birth to me right after he discovered penicillin and split the atom. "Other than Theodore, there are three known living Omega-level Metas. There's Millennium, a licensed Hero who, like Avatar was, is on the Sentinels. The Sentinels are a team of licensed superheroes headquartered in Astor City, Maryland." I doubted Mr. Priebus needed to say that part. Even Dad must have known who the Sentinels were. They were probably the most famous group of superheroes in the world. "Then there's the Rogue named Chaos. He's in prison in the federal Metahuman Holding Facility in Maryland after having almost destroyed the city of Chicago a few years back. Lastly, there is a five-year-old Omega-level Metahuman in Beijing, China named Liam Qiaolian." Mr. Priebus paused. "Actually it would be more accurate to say Liam is over seventy-five years-old. She's been in a self-induced coma for over seventy years. So, Millennium is the only active Omega, and the only one who is a Hero."

Dad let out a long breath. It was not every day you found out your son was one of the four most powerful people on Earth. Imagine how I felt. Hint: Not good.

"Okay, now that you've determined that Theodore is an Omega-level Metahuman, what's the next step?" Dad asked. He sounded tired. A wave of guilt washed over me. With Dad working as hard as he did to get out of debt, he had plenty on his plate as it was. The last thing he needed was to have to help me deal with something else. Especially when the something else was this big.

"After we finish talking, Floyd will help Theodore complete the registration process. We'll get his fingerprints, a retinal scan, get all of his contact information, that sort of thing. If Theodore does not intend to use his powers, he does not need to do anything else other than to make sure to keep his contact information current with the U.S. Department of Metahuman Affairs. The USDMA is the agency that runs this registration center and all the registration centers across the country. And, Theodore also has to be sure to not use his powers, of course. As you probably know, under the Hero Act of 1945, a Metahuman is only allowed to use his powers if he first receives a license to do so." Mr. Priebus settled back in his chair, with his hands folded over his big belly. He took on a professorial air. I could easily imagine him as one of my college professors. "The Hero Act was passed in order to protect the public from the powers of Metahumans. In 1945, an American Metahuman named John Tilly, concerned about the mounting casualties caused by World War Two, flew to Japan and used his powers to set off nuclear explosions in the cities of Hiroshima and Nagasaki. The Japanese surrendered shortly thereafter. To this day historians still argue about whether Tilly's actions made Japan surrender, or if it was on the brink of giving up anyway. To some Tilly is a hero who saved countless lives. It would have been a bloodbath had the Allies needed to invade the Japanese homeland to force their surrender. To others, Tilly was a homicidal madman who was meddling in events he barely understood.

"Regardless of which camp one falls into, one thing became clear as a result of Tilly's actions: Metahumans could not be allowed to run amok with no regulation or supervision. That was why the Hero Act was passed into law. The government did not want Metahumans using their powers unless they were trained to do so and unless they used them in the public interest. Most of the industrialized world has followed the U.S.'s lead and has put laws in place similar to the Hero Act. Under the Hero Act, all Metahumans must register with the federal government and must agree to not use their powers unless they first train and become licensed to use them. Registering, of course, is what you will be doing here today. Licensed Metahumans are known as Heroes; unlicensed Metahumans who use their powers anyway are known as Rogues." Mr. Priebus smiled slightly. "Or, in the more common vernacular, superheroes and supervillains.

Avatar and the Sentinels are licensed Heroes or superheroes. Chaos is an example of a Rogue or supervillain."

Mr. Priebus hesitated. "Actually, what I said about Metahumans not being allowed to use their powers unless they are licensed is not quite true. There are a few exceptions. For example, a Metahuman can use his powers under the supervision of a licensed Hero, usually for training purposes. But, those few exceptions aside, generally speaking, Metahuman power usage without a license is a felony."

"What happens to all of the information you get about me when I complete the registration process?" I asked. Mr. Priebus had said they would take my fingerprints. The idea made me uneasy. You know who had their fingerprints taken? Criminals. I was starting to feel like one, even though I had not done anything wrong. Why did this all have to be happening to me?

"Your registration information will be sent to the records division of the USDMA, as well as to the Heroes' Guild," Mr. Priebus said. "The Heroes' Guild is the association of licensed Heroes that all Heroes belong to. The Guild grants licenses to new Heroes and monitors and regulates the conduct of existing Heroes. The USDMA and the Guild keep information on Metahumans for a couple of reasons. One, if you decide to use your powers illegally, we will know where to look for you. Secondly, if something happens that involves a Metahuman's powers— a robbery or a murder or a terrorist attack, let's say—but we don't know who the Metahuman perpetrator was, having Metahumans' various powers on file will help us to figure out who is to blame. Unless there is reason to believe you have been involved in some sort of criminal activity, your registration information will be kept completely confidential and private."

"So what does Theo need to do if he should decide he wants to become a licensed Hero?" Dad asked.

"Not interested," I interjected before Mr. Priebus could answer. Dad waved at me to be quiet.

"First he would need to graduate from the Hero Academy. Some people call it Hero boot camp as it is run much like a military boot camp," Mr. Priebus said. "The Academy is designed to weed out the Metas who should not be Heroes and begins to train them in the use of their powers. Academy graduates go on to complete their training in one of two ways. The most prestigious way is to become an Apprentice to an already licensed Hero. Those Academy graduates who cannot get an Apprenticeship can instead complete their training in specialized Hero schools. After finishing an Apprenticeship or his time in Hero school, the potential Hero then has to stand for the Hero Trials. The Trials are a series of tests, both mental and physical, administered by the Heroes' Guild. The Trials are designed to ensure that a Hero candidate has the knowledge and skills to use his powers responsibly and to promote the welfare of the public. The majority of people who take the Trials fail them. That is the way the Trials are designed. We want to make sure that only the best of the best become Heroes."

"I'm not going to go through the Trials. I'm not going to the Academy or become an Apprentice or go to Hero school or any of the other crazy stuff you're talking about," I said firmly. "I have no interest in being a Hero or in using my powers ever again. They've gotten me into enough trouble as it is." I thought of my suspension from college and the fact that Donovan might wind up suing me. I also thought about the fact that Avatar had been murdered. If it could happen to a man like him, it certainly could happen to puny me. Use my powers some more and continue to get lied about, sued, or worse, killed? No thanks.

After Dad and I finished our talk with Mr. Priebus, he took us to another room in the center where we met with Floyd. Under Mr. Priebus' watchful eye, Floyd recorded my social security number and the contact information for me, Dad, and my closest relatives. He measured and recorded my height and weight. I was glad Jackie was not around for that part; how small I was made me feel like the world's biggest wimp. Floyd also took my fingerprints, palm prints, and footprints.

"Why do you need my footprints?" I asked Floyd as I took off my shoes and socks. "Aren't my handprints enough?"

"What if your hands get cut off? In a fight with a Rogue, for example," Floyd responded. He said it matter-of-factly, as if such a thing happened all the time. "The USDMA would still need a way to identify your corpse." *What if my hands get cut off? Corpse?* my mind repeated. *Yikes!* It hardened my resolve to never use my powers and to avoid any and everything Metahuman related. I did not want to ever find myself in a situation where my hands might get cut off. I was way too attached to them to want to see that happen.

Floyd had me dictate to him a detailed account of how my telekinesis manifested itself in the bathroom with the Three Horsemen. He made me give him such precise details I felt like I was reliving it. Floyd also took a handwriting sample, a retinal scan of me, recorded a voice sample, and made an impression of my teeth. With being fingerprinted and having my teeth examined, I felt like a combination of a criminal and a horse, as if my name was Secretariat and I had been caught robbing banks. Actually, it was worse than being Secretariat. If I had been Secretariat, at least they would have lined up some mares for me to be the stud to.

Thankfully they did not take another DNA sample; they already had two thanks to the blood Jackie had drawn from me. I did not think I would have been able to stand being impaled by yet another needle on top of everything else I had to deal with. My mind was already awhirl. Just a few days before I was merely a farmer's son and college student. Now, not only was I a Metahuman, but I was an Omega-level one at that. If only my powers included the ability to travel back in time. I would have gone back to before I walked into that USCA bathroom and not gone in. Hindsight really was twenty-twenty.

In addition to everything else, I had to sign a bunch of paperwork acknowledging that the Hero Act of 1945 had been explained to me, promising to keep the government advised as to my whereabouts, and swearing I would not use my powers without first being duly licensed as a Hero. I was even given a Metahuman Registration Number: 34589. I felt like I was being branded. At least they did not tattoo it on my forehead.

Jackie, Mr. Priebus, and Floyd all gathered in the center's waiting room to see me and Dad off once I had finished the registration process. Mr. Priebus seemed sorry to see me go. I felt like the prize exhibit in a zoo being released back into the wild.

As distracted as I was by everything that was happening, I was still sorely tempted to ask Jackie for her number before we left the registration center. I told myself I did not do it because there was not a chance to do so without Dad, Mr. Priebus and Floyd witnessing it. The truth of the matter was I could not work up the nerve. Instead of Jackie's telephone number, I instead walked out of the center with a handful of paperwork—copies of the documents I had signed plus brochures and pamphlets about the Hero Act, my obligations as a registered Meta, and the steps I needed to take if I wanted to obtain my Hero's license.

I looked the paperwork over as Dad drove us back towards Aiken County. The title of the pamphlet describing the process of becoming a licensed Hero was *So You Want To Be A Superhero?*

No, I did not.

CHAPTER FOUR

Three days after registering as a Metahuman, I was on my hands and knees in a field on the farm, digging up sweet potatoes. I was hot, sweaty, dirty, thirsty, hungry, and tired. Life as an officially registered Metahuman was not proving to be glamorous.

The mid-morning sun bore down on me. Normally I would be in class this time of the day, but I was still on suspension, so so much for that. It had rained the day before. The combination of the moisture and the implacable August sun made working in the field feel like working in a steam room. My long-sleeve cotton shirt stuck to my skin, wet with sweat. The inside of my wide-brimmed straw hat was soaked. I had on long-sleeves and the huge hat because if I did not, I would look like a boiled lobster by the end of the day. Dirt had gotten into my work boots. I felt the gritty soil between my toes every time I moved, digging into my tender flesh. My clothes looked like I had spent the morning making mud pies. I had been out here for over three hours so far. Breakfast seemed like an eternity ago. Each row of sweet potatoes was about four hundred and fifty feet long. I had finished not even half of the row I had started on earlier this morning. Including the row I now worked on, there were six rows of potatoes. It would take me two or three days to dig them all up.

The rows of sweet potatoes were at the bottom of a hill. On top of the hill was the single-wide, two-bedroom mobile home Dad and I lived in. When it rained, soil from higher on the hill ran off to where I was now, making this field some of the most fertile Dad owned. The problem was if it rained too hard, this part of the field got flooded and became completely unusable. I had seen times in prior years when where I now knelt was under a couple of feet of water, and stayed that way for months. That was one of the reasons I had no interest in following in Dad's and a long line of Conley men's footsteps and becoming a farmer. You could slave away on a crop for months, only to have all your hard work wiped out because it suddenly got too wet. Or too dry. Or too hot. Or too cold. Or some once harmless plant disease mutated into something far more harmful and killed your crops. Or locusts decided to swarm. Or deer got too plentiful and they ate most of your crops. Or any one of a thousand other things went wrong. Being a farmer, there were just too many things that were outside of your control regardless of how much you busted your butt working. You were like Goldilocks, praying that things would turn out just right so you could earn a living. That was why Dad was still in debt and was not financially successful despite the fact he worked like a dog seven days a week: things had gone wrong for him at the worst possible times. Four years ago it rained so much I had joked we should imitate Noah and build an Ark. Dad had told me to not be blasphemous. The fact that Dad's crops for the entire year had been ruined was not a joke, though. Though Dad did not wind up having to sell the farm to make ends meet, it was a close thing. That year I had eaten so many cheap canned beans for breakfast, lunch, and dinner, I had thought about opening a gas station. No thanks. I did not know what I wanted to do once I graduated college, but being a farmer was not it.

I stood up. My legs ached from kneeling in the dirt for so long. I wiped the sweat out of my eyes with my sleeve. My stomach rumbled. I glanced up to the top of the hill where our mobile home sat. The lunch I had made for myself the night before was waiting for me inside. I glanced up at the sun hopefully. I looked back down in disappointment. The position of it told me it was nowhere near noon despite the protests of my stomach. I wistfully looked at the house again. Lunch was so close by, and yet seemed so far away. When Mom was alive we lived in a brick rancher several miles down the road. After she died, in order to cut costs and to help pay down some of Mom's many medical bills, Dad had sold that house and the property it sat on and put a mobile home in one of his fields instead. Kids had called me white trash more times than I could count because I lived in a mobile home in the middle of a field. Dad always said that "anyone who calls you trash is trash himself and not someone worth listening to." Another Jamesism. I supposed he was right, but it still did not make me feel better about being called names.

I picked up my hoe and turned my attention back to the row of sweet potatoes I was working on. This variety of sweet potato plant had huge green leaves with purplish veins. The plants threw out tendrils of vines that got all tangled up, so the rows of plants were a huge interlocking jumble of leaves and vines, like a green blanket knit by a drunk Mother Nature. The tangle of greenery was so thick that you could not see the ground underneath it. I used the hoe to lift up a tangled mass of leaves and vines. I inspected the ground underneath the leaves carefully. Snakes liked to lie in wait for rodents under here and to take refuge from the heat of the sun under the leaves' shade. I was always careful to not pull up the plants without first checking to make sure I was not about to put my hand on a coiled up rattlesnake or copperhead. First I had gotten peed on, then I had gotten suspended, then I had found out I was an Omega-level Metahuman. Getting bitten by a poisonous snake would put the cherry on top of what was shaping up to be a terrible month. What would happen next? Would a nuclear bomb be dropped on my big, fat, sweaty head?

The coast appeared to be clear under the leaves and vines. I put the hoe down. I leaned down to grasp the next plant at its base, right where it entered the ground. The ground was slightly convex, a sign of the potatoes that were growing underground off the roots of the plant. I pulled the plant out of the ground, leaving behind a crater several inches deep. Several large reddish-orange potatoes were attached to the roots of the plant. I put the large unblemished potatoes into a bucket after brushing most of the dirt off of them. Those were the ones that Dad would sell to the customers he had accumulated over the years, including some small local grocery stores. The tiny potatoes went into a separate bucket for the rejects, as did the ones that were flawed in some fashion—bruised, partially eaten by gophers, split open, that sort of thing. Some of the potatoes grew with huge splits in them and looked like some kind of Frankenstein vegetable. I was unclear on why some potatoes grew like that; I only knew that lots of them did. The tiny potatoes and the ugly ones were perfectly edible, of course. But because of their size and how they looked, they were hard to sell. That was why I kept them separate from the large, attractive potatoes.

Some of these rejects would be given to my Uncle Charles, who lived about ten minutes up the road on his own small farm. Unlike Dad, who only grew fruits and vegetables, Uncle Charles had animals. The potatoes Dad gave him would be used to help feed his pigs. The potatoes not given to Uncle Charles Dad would give away to elderly people on fixed incomes who would be glad to have healthy, organic food. "Always help people when you can, Theo. Making others' lives better makes your life better," Dad always said. Another Jamesism. I should have written them all down and made them into a book. The problem was I did not know who would buy it. The Pope, maybe.

After pulling all of the potatoes off of the plant's roots and sorting them into the buckets, I dropped to my knees. I dug my gloved hands into the small crater left behind by the plant I had pulled up. There were almost certainly still potatoes in the ground that had gotten detached from the plant's roots. I rooted around in the wet ground like a pig searching for truffles, pulling out the potatoes I found there.

Was this how my life would unfold? Would I spend the rest of my days on my hands and knees toiled away in the hot sun? Dad did not seem to mind this kind of work, despite the fact farming constantly left him flirting with poverty. He had grown up on a farm in South Carolina— just a little bit up the road where Uncle Charles lived, as a matter of fact—and he would no doubt die on farm in South Carolina. I did not want that to be my life. That was why I was in college and why I read so much. I suspected there was so much more to life than digging potatoes and fretting about rainfall. I wanted to go places, see things, do things, the things I had read and dreamed about. What exactly I wanted to see and do, I did not exactly know. It was a like a worrisome itch I could not quite figure out how to scratch. Yet, at the same time, the wider world intimidated and scared me. I had spent my entire life in this small town on a farm. I knew little and had done less. Maybe I was not sophisticated or smart or strong enough to deal with the wider world. Maybe those kids who called me names were right—maybe I was just poor white trash and poor white trash I would remain until the day I died.

I was there on my hands and knees toiling away in the only world I knew while dreaming of worlds unexplored when a huge man wearing a costume, mask, and cape dropped out of the sky and landed in front of me.

CHAPTER FIVE

Startled out of several years' growth, I fell back on my butt with a panicked cry. I held a plant with potatoes dangling from the roots. I twisted, groping for the hoe. I twisted back around, clutching the hoe. I held it in front of me like a priest with a crucifix trying to ward off a vampire.

"What in the world are you doing?" the costumed man asked. His deep voice was accentless, like a television announcer's. The eyes behind his mask moved from the hoe pointed at him to the sweet potato plant in my other hand. If the hoe scared him even the slightest bit, he hid it well.

"Um, pointing a hoe at you? And, digging up sweet potatoes?" Thanks to my nervousness, my responses came out as questions. My fear at the man's sudden appearance was already starting to subside, but not my surprise. I now recognized the man. It was Amazing Man. I had seen him on television lots of times. He was a licensed Hero, and a famous one at that. One of the good guys. Whew! But why in the world was he here?

"I can see that. What were you planning to do with the hoe? Till me to death? Then again, I'd rather find you

40

clutching a hoe with an 'e' than the other kind. You're a little young to be clutching a ho." Amazing Man's steel-grey eyes looked amused. He waited expectantly. "That was a joke," he said when it was clear no laugh was forthcoming.

"Uh, I know. It was funny," I said, lying.

"Don't humor me, son. I'm a Hero, not a stand-up comedian. I know my strengths. I'll stick to my day job. But enough about filthy hoes of either variety. When I asked what you were doing, what I was really asking is why are you digging these potatoes up with your hands?"

"Oh," I said. "Well, my Dad and I don't have enough sweet potatoes planted to justify buying a machine to dig them up." I left out the fact we did not have the kind of money to buy a potato digger. Though such a machine could do in minutes what it took me days to do by hand, it cost thousands of dollars.

Amazing Man shook his head as if he was shooing away an annoying fly.

"That's not what I meant," he said. "What I'm trying to ask you is why aren't you using your powers to dig up the potatoes?"

"My powers?"

"Yes, your powers." Amazing Man's eyes narrowed. "You are Theodore Conley, aren't you?"

"Theodore Conley?" I hesitated, completely flustered. What was a world-famous Hero like Amazing Man doing here? "Uh, I guess so. I mean yes. Yes, my name is Conley Theodore. No, that's not right. I mean Theodore Conley."

Amazing Man looked puzzled for a moment. Then his eyes softened. He bent over a bit, looking me squarely in the eye.

"Theodore," he said, speaking very gently and carefully enunciating, "you don't by any chance go to some sort of special school do you?"

"What? Special school? No." It dawned on me what he meant. He thought I was mentally challenged. I could

41

hardly blame him. "No," I said again, more firmly this time, trying to sound smart. Then again, how smart could you sound saying a two letter word, even if that word was IQ?

I realized that I still held the hoe out in front of me like it was a sword. I knew enough about Amazing Man to know he was not going to hurt me. Besides, if he was inclined to hurt me, a hoe would not stop him. A bazooka wouldn't stop him. He was super strong, he could fly, he was nearly invulnerable, and he could shoot powerful blasts of energy from his arms. Since I did not need them—plus I looked silly—I put the hoe and the potato plant I still clutched down. I got to my feet. As sweaty, dirty, and discombobulated as I was, I must have looked a mess. What a way to make a first impression.

"Sorry about the hoe," I said. "You caught me off-guard, is all."

Now that I was on my feet, I took a long hard look at Amazing Man. I did not feel badly about doing so as he was doing the same thing to me. He was tall, taller than even Dad. His costume was chrome blue and silver with black accents. The accents were arranged in such a way that Amazing Man looked like he was in motion even when he stood still. The costume was tight on his body, almost as if it had been sprayed on. Amazing Man's terrifically developed musculature made me want to lock myself inside a gym with a large supply of raw beef and creatine and not come out again until I put on at least twenty pounds of muscle. His white cape, worn asymmetrically over his right shoulder, was bordered with blue and black. It hung down to his calves. His chrome blue mask only covered the area around his eyes, leaving the rest of his head bare. His hair was long, slightly shorter than shoulder-length. It was the same white color as his cape. That fact, combined with the lines on his face, made me realize Amazing Man was quite old despite the fact he had the body of a Greek god.

"Well?" Amazing Man finally said, jarring me out of my starefest. I realized my mouth hung open. I closed it. I had been having a lot of jaw-dropping experiences lately.

"Well what?" I asked.

"Well, why don't you use your powers to dig up the potatoes?" Amazing Man said, speaking slowly again. He did not sound convinced I did not go to a special school.

"Uh, because I'm not supposed to? Because it's illegal?" Amazing Man made me nervous. Because of that, I kept putting simple statements in the form of a question. What was I, a *Jeopardy* contestant? "Also, I don't know how." A thought struck me. "Wait a minute—how do you know about my powers?"

Amazing Man made a slight dismissive gesture with his hands.

"How I know about them is not important. The fact I do know about them is. I know you are an Omega-level telekinetic. I also know that an Omega-level telekinetic has no need to dig up potatoes by hand." He gestured impatiently at the plants around us. "So hurry up and dig them up with your powers. Come along now, we haven't got all day."

"But I'm not supposed to. I'm not licensed to use my powers. Besides, I don't know how." I realized I had said that already. I sounded like a broken record. Apparently, that was the effect talking to a living legend had on me.

Amazing Man sighed. "I happen to know that, under Heroes' Guild regulations, an unlicensed Meta can use his powers while under the supervision of a duly licensed Hero who is also a member of the Executive Committee of the Heroes' Guild." He winked at me. "I know that because I wrote the regulation myself back when I served as chairman of the Executive Committee. Though I no longer chair the committee—the damned title carried with it too many silly responsibilities and busywork—I'm still on the committee. Never let someone talk you into chairing a committee, by the way. A committee is an organism with multiple heads, six or more legs, and no brain. Trying to lead a committee of Heroes is worse than trying to herd cats. Chairing a committee full of them reminds me of the man who got ridden out of town on a rail. 'If it weren't for the honor of the thing, I'd just as soon walk,' the man said." Amazing Man paused, looking at me. I think he again expected to me to laugh. I was having a hard time following. I was too taken aback by this whole situation to barely breathe, much less laugh.

"Anyway," Amazing Man said, clearly having decided to move on, "rest assured that as long as I'm supervising you, you using your powers is perfectly within the bounds of the law." He folded his arms across his massive chest expectantly. "So go ahead. Use your powers to dig up all these potatoes. Hurry along now, we're burning precious daylight."

"Like I said, I can't. I don't know how."

Amazing Man shook his head at me.

"There is no can't. 'Can't' isn't a word that should be in a Meta's vocabulary. There is only willingness to do something, or not to do something." That was eerily similar to something Dad always said. Also, it sounded like something Yoda said in *The Empire Strikes Back*. I guessed that meant I was Luke Skywalker. And here I stood like an idiot, fresh out of lightsabers.

I was not too thrilled about the idea of using my powers again, even if it was legally allowed. The last time I had used them, it had not worked out so well for me. Besides, I did not want to get accustomed to using them. Being a Metahuman was dangerous. Avatar's death had reminded everyone of that. If I could turn my powers off forever and forget I had them, I would have rushed to flick the switch.

On the other hand, it was hot, I was hungry and thirsty, and I was heartily sick of digging potatoes. Maybe using my powers would speed up the process of me finishing. Plus, though I had no interest in being a Hero, when one like Amazing Man came along and asked you to do something, I was inclined to do it. Saying no would be like saying no to a professor or a cop. A cop who could grind you to powder between his thumb and forefinger.

"Okay," I finally said doubtfully, feeling just as doubtful. "I'll try."

I looked down at my gloved hands. The faint waves of energy that had been rippling out from them ever since my run-in with the Three Horsemen was still there, even though the thick gloves. The pain I had felt was totally gone, though. I pulled the gloves off and dropped them on the ground. I extended my hands straight out in front of myself towards the plants like a zombie. I felt as foolish as I no doubt looked. I waited expectantly.

Nothing happened.

I waited some more.

Even more nothing happened.

Maybe I needed to say something to trigger my powers, like some superheroes needed to in comic books. I thought of trying "Shazam!" or "Flame on!" or "It's clobberin' time!" but none of those catchphrases seemed terribly applicable. Besides, I did not want to embarrass myself further in front of Amazing Man.

I looked intently at the stubbornly unmoving potato plants. I waggled my fingers a little at them. Still nothing.

Amazing Man watched me throughout this. "You're not performing a magic trick," he said finally. "You don't just wave a magic wand over something and expect things to happen. You've got to concentrate, to will what you want to happen to happen. You have the power to do it, you just have to learn to draw on it. Think of it like water at the bottom of a well—to get to it, you have to prime the pump first."

"How do I do that?"

"Honestly, I'm not sure. Every Meta is a little different," Amazing Man said. "What was going on in your head the first time you used your powers?"

I thought about the incident with the Three Horsemen. I remembered having a clear picture in my head of throwing the three guys off of me before my powers kicked in and did it. I told Amazing Man.

"All right, then do that again. Form a clear picture in your mind of pulling the potatoes and the plants out of the ground. Once you have that picture firmly in your imagination, will it to happen. Don't try to pull up a bunch of plants at once. Just try it on one plant first. You have to learn to walk before you can run."

Still dubious, I tried again. This time I focused solely on the potato plant closest to me. I visualized in my mind what it felt like to pull the plant out of the ground with all of the sweet potatoes buried underground still attached to the root.

At first, exactly nothing happened. Then, the more I concentrated and visualized, my hands started to tingle, and then to burn. Encouraged, I concentrated even harder. The plant I focused on started to quiver, like it was being blown by the wind. I swore I could feel dirt, potatoes, and the plant's stem in my hands. My hands felt like they had been set on fire. Suddenly the potato plant lifted up from the ground, bringing all of the potatoes attached to its roots with it. The plant rose up in the air until it was level with my outstretched hands. It floated in front of me like a tethered balloon.

"I did it!" I said to Amazing Man. I was amazed at myself. I felt myself grinning like an idiot. I was sweating, but not just from the heat. Though I had barely moved, using my powers had been an act of both focus and physical exertion, like trying to solve a difficult puzzle while running on a treadmill.

"That's a good first step," Amazing Man said. "Now, try to separate the potatoes from the plant."

I concentrated again, visualizing clearly what I wanted to happen. The potatoes that were unblemished and of the right size I pulled off the plant. I floated them into the bucket of potatoes Dad would sell. The marred and small ones I put into the reject bucket with my powers. With each potato, it got easier and easier. Using my powers seemed to be like learning to type—it seemed impossible at first, but once you got the hang of it, you marveled there was ever a time you thought it was impossible.

Enthused despite how much effort pulling up the first plant had taken, I turned to the next plants in the row. Could I do two this time? I tried it, going through the same visualization and concentration process I had gone through the first time. This time the two plants came out of the ground without hesitation. I pulled the potatoes off of them, sorting them into the appropriate buckets faster and with a surer touch than I had the first time. Sweet! I was getting better. I felt like Mickey Mouse in *The Sorcerer's Apprentice* from *Fantasia*, using magic to get his work done.

Less than an hour later, I was exhausted, but more pleased with myself than I could remember ever being. With Amazing Man standing next to me, I looked around in satisfaction. The field was now empty except for buckets full of potatoes. I had dug up all the potatoes with my powers. It would have taken me days to do it by hand.

"Not bad," Amazing Man said. "I have to admit that you catch on pretty quick. Now let's see you fly."

"Fly?" I said, confused. "I can't fly."

Amazing Man looked down at me. He seemed incredulous. "You're an Omega-level telekinetic. Of course you can fly."

"Wait, that's not the first time you mentioned I'm an Omega. How did you know about that? For that matter, you never told me how you even knew I had powers."

"Never mind how I know. I just know. Just like I know that you can fly. So fly."

I shook my head. Even though this was a world-famous Hero, I was starting to get exasperated with him.

"I'm telling you I can't fly. Don't you think I'd know if I could?"

Amazing Man shook his head right back at me.

"Didn't I tell you you have to erase the word 'can't' from your vocabulary? In the time you're taking to tell me how you can't do something, you could instead be figuring out how to do that something."

"Does it look like I have wings? I can't fly," I said stubbornly.

Amazing Man sighed.

"You know what I told my goddaughter when she told me she couldn't swim?" he asked. I said no. "I told her she could swim, but that she just hadn't swum yet. Then I picked her up and threw her into a lake." Moving as fast as a striking snake, Amazing Man grabbed me by my shirt. He pulled me up off my feet until I was eye level with him. His steel-grey eyes bore into mine. "Now go fly." He twisted. He flung me into the air like I was a baseball.

I rose like a rocket. My hat flew off my head. I heard screaming. I realized it was me.

Screaming seemed like a pretty good idea right now.

CHAPTER SIX

The wind whistled in my ears. My body twisted around as I rose, making me dizzy. The cloudless blue sky looked like an endless sea of water that would swallow me whole. The ground receded beneath me like I was in an airplane that had taken off.

The problem was I was not in a plane. A plane meant there would be tons of metal and plastic around me, all kinds of safety precautions and emergency regulations, and a well-trained pilot and co-pilot who knew what they were doing. There was no cocoon of technology around me, nor a flight crew who knew how to use it. There was only me.

No, scratch that. There was also Amazing Man. He was a Hero. There was no way he would let me plummet to my death. Because that was what I was doing now. Plummeting. I had reached the apogee of my rise, and I was now falling back towards the spinning ground far below. I knew the word apogee, but not how to fly. They taught me vocabulary in school, not how to defy gravity.

Though I looked for him like a drowning man looking for a life raft, I did not see Amazing Man anywhere. It was hard to see clearly with the rushing wind stinging my eyes, the spinning, and the panicking. Especially the panicking.

But, I was sure Amazing Man would save me. That's what Heroes did—they saved people. The thought calmed me for a moment. The calm soon frayed, and then completely got blown away by the roaring wind.

Uh, Amazing Man? I thought, willing him to appear. Nothing happened, and no one appeared.

Any time now, Amazing Man. The ground got closer.

This is not funny anymore, Amazing Man.

I really could use a hand here, Amazing Man.

I'm about to go splat, Amazing Man.

"HELP ME AMAZING MAN!" I shrieked. If he could hear me, he did not demonstrate it by showing up to save me. Meanwhile, the ground grew chest-tighteningly closer, seemingly eager to enfold me in its deadly embrace.

God helps those who help themselves, came a Jamesism spontaneously into my head. What a time for a cliché. On the other hand, Amazing Man was still nowhere to be seen. If I did not save myself from the bloodiest pancake impersonation ever, who would? On the other other hand, just because my powers worked on meathead football players and potato plants, that did not also mean they would also work on my own body. No, that was the wrong attitude to have. My powers would work on myself because, well, they just had to. Otherwise, bye-bye Theodore Conley. Do not pass Go, do not lose your virginity, do not collect two hundred dollars. A shame. That two hundred would have come in handy in hiring a hooker so I wouldn't die a virgin.

Besides, like Amazing Man said, you're an Omega-level Metahuman, I thought fiercely. *You got this.* My inspirational pep talk to myself would have been more believable had I not still been screaming my fool head off.

With an effort, I stopped screaming. It was serving no purpose other than to make my throat sore. *You got this, you got this, you got this*, I repeated to myself like a mantra. *Okay, visualize stopping yourself from falling.* At the last moment I realized that I did not want to come to an abrupt stop. I remembered my high school physics. Isaac Newton's law of inertia said that an object in motion stayed in motion with the same speed and in the same direction. Bringing my body to an abrupt stop would be like hitting a brick wall in a car going sixty miles an hour while not wearing a seatbelt—yeah the car would stop, but the driver would keep going at the same speed and in the same direction, namely through the windshield at sixty miles an hour. If I brought my body to a sudden stop at this speed, maybe my brain and other internal organs would just keep going. My organs would suddenly be like pâté inside my body. Or not. I just didn't know. I never had to stop myself from dying after being thrown into the air by a costumed lunatic before. But, better safe than sorry. Despite the fact I was approaching the ground at a sickening speed, I needed to slow myself gradually, not to stop abruptly.

With the image of me slowing down gradually firmly in mind, I concentrated hard. My hands burned. I felt myself slowing. I also saw myself spinning closer and closer to the Earth. Amazing Man had apparently thrown me so far that I was coming down on the neighbor's property. Mr. Gonzalez was a farmer too. His cornfield was below me. Cornstalks that looked like sharpened spears were beneath me, getting bigger by the second. I resisted the urge to freak out and bring myself to an abrupt halt. I continued to slow myself down gradually. Oh no! I was about to hit. *Oh my God, oh my God, oh my God!* My hands were on fire. Maybe the rest of me would soon be on fire too if I went to the wrong place. Heaven was promised to no one. I wondered, not for the first time, if Mom was there, waiting for me.

I squeezed my eyes tightly shut. I braced for the impact.

I wondered how much it would hurt.

CHAPTER SEVEN

Weird. It turned out that dying didn't hurt at all. No, that's not quite right. My hands hurt. They were on fire just like they had been after I tossed the Three Horsemen around.

Whoever heard of just your hands hurting after you died? Could it be I was not dead? It was dark. That was not a good sign. Graves were dark. No, wait. My eyes were closed. Maybe that was why it was dark. I opened them a crack, afraid of what I might see.

I peeked down at tall cornstalks. I opened my eyes wider. Silk hung from the ears of the attached corn like topknots. The stalks swayed gently in the breeze for as far as my eyes could see. I was hovering mere inches from them, suspended in the air like an acrobat in a circus.

I did it! I thought. I shook like a leaf, a combination of relief and excitement. Unless everything I had been taught about the afterlife was a complete lie, I had not died. And, I was flying. Well, not exactly flying. Floating, really. Baby steps. Step one: Don't die. Step two: Float. Step three: Fly. I was over halfway there. Sweet.

Okay, I had mastered floating. Now to actually move through the air. Maybe it was like swimming. I starting stroking my arms through the air, simultaneously scissoring my legs. I did move a bit, but I would hardly call it flying. More like an air crawl.

I stopped flailing my arms and legs, feeling and no doubt looking like a fool. God, I was an idiot. Had I already forgotten what Amazing Man had taught me? *Visualize what you want to have happen, concentrate, and then will it to happen,* I thought.

I craned my neck up, trying to get my bearings. Off in the distance was a line of densely packed trees. It was the forest that bounded the southern edge of Mr. Gonzalez's property. I would try to fly in that direction. I formed a picture in my mind of me zooming towards the forest. I concentrated on the image, willing my powers to make it a reality. My hands burned intensely.

Suddenly, like a bullet shot out of a gun, I rocketed towards the tree line. The wind burned at my eyes, making me squint. I pressed my legs together and my arms to the side of my body to cut down on the wind resistance. I skimmed over the cornstalks like a rock skipping over the surface of a pond. The line of trees rapidly approached, getting bigger, as if I was zooming in on it with a telescope. This was fun. Flying was easy. Being able to do it almost made it worth it to be a Meta—

Ow! Something hit my cheek, right under my left eye. Startled and in pain, I willed myself to slow to a halt. Soon I once again floated motionless above the cornstalks. I reached up to touch my aching cheek. My hand came away bloody. Something was in the blood on my hand. I looked at it closely. It was part of a shell of a large beetle, plus bits of beetle legs. I had obviously hit a beetle as I had flown. My cheek hurt as if I had been stabbed. My high school physics again came to the rescue, telling me what had happened. Force equaled mass times acceleration. I did not know how fast I had been flying, but I had been going really fast, fast enough to have traveled almost the entire length of Mr. Gonzalez's huge cornfield in just a few seconds. That rate of acceleration plus my mass equaled a heck of a lot of force when I had hit that beetle. An inch or so higher, and the beetle would have hit my eye instead. If that had happened, I could kiss my eye goodbye. Goodbye eye, hello eyepatch. Did girls like the pirate look? Doubtful. I had enough problems attracting them as it was. I had really dodged a bullet—uh, beetle. What if I had hit something bigger than a bug, like a bird? I would not have gotten off lightly with just a bloody cheek.

I started to shake a little as I realized how close I had just come to seriously hurting myself. Surely there was a way to avoid stuff like that happening. I chewed on my lower lip as I thought. I had the power to move things around. Could I repel them, too? Maybe set up a field around myself where things would bounce off of them?

I pictured what I wanted to do in my mind, concentrated, and willed it to happen. After a few seconds, I noticed the cornstalks below me swam a little in my vision, as if I was seeing them through a slightly cloudy lens. I glanced around at my body. The same waves that emanated from my hands now emanated from my entire body, forming a shield around me. Would it act to repel things as I had pictured? I willed my floating body to drop down slowly. When the cornstalks came into contact with the field around my body, they bent, not going through the field to touch me. It looked like it was working.

Encouraged, I lifted back up again so I was floating slightly above the corn. Setting my sights again on the forest ahead of me, I took off towards it, careful to maintain the repulsion field I had set up around myself. I actually saw things bouncing off of my field as I rocketed towards the trees again.

In seconds, I was past the corn and at the edge of the woods. I slowed to a halt. Concentrating mightily, I lowered myself to the ground, twisting in the air to try to touch down feetfirst. I shut off my powers and touched down on the ground. I stumbled a bit. I had made the mistake of not quite being on the ground before I shut off my powers. My arms windmilled. I regained my balance and caught myself before falling.

I grinned. I did it! I flew. Yeah, maybe I had not stuck the landing, but I bet the Wright brothers did not the first time they flew either.

"Not bad Theodore. Not bad at all," a voice said. "The force field was a nice touch. Unexpected, but good."

I spun around, startled. Amazing Man was behind me, leaning against a tree. My jaw dropped. That had been happening a lot lately.

"How'd you get here?" I asked.

"Same as you. I flew."

"I mean, how'd you get here so fast without me seeing you?"

Amazing Man shrugged. "I'm a Hero," he said, as if that explained everything. The flush of my excitement about flying abruptly wore off. I remembered why I had needed to fly.

"What's the big idea, throwing me into the air like that?" I demanded, angry. "You could have killed me."

"Could have." Amazing Man shrugged again. "Didn't."

"Why didn't you come save me?" The fact he was completely unapologetic made me even madder.

"I'll say it again: you're an Omega-level Metahuman. If you were not capable of saving yourself, might as well find that out now."

"But, but—" I didn't know what to say. I was madder than a wet hornet. If Amazing Man had not been so much bigger and older than I and a Hero to boot, I might have taken a swipe at him. He had scared me to death. Nearly literally.

Amazing Man stood up straight. "Let's fly back to where we left the potatoes," he said. "I'm no expert, but I'm guessing leaving them out in this hot sun is not good for them." He soundlessly rose into the air. His cape flapped a bit in the breeze. He looked down at me. "You coming, or are you going to stay here and sulk?" Honestly, I wanted to stay and sulk, but I hardly could say that. It would make me seem like a petulant child. Besides, he had a point about the potatoes. Being scorched by the sun would ruin them. I triggered my powers, rising to join Amazing Man in the air. It was easier to do it now. Practice makes perfect.

Amazing Man and I flew back to the potato field. The buckets full of potatoes needed to go into Dad's storage building. That cinder block building was on top of the hill, directly behind our mobile home. Since the full buckets were so heavy, I normally could carry only one bucket at a time up the steep hill. By myself, it would have taken me several trips to haul all the buckets up to the storage shed.

Amazing Man and I did it in one trip. He toted multiple buckets in each hand as if they were full of feathers instead of heavy potatoes. I floated the remaining four buckets in front of me using my powers as I walked. Using my powers was beginning to feel natural. If I could not figure out what else to do with my life, I could always rent my services out as a human forklift.

I arranged the buckets in the storage shed using my powers, putting the potatoes which would be sold in the back and the ones that would be either given away or fed to my uncle's pigs in the front. Amazing Man watched me do all this. Thanks to my powers, it did not take long. Amazing Man clapped his hands together once I was through.

"Well, now that that's finished, let's go," he said.

"Go?" I asked, puzzled. "Go where?"

Amazing Man looked at me like I had sprouted a second head.

"Go where?" he repeated incredulously, obviously puzzled himself. "Go teach you how to be a Hero, of course." Frown lines sprouted between his eyes. He craned his neck down and looked at me in the face more closely. "Are you quite sure your brain works all right?"

CHAPTER EIGHT

"**B**ut I don't want to be a Hero," I protested.

Amazing Man still seemed puzzled by my reaction. "What does what you want have to do with anything?"

"Since I'm the one who would have to learn to be a Hero, what I want has everything to do with it." I resisted the urge to stomp my foot. I could not believe I was talking to a living legend this way, but frankly I was still annoyed at him for throwing me into what had felt like orbit and letting me almost break my neck.

"Don't you understand that people like you—people like us—have a responsibility to the wider world? You should use your powers to help other people. To do that, you need to be trained. If you don't, you're letting your once in a generation powers go to waste. With great—"

"If you say 'with great power comes great responsibility,' I think I'll throw up. That's the biggest superhero cliché ever." I shook my head, thinking of what had happened with John Shockey and the Three Horsemen. "The last time I stuck my neck out to help somebody, I got abandoned by that somebody, suspended from school, and threatened with a lawsuit. You're going to have to find someone else stupid enough to help protect people. I've got my hands full helping myself."

"Does your father have guns?" Amazing Man asked.

"What?" I was confused by the abrupt change in subject. Did Amazing Man think he could make me be a Hero by threatening me with one of Dad's guns? "Yes. A few."

"Living out in the country as you all do, I would've been shocked if he did not. Does he know how to use them?"

"Of course. It would be silly to have guns around and not know how to use them. I know how to use them too. Dad taught me when I was little. What does that have to do with anything?"

"It's the same thing with you and your powers. Your powers are a loaded gun. You need to know how to use them, even if you have no intention of ever using them again once you learn. To learn to use them responsibly you have to become a licensed Hero. A responsible gun owner does not want to ever shoot someone, but he has to know how to do it. If he doesn't know how to use his gun appropriately, he's a danger to himself and everyone around him. The same is true of you. You have to learn to use your powers not only for your own safety, but for the safety of the rest of us. You are an Omega-level Meta. Letting you walk around untrained is like letting a toddler walk around with a loaded gun with the safety off." I thought of the Three Horsemen and how I had tossed them around and hurt them without even meaning to. I shook my head, trying to clear the thought from it.

"A gun is only dangerous if you pull the trigger," I said. "Yeah, it was pretty cool pulling up all these potatoes with my powers and learning to fly, but I have no intention of using my powers in the future. I'm not dangerous to myself or to anyone else."

"Your mere existence poses a danger. Aside from you, there are only three known living Omegas. One is a Hero.

58

Another is a supervillain and in a federal penitentiary. The third is in a self-induced coma and has been for over half a century. If I could find out that you are an Omega, others will as well. You can't keep something that big a secret. To continue with my gun analogy, you and the other Omegas are the only loaded guns in existence. One such gun, being a licensed Hero, is on the side of the good guys. The other two are out of the commission. That leaves you. Do you really think the people who crave power—and there are lots of them—will leave the sole remaining gun in the world alone? No. They are either going to try to use it for their own purposes or destroy it so no one else can. That's why Avatar was murdered a few months ago—someone wanted him out of the picture, to keep him from thwarting their plans. If they try to do the same thing to you, you have to be ready to defend yourself and the people you care about."

My blood curdled at his words. Destroy me? Yikes! Amazing Man was trying to frighten me. It was working.

"You're just trying to scare me into doing what you want me to do," I accused him. "No one cares about me. I'm just a—" I hesitated, almost calling myself a kid. Seventeen was hardly a kid, though I often still felt like one. "I'm just a nobody who lives on a farm."

"If no one cares about you, why am I standing in the hot sun sweating my balls off arguing with you?" Amazing Man's lips tightened grimly. "Yes I am trying to scare you. You should be scared. It's a big scary world out there with a lot of big scary people. They're not going to just sit around twiddling their thumbs while you're down here digging potatoes with your head up your ass."

"The fact that it's a big scary world is why I have no interest in becoming a Hero. Avatar was a Hero. Look what happened to him." I paused. In his own way, Amazing Man was as much of a bully as the Three Horsemen were. He was trying to push me around. "Am I correct in believing you can't force someone be a Hero?"

Amazing Man sighed. "Of course not. If someone trains to become a Hero, it has to be something he undertakes voluntarily."

"Well I'm not volunteering. I know what it's like to be a Hero. I watch the news. I follow your adventures. Heroes get hurt and killed all the time. Being a Hero is like painting a big fat bull's-eye on your chest and inviting the world to take potshots. You'll have to find some other patsy because you're barking up the wrong tree here. I'm not going to become a Hero and I'm not going to start training to become one." I folded my arms, feeling stubborn, my mind made up. "And you can't make me." I immediately regretted my last words. I realized how childish they made me sound. I meant them though. Yes, I wanted to do more with my life than continue the family tradition and become a farmer. That did not mean I wanted to become a Hero. There were far safer and less scary things I could do with my life. I would do one of them. Mom had already died far sooner than she should have. I had no interest in following in her footsteps by undertaking something that was liable to get me killed.

Amazing Man examined my face carefully. I did not flinch away from his gaze. After a while, he sighed.

"Your mind is made up then?" It was as much of a statement as it was a question.

"Yes," I said firmly. Amazing Man shook his head.

"I hope you change your mind before it's too late. If you do, get into touch with me again. Just call the Heroes' Guild National Headquarters in Washington, D.C. Tell them your name and that you want to talk to me. Those of us on the Executive Committee of the Guild rotate running Hero Academy, and this year I'm in charge of it. I'll see that you're enrolled in the Academy so you can begin the training process."

"I won't be getting in touch with you," I said, feeling more sure of myself now that it was clear Amazing Man was going to leave me alone. "I'm not going to change my mind about becoming a Hero. I'm not going to use my powers. I won't need to."

As I soon discovered, it turned out that I was wrong.

Dead wrong.

CHAPTER NINE

I soared high in the sky, feeling as free as a bird. There were no birds awake this time of night, though. Well owls, maybe.

It was close to midnight, almost a week after Amazing Man had paid me a visit. With each passing day, the fact I had met him seemed like a dream, like it had not been real. The fact I now knew how to fly was real enough, though. Even though I knew it was illegal to do so, I had gone flying every night since I had met Amazing Man. Flying was fun. It gave me a feeling of freedom, a feeling of there being no limits, that I had never felt before. I always did it at night so I would not be spotted. I also waiting until Dad went to bed before I did it. He went to bed early, usually around 9 p.m., so waiting until he was asleep before I left the house to go flying was not hard to do. He would not have approved of me illegally using my powers. Honestly, I felt a little guilty about doing it, especially since I had insisted to Amazing Man that I would not. But, it seemed like a victimless crime. Who was I hurting? It was not as though I was using my powers to rob banks or something. I was just using them to go for joyrides. Uh, joy-flies.

I had learned more about my powers in the nights I had spent flying. I had discovered that the force field I formed around myself while flying to avoid hitting debris did not allow air in. I found that out the first night I went flying. After flying over a large stretch of countryside high up in the sky, I had felt faint. I had nearly passed out and plummeted to the ground before it occurred to me what the issue was. The incident had taught me that Amazing Man was right about one thing: using my powers without being properly trained was dangerous. I had then figured out how to make my force field permeable enough to allow enough air in to let me breathe, but still have it solid enough to repel anything that might hurt me. I was quite proud I had figured that out all on my own. Who needed some dumb Hero Academy when you had good old common sense and trial and error?

It was a beautiful cloudless night. The moon was full and bright, making it easy for me to see. A sea of stars twinkled down at me. I was tempted to fly up as high as I could to see them even more clearly. Caution stopped me. How high up could I go before there was not enough oxygen to breathe? Also, if I rose high enough, would the world keep spinning independently of me, putting me in the middle of Europe when I came back down from my stargazing session? I didn't know. Maybe they were stupid questions. Since I didn't know, better safe than sorry. I felt like my science classes should have addressed issues like that at some point. Then again, my teachers probably never thought one of their students would be able to one day fly around like a Learjet without the Learjet. Maybe they addressed issues like that at Hero Academy. Risking my neck to train to become a Hero did not seem worth it to satisfy my idle curiosity.

There was a slight chill in the air, especially as high up as I was, so I had on a light sweater in addition to my jeans and tee shirt. I was miles away from the house, but I was up high enough to make out the two utility lights that shone over Dad's storage building. Out here in the country, there was not much in the way of artificial lights. I used the two lights to keep my bearings and to not get lost by flying too far from the house.

With each passing day, Amazing Man's warnings that I would wind up being the target of people who wanted to either use me or kill me seemed more and more like the cries of the boy who cried wolf. Especially up here, high in the sky, far removed from the cares and concerns of the mundane world. Up here, I felt invulnerable. Untouchable. No bullies would mess with me if they saw me like this. If the Three Horsemen could see me now, they would poop twice and die.

I was grinning at the image of that when something caught my eye. It looked like a shooting star, a streak of fiery light that flashed across my peripheral vision. This was no shooting star, though. It was too low. It had come not from the sky but from close to the ground, near where I had been keeping track of the utility lights by the storage shed. Then a fireball rose into the sky in front of where the shed was. It seemed tiny, not real, from this far away. Up close, though, it must have been huge. Red and orange flames came on the heels of the fireball, steady and distinct against the background of the dark ground.

It took a moment for my brain to process what was happening. Where it was happening. The fireball had erupted in front of the storage shed's utility lights. From where our mobile home was.

My heart rose to my throat.

Dad!

I was in motion before I even consciously thought about it. I turned in mid-air and rocketed towards our house. I flew faster than I ever did before. I must have broken the sound barrier getting there. Some of our neighbors reported hearing booming sounds and shattered car and house windows afterward.

I slammed to a stop high in the air over our mobile home. It was on fire from end to end. The house was a long rectangle. The middle of it had a huge charred hole in it, out of which flames and smoke shot up into the night sky. There was an ear-numbing roar and intense crackling and popping, like that of a huge bonfire. It was a scene straight out of Hell. Even at this distance, I felt like I would also burst into flames. The heat coming from the house was that intense. It did not matter. Regardless of the heat, I had to go in after Dad.

Right as I was about to fly into the inferno, I saw someone floating above the house, on the other side of it from where I was. He had on a pitch black suit that covered him from head to toe. There were luminescent ragged lines on the black suit. It reminded me of the pictures I had seen of lava right as it was breaking through the Earth's crust. The man's body was glowing, half orange-red, half light blue. A Meta obviously. A Hero presumably. Thank God!

"Hey!" I cried out to him. My voice was panicked. "Can you help me? My Dad is inside."

The floating figure looked over at me. He floated closer.

"Are you Theodore Conley?" he called to me. How did he know my name?

"Yes, yes," I cried impatiently. What was he waiting for? "My Dad. I think he's still inside. Help me!"

"I assumed you were inside asleep, kid," the man said. "My bad. Easily corrected error, though." He raised his left hand, palm out. "I promise it'll be quick."

There was a flash of blue light. Something formed around me, shutting out the fiendish light from the fire. It felt like I had been plunged into a frozen lake. I suddenly felt impossibly heavy. Dread stabbed at my heart as I realized what had happened. I was encased in ice. I could not stay airborne. I was too heavy. I plunged toward the ground.

My mind roiled as I fell. That was no Hero. Obviously.
How stupid could I be? As I plummeting out of the sky,
freezing, I felt sick to my stomach. My stupidity might
have gotten Dad killed.

It was about to kill me.

CHAPTER TEN

I wished I could say I meant to raise my force field as that Meta shot his cold beam or whatever in the heck it was at me. I wished I could say it, but I could not. It was pure dumb luck that I raised it, an instinct triggered by fear. If it were not for my force field, I had no doubt I would have been frozen to death before I even hit the ground.

Though I felt like a human popsicle, I was not dead. Not yet at least. Hitting the ground after falling from as high as I was would change that soon enough.

I tried as hard as I could to shatter the ice around me. I strained against it both with my body and with my powers. No good. I was as secure as a fossilized fly in amber. And, about to be just as dead. I tried to lift myself back into the air with my powers. After a terrifying moment, I gave up on that too. Too heavy. Damn it! I could not die. Who would save Dad?

I changed tactics. I tried to slow my rate of descent at least a little. My hands burned with a now familiar sensation. Would it be enough? I ground my teeth together, bracing for the impact.

I hit the ground hard. It felt like everything inside my

body bounced around. The impact reminded me of the time I had gotten rear-ended in my car by a speeding pickup truck. Everything ached. But, I was alive. Even better, the impact had cracked the ice a little. Straining against the ice with my powers, I could feel little fissures spreading through the ice thanks to the force with which I had hit the ground. I focused on them with my powers, willing them to get bigger. It was like trying to open dozens of crates simultaneously with dozens of crowbars.

My head hurt with the force of my concentration. I felt the ice starting to give way. I heard popping and cracking. I just had to get free. I pushed with all my might. The ice shattered. Shards exploded away from me like I was at the center of a bomb.

I lay halfway in the ground in a small crater caused by my impact with the ground. I quickly got up. My head swam, making me see double. Two infernos filled my vision. I shook my head, trying to clear it. The two infernos snapped together into one hellish sight, that of my house burning with Dad inside. I leapt out of the crater. I ran as quickly as I could towards the fire. I limped. My right leg was not working right. Pain stabbed at me like a rusty knife every time I put my weight on it. I tried to ignore it.

A flash of light from above. I dove to the right. A fireball scorched the ground where I had been an instant before. That blasted Meta again. The fireball did not simply go out. Instead, it ignited the ground where it hit. The fire spread faster than any normal fire I had ever seen, encircling me, covering me in a dome of flame as quick as a wink. The dome started to shrink, closing in on me. My skin burned. It felt like I had been plunged into an oven and I was about to be cooked.

I activated my force field again, using the one that kept everything out, even the air. I was not up to flying out of the fiery cage. Instead, using a short burst of my powers, I threw myself out of the fiery dome like a tossed ball. I landed on the other side of the flames, free of their confines.

The Meta glowed above me, glittering like a snake's eye. It was now obvious he wasn't going to let me into the house without interfering again. I knew I would have to take him out in order to get into the house to save Dad.

There were plenty of things around I could have thrown at the Meta to incapacitate or kill him—trees, utility poles, a tractor, my car, trucks, a bunch of things. The problem was, even at my best, I was not proficient enough in the use of my powers to pick up stuff that heavy. Maybe if I had trained in them. But, I was neither trained in their use nor at my best.

Wait! The utility poles. The Meta was near them. I exerting my will on the power lines that ran from the poles. I snapping them. I whipped them at the Meta like a cowboy lassoing a steer. They wrapped around him like an anaconda wraps around its prey. I made a line snake towards the Meta's neck. I did not know the best way to incapacitate someone, but I knew you could choke someone unconscious by his neck.

The Meta fought against the constricting lines for a moment. Then he relaxed. I thought I had him. Wrong again. The Meta's entire body glowed red-orange. The lines binding him melted off like ice thrown into a furnace. The molten metal and plastic dripped off of him like perspiration.

The Meta raised his hand again, pointing his open palm at me.

"It's nothing personal, kid. I've got a job to do is all," he said. His voice was gravelly, like he was a long-time smoker. "You're starting to annoy me though. Hold still and I'll make this nice and painless." The Meta's palm glowed brighter, like an exploding star. I braced myself. I was not strong enough to defeat this guy. I had failed both myself and Dad. I deserved what I was about to get.

Unexpectedly, the Meta cocked his head to the side.

Then, I heard it too. Sirens. An instant later I saw flashing lights from a series of vehicles pulling into the driveway of our property. The Meta shook his head.

"You are one lucky sonofabitch, kid," he said. "I was told to make your death look like an accidental fire and to make sure there were no witnesses." He nodded his head at the approaching vehicles, cops and fire trucks, that were almost on top of us. "That looks to me like an awful lot of witnesses." He lowered his glowing hand. "Rain check? Rest assured that this is not over. We'll see each other again when there aren't so many others around. Until then."

The Meta quickly rose straight into the air until he was only a pinprick of light. Then he streaked off into the distance as a bright blur against the night sky.

I did not watch his entire departure. I was too busy racing towards our burning home.

I flicked on my impermeable force field to protect myself from the flames when I got close. I plunged inside, hoping I had enough air in the small bubble around me until I found Dad. I did not even have to go through a door as the fire had burned holes in the walls. Most mobile homes were built cheaply. Ours was burning like a lit box of tissues.

The inside of our house was a scene from Dante's *Inferno*. There were not many places to search for Dad as our small house contained only two bedrooms, a bathroom, and an open area that served as both living room, dining room, kitchen, and laundry room. Thanks to how small the place was, despite all the smoke and the flames, I found Dad in seconds. He lay unmoving on the floor outside his bedroom, near the front door. Maybe he had been trying to make it outside.

Normally I would not have been strong enough to lift Dad. But now, my surging adrenaline enabled me to do it, along with a bit of an assist from my powers. I carried Dad out through a gaping hole in the side of the home. I carried him as far as I could away from the blaze before collapsing in exhaustion in the grass outside. Dad fell out of my arms into the grass face first. He did not move. His clothes were burning. I feverishly stripped off my sweater. With it, I frantically smothered the flames that licked Dad's body.

I turned Dad over. No, no, no, no, no, no. Over half of Dad's face was gone. His skull poked out of his burnt skin, white against charred black. My vision blurred, making Dad's face an impressionist's painting of a Halloween mask. I knew it wouldn't do any good, but I checked for a pulse anyway. I had a hard time doing it as I was mostly blinded by tears.

I could not find a pulse. It was not there to be found.

Amazing Man had warned me. I had been too stupid—too scared—to listen. And look at what happened. Now Dad was dead. It was all my fault. If I had left with Amazing Man to go be trained, that Meta would not have targeted our house as I would not be here. And, if I had training and then that Meta had come after us, I could have stopped the Meta before Dad died.

Dad always said life was not fair and that I might as well get used to it. I looked down at Dad's charred remains. How could I ever get used to this? I knew I never would.

That was how the cops and firefighters found me—holding Dad's burnt body, my tears trying too late to extinguish the fire that had consumed much of him. At least that's what they later told me. I did not remember seeing them. They also told me they had to pry Dad's charred dead body out of my hands. I did not remember that either.

What I did remember was the Meta's last words to me. "Rest assured that this is not over," he had said. "We'll see each other again." He was right about that. This was not over. We would see each other again. As I held Dad's lifeless body, I swore to him that Meta and I would see each other again. I would make sure of it. Someway, somehow, someday, I would.

And when we did see each other again, when I looked upon that murdering piece of filth again, I would be ready for him. Unlike when we first met, it would not be me who needed rescuing. No cop or firefighter would delay or stop our reckoning. I would learn to use my powers. No, not just learn to use them. I would embrace them. I would get so good at using them that Meta would not stand a chance against me. I would get myself ready for the happy day I met that Meta again. If I needed a Hero's license to accomplish that, so be it.

And when I did meet that Meta again, I would erase him from the face of the Earth so thoroughly not even an electron microscope would be able to find his remains.

As God as my witness I would.

CHAPTER ELEVEN

I was hospitalized for several days due to smoke inhalation, burns, and a few other things. My time spent in the hospital was a blur, like my mind was disconnected from my body. My mind was in the morgue with Dad.

Once I was discharged, I dropped out of college of course. Sitting in classrooms all day learning about syllogisms and the themes that ran through *Huckleberry Finn* seemed pretty stupid and pointless in light of what had happened. Besides, learning about those things would bring me no closer to finding the Metahuman who killed Dad. As far as I was concerned, finding him was the sole reason for my existence. Nothing else mattered.

I contacted Amazing Man through the Heroes' Guild. I told him what happened, and that I wanted to train to become a Hero after all. Amazing Man was upset about the sudden appearance of the Meta who killed Dad. He said there clearly was a leak at the center which had registered me, and that he would make sure heads would roll. Though he did not say so, I got the impression Amazing Man himself had found out about me and my Omega-level powers through the registration center. The information about me the registration center had was supposed to be held in the strictest of confidence. It was not to be the last time I learned the phrase "government secrecy" was an oxymoron.

As Amazing Man and Mr. Priebus had told me, the first step towards my goal to become a licensed Hero was to enroll in the Hero Academy. In the few months until the Academy was set to start up again, I stayed with my Uncle Charles and his wife Beth. Amazing Man arranged it so a series of Heroes took turns safeguarding me when he could not do so himself. Despite the fact I knew about the exploits of some of those Heroes—Scorpion, Delphic Oracle, and Medusa, for example—I did not enjoy constantly having a chaperone. I did not complain or try to get away from the Heroes, though. For now, I needed them. I had proven myself incapable of defending myself and the people I cared about. There was no way I was going to risk getting myself killed before I learned to properly stand up for myself and avenge Dad. Someone had to find the Meta who killed Dad, and that someone was going to be me. I had to stay alive long enough to do it. After I accomplished that, frankly I could not have cared less about what happened to me.

To enroll in the Academy, you either had to be an adult or have the permission of your legal guardian. Since I was only seventeen, that meant I needed the permission of Uncle Charles, who was now my closest living relative. He refused to let me go. He said it was too dangerous and that my parents would not have approved. I was pretty sure his real concern was that he expected me to stick around to be a farmhand on his farm whom he would not have to pay in light of the fact he would be feeding and housing me.

I spent the evening seething in frustration after that conversation with Uncle Charles. The next day, I got busy. I found a lawyer, Cathy Jenkins, who was willing to represent me pro bono as the only money I had was a couple of hundred dollars in savings from birthday money

I had gotten over the years. Finding and retaining Ms. Jenkins was not terribly hard. We lived in a small community where not too much happened. My father dying in that fire was huge news. Ms. Jenkins was more than happy to help an orphan. Most people were inherently good and would help you if they had a chance. Dad had taught me that. Another Jamesism. Though I had often rolled my eyes at them when he had said them to me, I would have given anything to hear him tell me one again.

Ms. Jenkins filed with the local court on my behalf a petition to have me legally emancipated and declared an adult. I think Amazing Man might have pulled some strings because we got a hearing on the petition in a little over a week rather than the months Ms. Jenkins had told me it normally took. That was a tense week waiting for my hearing while still living with Uncle Charles and Aunt Beth. Having to live through the tension in the house wound up being worth it. After a brief hearing, the judge emancipated me and declared me an adult. I sent in my paperwork applying to the Hero Academy that same day.

By law, the Academy was required to accept anyone who applied as long as he passed a mental and physical capacity exam as well as a background check. The background check did not worry me; I had never gotten so much as a speeding ticket. But, I had to again go to the Metahuman Registration Center in Columbia for the physical and mental exam. It was weird going there without Dad, not to mention intimidating. I still was not used to driving in a town bigger than Aiken was. I did not go there alone, though: one of my Hero guardian angels rode shotgun.

I hoped the very cute Nurse Jackie would be the one to conduct the exam. No such luck. A very male, very hairy, and very not cute guy named Doctor Martel did it instead. After I took the mental exam, Doctor Martel then examined my body so thoroughly that it kind of felt like I lost my virginity that day. He did not even have the decency to buy me dinner first.

At the end of it all, Doctor Martel cleared me to enter the Academy. I caught a glimpse of what he wrote on his report about his physical examination of me. He said I was "underdeveloped, but healthy." I hoped that was not what the girl I eventually lost my virginity to would say. Before I left the registration center, Doctor Martel gave me a thick Heroes' Guild publication. It was the manual for the Hero Academy. He admonished me to read it before I reported to the Academy. I thought I had left homework behind when I dropped out of college. I apparently was wrong.

Dad's farm and all of his equipment I sold to Uncle Charles. Ms. Jenkins advised me that the amount Uncle Charles offered me was well under market value and that I could do much better if I found another buyer. I did not need her to tell me that Uncle Charles was cheating me. I knew. I did not care. After all, I was not going to farm the land myself. The sooner I could sell it, the sooner I could start my training and find that Metahuman murderer. Uncle Charles' behavior did make me finally realize why he and Dad were never particularly close, despite the fact they had lived less than fifteen minutes away from each other. Dad never would have cheated anyone, much less a relative.

The manual Doctor Martel gave me said the grounds of the Academy were known as Camp Avatar. The grounds had been named that shortly after Avatar's death in his honor. Camp Avatar was in Oregon, right outside of Portland. I had never been to Oregon before, of course. I had never been much of anywhere. I used some of the money from the sale of the farm to buy a plane ticket to Oregon. I had thought about flying there using my powers, but I had discovered using my powers drained me. I did not think I could sustain a cross-country flight. At least not yet. Maybe one day.

The flight to Oregon was my first plane ride. It was to be the first of many firsts.

***

The bright overhead lights of the barracks flicked on. I had not gotten to Camp Avatar until late the night before. It felt like I had only been asleep for a few minutes.

"Everybody up! Put your uniforms on and stand at attention!" a deep masculine voice cried out. The words barely registered on my consciousness. I was exhausted. Groaning, I rolled over. I pulled the cot's sheets over my head to blot out the harsh lights. The cot was both hard and lumpy. If this was a dream, it sucked.

A few seconds later, I found myself twisting and falling. Crying out in surprise, I caught myself with my hands, barely keeping myself from face-planting into the cold floor of the barracks.

"What's the big idea?" I said, still groggy. I looked up to see the retreating back of Carbon Copy, one of the assistant drill instructors at Hero Academy. He wore the black mask and costume all the drill instructors here wore, along with a short white cape that extended down to the middle of his back. If he had heard me, he gave no sign. He was too busy doing to other stragglers what he had done to me, namely tilting their cots up to dump them on the floor. Other versions of Carbon Copy were doing the same throughout the cavernous room.

I got to my feet, relieved that Carbon Copy had not heard me. Even in the few short hours I had been at Camp Avatar, I had learned it was not a good idea to be lippy to the Heroes on staff. I opened the Academy-issued chest at the foot of my cot. It contained everything I owned in the world except for the money from the sale of the farm. That I had parked in my savings account until I figured out what else to do with it. I hurriedly tugged on the uniform the Academy had issued to me the day before when I arrived. It was a two-piece outfit that was red on top, black on the bottom. The colors reminded me of the uniforms *Star Trek* security officers wore in the original television series. Those officers always seemed to wind up dying within five minutes of showing up somewhere. I hoped the same would not happen to me.

The Academy uniform unfortunately fit me like a glove. I say unfortunately because a lot of the other guys in the room made me feel like a child in light of how big and muscular they were. Like me, the other trainees—that was how they referred to those of us enrolled in the Academy when we had not done something to justify a less flattering name—were hastily getting dressed under the watchful eye of Carbon Copy. Well, "eyes" really since there were several versions of him stalking the room like a lion ready to pounce on a wounded deer.

I already had my black mask on as I has slept in it. The mask was small, rounded, and only covered my eyes and the space between them. It was a domino mask, a term I had learned for the first time when I had been issued the mask along with my boots and uniform. My mask was so comfortable I had already mostly forgotten I had it on. I had no idea what held it onto my face. Fear of pissing off the drill instructors, maybe. I, like all the other trainees, had been instructed to always keep the mask on unless we wanted the other trainees to know we really looked like. Apparently there was some technology imbedded in the mask that obscured the true features of its wearer. What I needed was one that made me look like Brad Pitt.

My head was cold as I pulled on the black boots the camp had also issued me. I, like the other trainees in the room, was as bald as a cue ball. My head had been shaven right after I arrived at camp. I did not realize how much hair served to keep your head warm.

Once we were all up and dressed, Carbon Copy ordered us to line up in two lines facing each other in the center of the barracks. He told us to make sure to stand a foot away from each other. There was much jostling as this was done, punctuated by the shouts and curses of the various forms of Carbon Copy. After we were all lined up, the door to the barracks opened. Above the door was emblazoned the Academy's motto: Society Before Self.

In trooped another group of trainees, all dressed as we were. They were all women. The tightness of their uniforms made their sex delightfully all too obvious. Most of them had short hair that was pinned up. The few with long hair had it up in various forms of buns as per the guidelines in the Academy manual. Females were housed in separate barracks across camp from the rest of us. I counted them as they marched in single-file and lined up along with the rest of us. Twenty-three total. There were more male trainees than female ones, certainly more than twice as many. I did not know exactly how many. Nor did I care. The guys did not have breasts, after all. We were far less interesting to look at and count.

Once we were all lined up, the various versions of Carbon Copy went to the front of the barracks by the door. One after another, they walked into another version of Carbon Copy standing there, soundlessly merging into him like a falling raindrop merges into a puddle of water. It was freaky to watch. Not that I needed it, but it was further proof I was not in South Carolina anymore.

The door of the barracks opened again. Amazing Man strode in, dressed in his usual silver and chrome blue costume. It was the first time I had seen him in weeks. He was followed by two drill instructors in their standard black uniforms, one female, one male. The woman was pretty hot. The three of them stood near Carbon Copy, with Amazing Man at the front. Amazing Man was the tallest of the group. The drill instructors' short white capes looked cool. I wondered if they would let me wear one with my uniform.

There was the faint murmur of whispers up and down the line of trainees.

"The next person who makes a sound will have his head twisted off and used as a toilet," the female drill instructor said in a raised voice. She said it flatly and unemotionally, like she was telling us it was about to rain outside. Everyone shut up. Although no one had seen the woman before as far as I knew, there was something about her that commanded obedience. I immediately went from thinking the woman was hot to being wary of her. I liked my head right where it was, thanks very much.

"As many of you know, my name is Amazing Man," he said once everyone had quieted down. His voice carried throughout the barracks even though he did not seem to be speaking particularly loudly. "Welcome to Camp Avatar. I am the head of Hero Academy. The grounds of the Academy are named after one of the greatest Heroes the world has ever known, who as you know was recently killed. Every civilization throughout history has had elite fighters, men and women society calls on to protect and stand up for it in the darkest of times. And to die for it, if necessary, just as Avatar did. The Roman Empire had its legions. The Aztecs had the Jaguar Warriors. The Japanese had the samurai. The United States military has the Seals and the Green Berets. We have you. Or rather, who you aspire to be—Heroes. Our mission at the Academy is to train each of you to become a Hero, to give you the tools you will need to wrestle with an uncertain and dangerous world. Your path will not be easy. Nothing worthwhile ever is. But, if you work hard and earn your place among us Heroes, I will be proud to call you my brothers and sisters."

With that, Amazing Man turned with a swirl of his long white cape. He left the barracks. For a bit, no one moved or said a word. You could have heard a pin drop, it was that quiet.

Then, the masked female instructor Amazing Man had walked in with stepped forward. She started to walk slowly between the two lines of us trainees. She was tall for a woman, and her shoes made her taller still. Her high-heeled, almost knee-high boots clicked loudly against the hard floor. They were black, shiny, and sexy. I did not have a shoe fetish, but I could learn to have one looking at her. She had alabaster skin, with a build like a fitness model and the looks to match. Her long glossy black hair was done up in a sock bun. Like Carbon Copy, she had on an all-black costume; unlike him, she filled it out far more interestingly. Her black mask was shaped like mine was. Her short white cape was bordered with red.

As she walked, the woman looked at each of us as if we were dog turds she had found at the bottom of her shoes. She shook her head slowly and sorrowfully as she surveyed us.

"I don't know what I did in a past life to deserve this," she said. Her voice was deep and throaty. "Whatever it was, it must have been a doozy. I have never seen such a pathetic and unlikely group of wannabe Heroes in my life. Apparently the only Metas who want to become Heroes these days look like they have a combination of mental retardation and consumption. Oh well. You work with the raw material you're given, even if it looks like raw sewage. God help me." She said it all as if she was talking to herself, but her voice carried. I was sure everyone heard her. I knew I did. Her words made me feel even punier than I already did in my tight uniform.

"My name is Athena," the woman said in a louder voice. "But you haven't earned the right to call me that yet. As far as you wet behind the ears infants are concerned, I have three names: ma'am, yes ma'am, and no ma'am. Is that understood?" A handful of people mumbled. Not me. I kept my trap shut. I had not forgotten that Athena had threatened to twist people's heads off if they spoke.

Athena shook her head at the tepid response. "You people make me believe in reincarnation. Nobody could learn to be this stupid in one lifetime." She raised her voice to a roar. "I asked you infants if you understood." The barracks thundered with "Yes ma'ams." Mine was among the loudest now. I had no interest in being singled out for attention by this woman. I had gone from thinking Athena was hot to being wary of her to being absolutely terrified of her.

"I am a licensed Hero," she said loudly. "I am also the senior drill instructor here at the Academy. Amazing Man, as you have heard, is the head of the Academy. As far as you infants are concerned though, he is God and I am his chief prophet. Near the door are Carbon Copy and Sprint, two of the drill instructors here. You will know who the drill instructors are because we all wear the same black costume and the same short white capes. If we or Amazing Man tell you to do something, you had better be doing it before the words are completely out of our mouths. If you don't, I will make you wish you had never been born. I will hurt you so badly that your ancestors will feel it. I will make your horny granddaddy rue the day he ever went into that two-dollar brothel to knock up your grandmother." Athena glared at us balefully. I believed her.

"Our mission here is to train each of you to become a Hero. In the very unlikely event you prove yourself worthy, most of you will leave here to apprentice with an already licensed Hero to complete your education and training. Most of you will not prove worthy. That is as it should be. Becoming a Hero is not a right. It is a privilege earned with blood, sweat, and tears. This is not the namby-pamby, soft, politically correct world you infants come from. There are no medals for participation here, no praise for merely showing up, no quotas, no grading on a curve because of what somebody's ancestors did to your great-great-great grandfather, and certainly no affirmative action. I don't care what color you are, what your religion is, who you sleep with, how much money you have, who your daddy is, or what a special snowflake your momma wrongfully told you you are. You're all equally worthless here until you've put in the work to prove to me you're worthy of wearing a Hero's cape. The women and men who have earned their right to wear a Hero's cape have fought off supervillains bent on world conquest, repulsed aliens who wanted to enslave humanity, averted catastrophes, and saved more people than you can ever count. You will not sully that proud tradition by either word or deed. A Hero never lies, cheats, steals, compromises, or quits. And neither will you. If you do, I will shove my foot so far up your butt you will think you're having anal sex with a sequoia. I will—" She stopped, suddenly shoving her face into mine. "Is something funny infant?" she yelled into my face. A bit of her spit hit my face. I realized with a start I had grinned at her sequoia remark.

I wiped the grin off my face, but not the spittle. I knew better.

"No," I said. "Uh, I mean no ma'am."

"What is your name infant?" She had to bend down a bit to put her face into mine. I felt like the infant she called me.

"Theodore—" I closed my mouth abruptly. I had almost added my last name. I remembered reading in the Academy manual how I should not reveal my real name. Most of the people in the Academy would not become Heroes, and we trainees were supposed to keep our real names private. "My friends call me Theo," I added instead, immediately regretting it. It sounded lame, even to me.

Athena rolled her eyes heavenward so hard I thought I could hear them moving.

"Does it look like I want to be your friend, Theodore?" she yelled. The way she said my name, it sounded like a curse word.

"No ma'am."

"Theodore means 'gift of god' in Greek," she said. "Do you think you're god's gift to the rest of us?"

"No ma'am." I had not known that about my name.

"Then why did you choose Theodore as a code name?"

Too late I realized my mistake.

"It's not a code name ma'am. It's my real name." The look in her eyes made me think she already knew that. I had a sudden flash of suspicion that she knew all there was to know about me and everyone else in the room.

"Didn't you read in the manual you were given that you were supposed to select a code name?"

"Yes ma'am. I forgot," I said honestly. What with leaving home for the first time and all of the information packed in the Academy manual, I had not given any thought to what my code name should be. I suspected Athena was not interested in my excuses, so I did not elaborate on why I forgot.

"You forgot?" Athena repeated mockingly, drawling the last word. She suddenly had a deep Southern accent. I realized she was imitating me. Did I really sound like that? "Where are you from, Theodore?" she drawled in the same mocking accent. I felt all of two inches tall.

"South Carolina, ma'am."

"South Carolina, ma'am," she repeated in the same accent. "Since you can't be bothered to pick a code name on your own, I'm going to select one for you. For the duration of your training, your name is Carolina. Does that suit you, Carolina?" It did not, but I was certainly was not going to tell her that. Besides, I was starting to get irritated. I did not like being made fun of. I had gotten made fun of far too often in my life.

"Does a bear shit in the woods?" I asked in response. There was a whisper of a smile of Athena's face. It disappeared so quickly I thought I had imagined it, replaced by the same scowl she had been favoring me with since I had drawn attention to myself.

"Carolina, report to my quarters at oh seven hundred hours tomorrow morning. Between now and then you will memorize the page of the manual that discusses how you were to select a code name. You will recite that page to me by heart. Perhaps that will aid in your reading comprehension. And, since you're so interested in excrement, after that you will clean the men's latrine. I want to be able to eat off the toilets by the time you're finished."

Athena moved on before I could get out a dismayed "Yes, ma'am." She started to berate someone who had laughed at my bear comment. He was a light-skinned black guy a few people down from where I stood. He told Athena his name was Myth. I hoped she would make him help me clean the latrines.

Misery loves company.

CHAPTER TWELVE

Athena and the other drill instructors led us outside after Athena berated Myth and then finished giving the rest of us the world's worst pep talk. The way she talked, we trainees were too stupid to come in out of the rain, much less to become Heroes.

Outside, Camp Avatar looked exactly like that—a camp. It was as if someone had cut down a huge circle in the middle of a massive Oregon forest, and then plopped down several buildings in the middle of it. With much cursing and questioning of our intelligence, the instructors lined us up in rows in front of them, near the edge of the surrounding woods. Once we were finally in place, Athena surveyed us with her hands on her hips. She looked disdainful.

"Well, you've already proven yourselves too stupid to line up properly," she said. "I've half a mind to tell you all to go home and to start off fresh with a more likely group of trainees. Can any of you infants at least fight?" No one said anything. Everyone was so quiet, I could hear someone's stomach rumbling. Athena's face grew even more contemptuous. "Come on. Nobody? I'm not asking you to take on all the drill instructors at once. Just little ol' me. Surely there's somebody among you who's not scared of a woman."

"I ain't scared," came a voice from behind me.

"Oh good, someone who's not a complete coward. I was starting to think I'd have to give you all a testosterone transfusion. Step up so I can see you," Athena said. A hulk of a man squeezed from out of the lines and stood before Athena and the rest of us. Though he did not look to be much older than I, he was well over six feet and a half tall, and as broad as the side of a barn. He was a mountain of a guy. Even his muscles had muscles. He made the Three Horsemen look like malnourished children.

"What's your name?" Athena asked the massive guy. As tall as she was, he towered over her.

"Brute," he said. Of course that was his name. As far as I was concerned, a guy that size could call himself Tinker Bell and I would happily call him that with a straight face.

"And your powers?"

"Strength." It came out as more of a grunt than a word. Brute did not seem like the sharpest tool in the shed. Maybe when you were the size of a shed, you did not have to be. He was white, hairy, and had a low, sloping forehead and a jaw that jutted out. His jaw looked like it was designed to chew boulders. Brute looked like the missing link between modern humans and our caveman ancestors.

"Looking at you, I can't say I'm surprised super strength is your power," Athena said. "All right Brute, attack me."

Brute hesitated. "You sure? Don't wanna hurt you." Athena smiled at him condescendingly.

"It's adorable that you think you could. Just attack."

A confident smirk sprouted on Brute's big dumb face. He twisted his head from side to side. His neck popped a few times. It sounded like exploding firecrackers.

With no further warning, Brute suddenly rushed Athena. His hands were outstretched. I thought Athena was about to be ground to a pulp. I did not feel too badly for her; I was looking forward to her getting her comeuppance for her cockiness and dubbing me Carolina.

What happened next happened too fast for me to completely follow. But what I think happened is this: Athena stood rock still as Brute rushed towards her. Right as he was about to grab her, she stepped out of the way, grabbing one of his extended arms. She turned and twisted, using Brute's momentum against him to throw him over her back. Brute flipped in the air. He then hit the ground back-first with a bone-rattling thump. He moaned weakly and stayed down.

Athena stood over Brute. She bent over and looked at him carefully.

"I'm pretty sure I just knocked the breath out of you and didn't really hurt you," she said to him, not unkindly. Not a hair on her head was out of place. She was not even breathing hard. "But we'll take you to the infirmary to check you out just to be sure. If you're all right, I'll start teaching you how to channel your strength rather than merely rushing forward blindly. Carbon Copy, will you do the honors?" Carbon Copy nodded. Two identical versions of him stepped out of the Hero. It was like watching a cell divide under a microscope. The two new versions of Carbon Copy grabbed a stretcher. They loaded Brute on it with the help of a couple of trainees they drafted for the purpose. Struggling a bit under Brute's dead weight, the two Carbon Copies lifted Brute off the ground. Then, with the stretcher between the two of them, the Carbon Copy versions trudged slowly off towards the infirmary.

Athena turned her attention to the rest of us again. An arrogant smirk was back in her face. It was in stark contrast to how she had just sympathetically spoken to Brute.

"In case you all were wondering, unlike Brute I'm not super strong," she said. "Nor am I super-fast, nor do I have super reflexes. What I just did there to Brute any of you can do. You will be able to do it by the time we're done with you. If you don't wash out first, that is. All right, despite the fact he was as graceful as his name implies, at least Brute was not a coward. Anybody else with the stones to fight me?"

I knew better than to volunteer. I had little doubt after that display with Brute that Athena could handle me with one hand tied behind her back. With both hands tied behind her back, maybe. And, I had not even seen her use her powers yet. I marveled at the ease with which she had handled Brute. If I could learn to fight like her, I bet I would be able to handle the Meta who had killed Dad.

"I'll take a stab at it," came another voice from the ranks behind me. A wiry little guy stepped forward. He was short and small, even smaller than I. Even so, he walked with a confident strut. He reminded me of the bantam roosters Uncle Charles kept on his farm.

"Name?" Athena asked.

"Nimbus," the wiry guy said.

"Powers?"

"I can fly, plus I can shoot energy beams. What about yours?"

"You'll find out soon enough," Athena said. "That is your first lesson of the day—never volunteer to an opponent what your abilities are. It gives her a chance to prepare for you. Are you ready?"

"Born ready," Nimbus said.

Without no further ado, Athena sprang towards Nimbus like a pouncing cat. She was fast. But, Nimbus was faster. A white and yellow energy field suddenly surrounded him. He rocketed up above us, leaving Athena clutching at air where Nimbus had been an instant before. Nimbus turned in mid-air. His clenched fists stretched out in front of him, pointing towards Athena. A blast of the same yellowish-white energy that surrounded Nimbus shot out from his fists towards Athena. Athena moved to the left, easily dodging the blast. It hit the ground with a loud concussion, making my teeth rattle. An odor like what you smelled after a lightning strike filled the air.

Something long and narrow appeared in Athena's hand out of seemingly thin air. She spun whatever it was quickly at her side, like she was turning a jump rope. She released the spinning object, sending it shooting towards Nimbus overhead. He tried to dart to the side to avoid it. Too late. The object wrapped around him like a piece of wound string. Now that the object was still, I recognized it. It was bolas, a weapon with weights on the ends of interconnected cords. I had seen pictures of them, but I had never seen one in action before.

A visible spark of current ran along the length of the bolas. Nimbus cried out in surprise and pain. The glow of energy around him flickered for a moment. He fell slowly out of the sky, like a punctured helium balloon. He crumpled onto the ground. Athena quickly moved over to where he had fallen and stood over him. She rolled him over with her foot, pressing her boot against his chest. Nimbus struggled against both his bonds and her boot. A sword flickered into existence in Athena's hand. She held the point of the sword against Nimbus' neck. Its blade looked razor sharp. Nimbus stopped struggling.

"You have a bolas wrapped around you," Athena said to Nimbus, her voice raised so we could all hear her. Despite her raised voice, her tone was conversational, like she was describing what the weather was like. "It's electrified to disrupt the powers of most Metas. As you should have surmised by now, my Metahuman power is the ability to generate any known weapon. From anything as simple as this sword here to a nuclear bomb." She paused. "Do you yield?" she asked Nimbus.

"I suppose I don't have a choice," he said. He sounded frustrated and somewhat deflated.

"No you don't," Athena said. "Not unless you want your throat sliced open." The sword in her hand and the bolas around Nimbus disappeared. Athena helped Nimbus up. He brushed himself off while shaking his head. He returned to our ranks.

"If that's the best you infants can do, I and the other instructors have got our work cut out for us in trying to make you into anything resembling Heroes," Athena said to us. "It'll be like trying to carve a statue out of a steaming pile of dog-doo. If no one else wants to embarrass themselves, let's get to work. Split up into—oh wait, here's a new masochist after all."

One of the trainees had quietly stepped out of the ranks and in front of Athena. She was of average height, slender and toned, and maybe a little older than I. She had shiny black hair that was up in a braided bun. Her skin was olive-colored. Her skin tone, along with the aquiline shape of her nose, made me conclude she was of Indian descent. The Asian kind of Indian, not a Native American. This trainee was pretty, but evidently not too bright. You would not have caught me volunteering to take on Athena. A wise man learned from the mistakes of others.

"Name?" Athena asked of the trainee.

"Smoke," she said. Her voice was clear and firm, with just the slightest hint of an accent.

"Powers?" Athena asked.

Smoke smiled a bit. "Stylishness," she said. She seemed entirely sure of herself. Then again, so had Brute and Nimbus.

Athena actually smiled back at her. I thought the expression might break her face. I had thought it was permanently etched with a scowl.

"See?" Athena said to the rest of us. "That is the way you should answer that question when an opponent asks. Don't volunteer information."

Athena and Smoke separated from the rest of us a bit, getting close to a copse of tall trees.

"Ready?" Athena asked. Smoke nodded. Athena quickly closed the gap between her and Smoke. Smoke remained still. Athena let loose a roundhouse kick that I thought was going to take Smoke's head off. At the last moment, Smoke's head became translucent and misty-looking, like it was made out of a grey cloud. Athena's kick passed right through Smoke's head like it was, well, smoke. Athena was thrown off-balance and staggered, struggling to regain her balance since her kick had unexpectedly met with no resistance. Smoke hit Athena with two quick punches in the torso. Athena danced back out of Smoke's reach. Smoke pushed forward towards Athena. Her whole body became gaseous and pink, and it spread out to engulf Athena's body. Athena tried to move out of the gassy area, but Smoke's gaseous form followed like she was Athena's second skin. Athena coughed, staggering slightly. She looked up. She was under a thick branch that was high up on a tree. Athena lifted her hand. A bulky, silver-colored gun with a grappling hook on the end of the barrel suddenly appeared in her hand. Athena pulled the gun's trigger. The grappling hook shot out of the gun with a loud blast. A long and thin metallic cable extended out, running from the end of the ascending grappling hook back into the gun. The grappling hook wrapped around the overhead tree branch.

Holding onto the bulky gun with both hands, Athena quickly ascended out of the gaseous area Smoke had formed. Tendrils of pink gas ran down from Athena's body as she shot upwards. Once she was clear of the gas, Athena let go of the gun. Athena fell towards the ground in an arc, clear of the gas. Athena landed, rolling gracefully to her feet. She turned towards where she had left Smoke's gaseous form behind.

Still in vapor form, Smoke surged towards Athena. A backpack containing two big tanks formed on Athena's back, connected by black tubing to a gun-like wand in her hands. Athena suddenly looked like a Ghostbuster wielding a proton pack. Athena aimed the wand in the direction of the approaching gas. A jet of flame licked out of the wand Athena held. The thing on Athena's back was obviously a flamethrower. The flame did not hit Smoke as Athena was not aiming it directly at her. Rather, the stream of flame extended out like a fiery tongue slightly above and to the right of the mass of Smoke's gas. The mass of gas visibly recoiled from the flames near it. The gas collapsed in on itself, away from the flames, quickly coalescing into the form of a figure. Smoke reappeared, crouching on the ground.

As soon as Smoke became corporeal again, Athena's flamethrower disappeared, leaving behind the smell of fuel in the air. Another gun appeared in Athena's hands, this one looking a bit like a sawed-off shotgun, only far more high-tech looking. Athena fired the new gun at Smoke's crouching body. There was not the usual sound of gunfire I would have expected. Rather, there was more of a low whistling sound as a mass shot out of the end of Athena's gun. The mass expanded as it flew towards Smoke. It was a net. The net landed on Smoke. It constricted around Smoke like it was an animal trying to squeeze her to death. Visible sparks of current ran along the webbing of the net. It looked similar to the current that had neutralized Nimbus. Smoke struggled against the netting. But, the more she struggled, the tighter the net constricted around her.

Athena walked up to Smoke's struggling form.

"Do you yield?" Athena asked. She had to ask again before the question seemed to sink into Smoke. Smoke stopped struggling against the net. Smoke nodded.

The net around Smoke disappeared as if it had never existed. Smoke stood. She shook her head both ruefully and with appreciation.

"How did you know I was flammable when I was in my knockout gas form?" Smoke asked Athena.

"I've encountered that gas before," Athena said. "I recognized the smell. Who trained you? You clearly have combat experience."

Smoke hesitated for the briefest of moments before answering. "Doctor Alchemy," she said. She said the name almost like a challenge, as if she expected Athena to make something of it. There were audible gasps in the ranks of trainees behind me. There was some ugly muttering until Sprint yelled at us to shut up.

Like others obviously had, I recognized the name Doctor Alchemy. It would be more surprising if I did not recognize the name. Doctor Alchemy was a supervillain. Actually, that understated the reality of the situation. Saying Doctor Alchemy was a supervillain was like saying George Washington was a President: it was technically true, but still understated the facts of the matter. If there was a Mount Rushmore of supervillains, Doctor Alchemy would be on it. In his own way Doctor Alchemy was as famous as Avatar, though maybe it would be more accurate to say Doctor Alchemy was infamous rather than famous the way Avatar was. Among other things, Doctor Alchemy was the supervillain who had tortured and killed Wildside, a very popular and well-respected Hero. That killing and other monstrous deeds had made Doctor Alchemy one of the most hated of all the supervillains.

Why in the world was someone who had been trained by a supervillain like Doctor Alchemy at the Academy?

"I see," Athena said simply in response to Smoke's revelation. "Doctor Alchemy trained you well then. You're the only one today who even came close to giving me a run for my money. Return to the ranks." Smoke did so. A few trainees gave her dirty looks.

Athena proceeded to lead us through a series of rigorous body-weight exercises. I was relieved when they were finally over. My arms and legs were rubbery. My torso burned. I was exhausted and dripping with sweat. I could have used a nap. I did not get one though, as the day was not nearly over. The body-weight exercises were apparently just a warm-up. Half of us trainees were sent to the gym with Carbon Copy. It was housed in a building on the other side of the camp. The rest of us, including me, went for a run through trails in the surrounding woods with Sprint and Athena. Lucky us.

We did not run to the Moon and back, but it sure felt like it. Athena encouraged us during the run, if you could call what she said to us encouragement. I did not know how she ran just as far as we did in heels, but she did. As she easily kept pace with us, she questioning our parentage, our hygiene, our ability to fight anything more formidable than a one-legged elderly woman on dialysis, and our worthiness to breathe the same air as her and Sprint. Her ability to belittle us without once using a curse word was remarkable. I might have admired it had I not been one of the targets of it. Sometimes Athena ran backwards as she singled out a straggler for special attention. I knew because I was one of those stragglers. I was not used to running that hard or that far. I was convinced that my lungs would collapse and that my heart would explode.

And oh, did I mention that about halfway through the run it started to rain? Hard. After a while, I didn't know if I should continue running or start swimming.

Once we runners returned to Camp Avatar, our group hit the weights in the gym under Athena's critical eye and even more critical mouth. The other half of the trainees who had lifted weights while we had run left to go for a run with Carbon Copy. Other than the few of us trainees who were gifted with superhuman endurance, most of us looked like we were going to be sick. A few of us were.

I sat on a weight bench with a trash pail pressed between my legs. I felt like I had just thrown up every meal I had in my entire life. As I tried to recover from throwing up what felt like all of my internal organs, I looked over at Athena. She was encouraging a pudgy and pasty trainee who lay on a bench and was struggling under a loaded barbell. By "encouraging," I mean she was berating him. Despite having run with us, Athena looked as fresh as a daisy as she yelled at the guy. I looked down between my legs. I wondered what a daisy would look like with a pailful of puke dripping down it. Could I send it over to her with my powers without her knowing where it came from?

Then I remembered how easily Athena had dealt with Brute, Nimbus, and Smoke. I shuddered at what I had thought about doing. Exhaustion and puking my guts out had made me go temporarily insane.

As if she could read my mind, Athena looked over her shoulder at me.

"Enough goldbricking, Carolina," she barked at me. "Get up and shake a leg. Those weights won't squat themselves."

Suppressing a groan, I put the trash can down. I got up. My legs were wobbly. My body felt like an old man's. Then I had a sudden terrifying thought:

What if Athena actually can read minds? God help us!

CHAPTER THIRTEEN

At the end of the first day, we trainees assembled in the mess hall for dinner. None of the instructors were present. Enough food to choke a herd of elephants was arranged in the center of the hall buffet-style. Long tables were arranged around the room, with bench seats on either side of them. Each trainee had been issued dietary guidelines that were specially tailored to each of our bodies based on our earlier physical examinations. My guidelines were a page long and talked a lot about my metabolic rate, carbohydrate loading, amino acid diversification, and a bunch of other stuff that sounded like bro science. But it could all be boiled down to a one sentence mandate: Eat more, and more often.

Even so, I would have thought I would be too tired to eat when I dragged myself into the mess hall. My body felt like I had competed in the Olympics right after having run a marathon backwards. But, when the smell of the food hit me, I realized I was ravenous. I inhaled my first plate. I was not sure if I even chewed. I might have just swallowed the heaping pile of food whole, boa constrictor-style.

I got up from the table, fixed myself a second helping, and returned to my table. Everyone knew me thanks to

Athena yelling at me. They all called me Carolina. I did not correct them. When Athena had dubbed me that, I thought the name would then be used by my fellow trainees to make fun of me. That was not the case. They called me Carolina endearingly, like it was a cool nickname. I never had a cool nickname before. I was usually on the outside of social circles looking in. I got called names, not nicknames. That was not the case here. Though we had not even spent a full twenty-four hours together, we trainees had all been through a lot together already. Besides, we did not have the energy to waste by picking on one another. We focused our energy on a common enemy: the drill instructors, especially Athena. Since I had been the first to be singled-out by Athena, everyone seemed to like me even though they knew nothing about me. It was a "the enemy of my enemy is my friend" kind of thing. I was popular for the first time in . . . well, ever really. I wondered how long it would last.

"Next time, I'm gonna screw her head off her body like it's a beer cap," Brute said about Athena. He went on to detail what he would do to her next. There was a lot of smashing and stomping involved. Brute was one of the dozen or so trainees at my table. It turned out Brute had not been hurt when he had been slammed to the ground by Athena, so he had worked out with the rest of us after being cleared by the infirmary's doctor. I seriously doubted Brute would be able to do as he said. I did not think he would be up to doing anything to Athena she didn't want him to do, even after he trained more. Too much brawn, not enough brains. Besides, he was talking too much about what he would do to Athena. Like Dad always said, the biggest talkers were usually the smallest doers. I of course kept my thoughts about Brute's threats to myself.

Some of the guys at the table jumped in on what Brute said to add what they would also do to Athena and other the drill instructors. The statements were vulgar, funny, biologically improbable, almost certainly illegal, and unlikely to ever occur. I threw in my two cents as well. It felt good to blow off some steam. The camaraderie felt good too. I was not used to it.

"Some of the girls got together and told Athena the girls shouldn't have the same physical requirements the boys do," Smartphone interjected. She was a big blocky girl with short platinum blonde hair. "I was there when they did it. They told her it wasn't fair."

"What did Athena say about that?" I asked.

"She said, and I quote, 'If you want fair, enroll in a fancy women-only liberal arts college, take your teddy bears, blankies and trigger warnings to their most comfy safe space, and watch an *Oprah Winfrey Show* marathon about how to actualize your best self. If you want to be a Hero, you'll do exactly what the males have to do, and you'll shut up while you're doing it. Supervillains won't go easy on you because you're female. You're here to be trained, not coddled.'" Smartphone had an eidetic memory. If she said that was what Athena had said, I believed her.

An argument soon broke out about whether the physical requirements should be lowered for females. I did not have a dog in the fight. Besides, I was hungry again despite having polished off my second plate of food. So, I got up and fixed myself a third plate from the buffet table. As I did so, I noticed Smoke sitting at the far edge of a table at the end of the mess hall. While she was not alone at the table, the six or so others at the long table sat on the other end of the table far from Smoke. They were carefully ignoring her. The fact Smoke had trained with a notorious supervillain clearly had not gone down well with the other trainees.

I felt badly for Smoke. I knew what it was like to not feel like you a part of the larger group. When I was in the fifth grade, I had run for class vice-president. The election rules had said I had to have a campaign manager, which involved zero work other than the fact you would have to say you were my campaign manager. Not a single kid in my class would agree to be my campaign manager. I had been that big of a social outcast, mainly because I was more than just a little nerdy and because I was seen as little more than the dirt my Dad farmed on. I never forgot that incident and others like it that happened throughout my life. More to the point, I had never forgotten how those incidents had made me feel.

That was why, though I knew I was risking my newfound and unaccustomed social cred, I took my plate over to Smoke's table.

"Hi!" I said to her. I was quite the smooth talker. Cary Grant from one of those old movies did not have anything on me.

Smoke looked up at me. Her eyes were hazel, and quite the contrast to her darker skin. I was struck again by how pretty she was.

"Hi yourself."

"Do you mind if I join you?"

Smoke glanced around. The people on the end of the table were staring at us from the corners of their eyes while pretending not to. "Aren't you scared of catching my cooties?" Smoke asked me. "I seem to have a particularly virulent strain of them."

"I'm a Hero trainee. I'm not scared of cooties. Cooties are scared of me." I winced, and sat down. "That sounded way cooler in my head, by the way."

"I would hope so." She smiled at me. Her teeth were white and even, like she had spent a lot of money on dental care.

"The name's Carolina," I said, extending my hand over the table. I winced again. I sounded like a character in a bad Western. Smoke took my hand.

"I know. I saw your run-in with Athena. My name's Smoke."

"I know. I saw your run-in with her too. You have a bit of an accent. Where are you from?"

"You're one to talk about accents Mr. South Carolina," she said with a slight smile. "I was born in Gujarat." My face must have looked blank because she added, "It's a state in western India. I was raised here in the U.S., though."

We fell silent. I was at a loss for what else to say. I had not planned this out beyond the go over and say hello stage. I looked down at Smoke's plate. There was no meat there, only vegetable-based dishes.

"Are you a vegetarian?" I asked, grateful for the lifeline.

"Yes. I'm Hindu. I very occasionally eat meat, but I generally avoid it."

"Not me. I'll eat anything as long as it's dead. Sometimes even if it's just moving slowly."

"Note to self: don't die or move slowly."

We both laughed. The ice was broken. I asked her about Hinduism. I had never met a Hindu before. We talked for a long while about that, life in India, and a bunch of different things as the conversations of the other trainees swirled around us. I wanted to find out the story about her being trained by a supervillain, but I did not want Smoke to think that was why I approached her. So, I did not ask. Besides, after talking to her for a while, I did not care if or why Smoke was trained by a supervillain.

I liked her.

***

Several trainees quit the Academy that first night, including most of that group of girls who had asked Athena to have different physical standards for males and females. We all had the right to quit, at any time and for any reason. It said so right here in the Academy manual, part of which I stayed up late memorizing after lights out using a pen light Carbon Copy lent me. The manual made clear that if you did quit the Academy, you could never return. You certainly could never go on to become a licensed Hero.

Honestly, lying there in the dark straining my eyes reading, I kind of felt like quitting too. Despite the fact I had enjoyed my chat with Smoke and the camaraderie of the other trainees, I was not used to being yelled at, embarrassed, humiliated, and pushing my body like I was a slave on a cotton plantation. Everything on my body hurt except my eyelashes. Even they did not feel quite right.

I might have quit had I not had a picture of the Meta who murdered Dad firmly in my mind's eye, like a target I was aiming at.

After finally memorizing the page I needed to recite to Athena the next morning, I flicked off the pen light. The room was dark. Some of the guys in the barracks were snoring. Dad had snored too. The familiar sound made me sad. It also made me very homesick for a home that no longer existed. Though I was surrounded by dozens of people, I felt both alone and lonely.

I rolled over in my cot. I winced as I pulled the thin cover over my head. Muscles I did not even know I had hurt. I buried my face into my pillow. I felt sorry for myself. I am not proud to say I cried a little before finally drifting off to sleep, but that's exactly what I did. I prayed no one heard me.

In my troubled dreams I saw, as I often did, the masked face of the Meta who killed Dad.

CHAPTER FOURTEEN

Reveille sounded at 0600 the next morning. I tried to sit up in my barracks cot. My body refused. I was sore all over, but especially in my legs. I could barely move them. I felt like a well-tenderized steak.

The world spun. Suddenly I was on the cold floor. I looked up to see Carbon Copy walking away, doing the same thing he had done to me to others who had not gotten up promptly. If I had been able to move my sore arms, I might have tried to choke him.

At exactly 0700 hours, full from breakfast and feeling only slightly less like death warmed over, I stood in front of Athena in her quarters. Her furnishings were unsurprisingly spartan and cold. I recited to her the page of the Academy manual she had made me memorize. She read a book as I spoke, not even looking at me. I wondered if she was even listening. I also wondered if she was reading about the Spanish Inquisition. Looking for tips, maybe. I sneaked a peek at her book as I recited. It was in another language. It could have been Spanish. Then again, it could have been Inuit. I only knew English. Even with English I sometimes questioned my fluency.

I finished my recitation. There was silence for a few

moments, which was broken only by the sound of Athena turning the page of the book she was reading.

"You left out the word 'appropriately' from the last sentence of the second paragraph," Athena finally said, still not looking at me. I was dubious; I had lost a lot of sleep perfecting my memorization of that page. I was not about to argue with her though. "But for now, that's close enough. I expect perfection the next time, Carolina. Remember that details matter. A small detail can mean the difference between life and death. You can go now. I believe the men's latrine awaits you. Be sure to only use your powers to clean it."

"My powers?" I didn't know I was allowed to use them here without a Hero looking over my shoulder as I did so.

"Yes, your powers. We're here to teach you how to be a superhero, not how to be a maid."

I hesitated, unsure if she was finished with me. Athena looked up. She made a shooing motion with her book. "Why are you still here? Go."

So, I went. I was met at the men's latrine by the tall, light-skinned black guy who had laughed at my bear pooping in the woods remark the day before. After dressing him down, Athena had told him to clean the latrine along with me.

We were both armed with cleaning supplies from the camp's supply building. We went inside the latrine. Both of us immediately winced. The smell that greeted us would have gagged a hog. I held my hand up to my nose. It helped, but not much. I wanted to close my eyes too. The filth we saw looked like something out of a horror movie. I had used the latrine yesterday, but it was way worse in here today than it was yesterday.

"Were these guys raised in a barn?" I asked. "It's a real shitstorm in here."

"No shit, Sherlock," the other guy said. I laughed, then caught myself.

"Don't make me laugh. I can't hold my breath and

laugh at the same time. You'd think the Heroes who run this place would be able to afford cleaning people."

"I asked Carbon Copy about that before I came here. He looked at me like it was a stupid question and said, 'You trainees are our cleaning people.'"

"Wow," I said. "The shit really does roll downhill doesn't it?"

"You ain't shittin'. The problem is, I'm no expert on cleaning bathrooms. I don't know shit from Shinola."

I grinned at him. "How many puns do you think we can come up with to help us put off cleaning this place?"

"A shit-ton," he said. He grinned back at me. "I'm Myth, by the way." He was dressed like I was, in his trainee uniform and mask. Like all the male trainees, his head was shaved. He was a couple of inches taller than I, and a bit older as well. His skin was the color of a light brown leather. His hands were covered with long, straight black hair. I wondered if he was hairy all over. If so, he might look like part wolfman naked.

"I'm Carolina." We shook hands.

"Yeah, I know. I heard yesterday when Athena got up in your face. If it's all the same with you, I'll call you Theo. I don't want you to think I'm making fun of you by calling you Carolina. You can't help how you sound. It's like making fun of someone from England for speaking with a British accent."

"Of course you can call me Theo," I said. I liked Myth already. I looked around again. I did not like the task facing us, though. "I wonder if the females' latrine is this gross."

Myth grinned. His brown eyes danced behind his mask. "I don't know. But, I'm willing to do a surprise inspection and find out if you are."

I glanced down at the bucket of cleaning supplies in Myth's hand. "Athena told me we have to use our powers to clean this place. What can you do?"

"I can assume the appearance and ability of various

mythological creatures. I've only mastered a few shapes, but the more I practice and study different cultures' myths, the more creatures I can turn into."

"That's pretty cool," I said honestly. "How did you find out you could do that?"

"I was watching *Game of Thrones* one night, and there was a scene showing dragons. I thought, 'You know, it must be pretty cool to be a dragon.' And then, all of a sudden, I was one." He shook his head at the memory. "Almost scared my mother to death. When I opened my mouth to reassure her it was me, I accidentally almost cooked her to death too by breathing fire. Not to mention caving in the roof of our house. What about you?"

"I'm a telekinetic. My powers manifested themselves when I got into a fight in my college bathroom."

"And here you are in a bathroom again. It's the Metahuman circle of life." Myth looked around, disgust evident on his face. "'You should become a licensed Hero,' they said. 'It will be exciting,' they said. 'You'll be able to help a lot of people,' they said." He shook his head ruefully. "If they could see me now, surrounded by piss and poo. I feel like Hercules at his Fifth Labor."

"What?"

"Sorry. I read a lot of mythology because of my powers. I forget sometimes not everybody is a walking fountain of myth trivia. During the fifth of the Twelve Labors of the Greek and Roman demigod Hercules, he had to clean out the Augean Stables, which had not been cleaned out in decades. He diverted the path of a couple of rivers to wash out all the filth." Myth snapped his fingers. "Actually, that gives me an idea." He sketched out his idea to me. We agreed to try it.

As I watched, Myth closed his eyes. He started to glow a bit, like the hands of one of those glow-in-the-dark watches. He started to shrink in on himself, like a collapsing building. Glossy and wavy black hair sprouted out of his bald head, growing until it reached well past his shoulders. His body became more rounded, more feminine. His hips swelled; full breasts formed. The rest of his body became even more slender than how Myth had started out. His skin went from brown to a blueish-green. The shape of his face changed, becoming more angular, with a smaller nose and poutier mouth than Myth had started off with.

The slight glow Myth had been giving off during his transformation stopped. He—or rather, she—opened her eyes. Unlike the brown eye color Myth had started with, these eyes were azure and pupilless, surrounded by long, thick eyelashes. Her skin and Academy uniform had beads of water on them, as if she had just stepped out of a pool.

Much shorter now, Myth looked up at me. She saw the look on my face. She stomped her foot in a way I can only describe as daintily.

"Stop staring at me like that," she demanded. Her voice was high, like an anime character's. "This is what a Naiad—a water nymph—looks like."

"Oh I don't doubt it," I said. I was trying not to laugh. Myth balled her tiny fists.

"If you so much as giggle I swear I'll punch you in the throat." It was like being barked at by a Chihuahua.

"I'm not sure you can reach that high," I said. "You're very pretty when you're angry. If this whole Hero thing doesn't work out for you, you can always try Little Person beauty pageants." Myth raised her small clenched fist threateningly, advancing a step. Laughing, I backed up. I tripped on one of the mops we had brought, and fell backwards. Acting instinctively, I caught myself with my powers. I didn't hit the ground, and instead floated a couple of inches off the floor.

Myth laughed too. "That's what you get for insulting a lady," she said with mock dignity, flipping a lock of hair out of her eye. She laced the fingers of her tiny hands together and cracked them. "Okay, let's get down to work."

Myth stretched her hands out in front of herself like a maestro about to conduct an orchestra. In the meantime, I righted myself with my powers, and stood back up again. Even though I had not used my powers since my fight with the Meta who killed Dad, I had stopped myself from hitting the floor without even thinking about it. Maybe using them was like learning to ride a bicycle—once you learned how to do it, you never forgot.

As I watched, Myth's azure eyes grew brighter, as if they were lit up by a light from within Myth's body. All of the faucets over the various sinks in the latrine turned on. I heard the simultaneous flushing of all the toilets. All of the showers turned on. Then, the water from the faucets and showerheads started whipping around the room, like the latrine had turned into a giant dishwashing machine. Myth and I remained dry, though. Myth apparently had formed a small bubble around us that she was not letting the water penetrate. Watching all of the powerful jets of water spraying around the room reminded me of what it was like to sit in a car when your vehicle went through one of those automatic car washes. The roar of the water around us was terrific, like standing at the bottom of a waterfall.

After a minute or two, Myth shut off the faucets and the showerheads. She lowered her arms. The light of her eyes faded. The sudden relative silence was deafening. The only sound was that of water flowing out of the floor drains of the latrine. Already the place looked much cleaner.

It was my turn. I activated my powers again, picking up the various containers of cleaning powder we had brought with us. While still standing near Myth, I used my powers to move the containers of cleaning powder all throughout the latrine, upending the containers to sprinkle powder everywhere. I did not have control enough over my powers to pick the powder up directly instead of using the bulky containers it was contained in. Maybe I would be able to pull that off after I practiced in the use of my powers some more. I had come so far already from when my powers first manifested in the bathroom with the Three Horsemen. That incident seemed like it happened in a world far away from where I now stood.

Once the cleaning powder was distributed everywhere, I picked up with my powers the brushes and mops we had brought. Still using my powers, I got busy mopping and scrubbing everything in the latrine. I was able to keep five things going at once; anything more seemed to be too much. Again I wondered if I would get better the more I used my powers. Digging up those sweet potatoes with Amazing Man had been good practice for this.

"You missed a spot," Myth said in her high voice. She pointed at a sink I had just cleaned with one of the scrubbing brushes. While my mops and brushes did their magic, Myth had been leaning against a wall near me with her arms crossed, whistling. I recognized the tune. It was *Whistle While You Work*.

"You can always grab a brush and help, you know," I said through gritted teeth. Keeping all these mops and brushes going was hard, as hard in its own way as the weight room workout I had gone through the day before. Myth shook her head.

"Nope. Can't. Though I'd love to help, Athena said to use our powers to clean this place. I do as I'm told. I'm a stickler for following orders. I'm well-known for it. I even thought about naming myself Stickler instead of Myth. Besides, it was my idea to clean the place this way. I'm the visionary. The job creator. You're the little guy who goes out and executes my bold vision. That's capitalism. I'm too busy supervising you and thinking about the big picture to pick up a brush myself." Myth lifted her hand to her mouth and yawned into it. "Supervising is a tough job, but somebody's got to do it."

"I don't know how you work as hard as you do." Sweat was pouring off my forehead due to the effort it took to keep the brushes and mops going. "The sacrifices you make for the team are remarkable. You're truly selfless."

Myth made a great show of examining her nails and buffing them on her uniform. "I think so too, but I didn't want to be immodest and come right out and say it."

"Both modest and beautiful? You're going to make someone a terrific wife someday," I said. Myth picked up a wet sponge and sent it rocketing towards my head. I saw it in time, stopped it in mid-air with my powers, and sent it shooting back at Myth. It hit her dead in the middle of her face. She sputtered, wiping suds away.

"See, my mistake there was throwing something at a telekinetic," she said, as if to herself. "It's like throwing slop at a pig. Next time I'll know better." I stuck my tongue out at her triumphantly. I picked up the mop I had let fall when I had turned my attention away from it long enough to hit Myth with the sponge.

After a while, I finished. I had mopped and scrubbed every inch of the latrine. I retrieved all the brushes and mops, floating them over to us. Myth was up to bat again. As before, she used the water manipulation powers of her Naiad form to spray every nook and cranny of the latrine with jets of water. She again used her powers to shield us from getting wet. Once everything had been rinsed, Myth let the water drain away. What did not drain away on its own she "encouraged to evaporate," as she put it.

One she finished drying everything, Myth closed her eyes again. Her body again glowed. It slowly stretched out and morphed back into Myth's male form. In a few moments he was his normal human self again.

"I think I liked you better with boobs," I said.

"That's the creepiest thing anyone's ever said to me." Myth was a bit pale, and looked as tired as I felt. Apparently him using his powers drained him as much as me using mine drained me. Though using my powers to clean the place had been hard, hanging out with Myth also made it kind of fun.

We took a moment to look around and admire our

handiwork. Every surface of the latrine gleamed and looked like new. The latrine smelled like someone had brought a pine tree into a sterilized hospital ward. Though we were tired, it had taken us a far smaller amount of time to clean the latrine with our powers than it would have taken us had we done it by hand.

Myth and I high-fived one another.

"Not bad, Theo. Not bad at all," Myth said. "If we ever have to face a supervillain named Pig Sty, he won't stand a chance against us."

We went looking for Athena. We found her in a huge clearing on the camp's grounds along with the rest of the instructors. They were drilling the other trainees in the use of their powers.

"We finished cleaning the men's latrine," I said to Athena. "Do you want to come inspect it?" Athena looked at me as if what I asked was the stupidest question she had ever heard.

"Like I said yesterday, a Hero does not lie or cheat," she said. "Are you two telling me the latrine is as clean as you can make it?"

"Yes ma'am," Myth and I said.

"Then I'll take your word for it. Now fall in and stop tugging at momma's skirt. I'm busy." She turned away from us and resumed yelling at a young female trainee. The girl's eyes glowed red like a demon's behind her mask. Her lips were quivering. She looked like she was about to cry. "Shoot the target," Athena yelled at her. "Not everything but the target. Sweet Jesus! Pretend like it's a Rogue trying to kill you. If you can't hit him, at least get close enough to make him nervous and think twice about attacking you." Red energy beams blazed out of the girl's eyes with a low humming sound. Off in the distance, the ground exploded where the beams of energy hit it. She had missed the target she had been aiming at by a country mile.

Athena shook her head in disgust. "Congratulations," she said to the trainee. "You missed the Rogue rushing towards you. You're now dead. Is your plan to come back as a ghost and scare him to death?"

As ordered, Myth and I moved away from Athena and the young trainee to get into line. "What do you think about her?" I asked Myth about Athena once we were out of her earshot. Myth shuddered.

"I try not to," he said.

***

After training with our powers, as the day before, half of the trainees went for a run and the other half of us hit the weights in the gym. When the runners got back, they swapped places with those of us in the gym.

After what seemed like forever, dinnertime finally arrived. As with the day before, all the trainees assembled in the mess hall to eat. As there were no drill instructors present, the bulk of the talk was about them and what kind of parents gave birth to such monstrosities. While I agreed with the general sentiment, I was starting to respect Athena and the other drill instructors, much the way a deer respects a lion. If I possessed the kind of skills and experience those Heroes had, I had little doubt I would have been able to stop the Meta who had killed Dad.

One day, I thought. *One day*.

I again sat with Smoke during mess. Myth joined us. I was happy to see that Myth and Smoke hit it off. Everyone else gave Smoke a wide berth. She noticed it—it would have been hard not to—but did not seem to mind. She did not seem to mind much. She gave the impression that if she had been on the Titanic when it hit that iceberg, she would have shrugged, finished her dinner, and then calmly made her way to the lifeboats. Though she was only a little older than I, her composure made her seem much older than the rest of us trainees.

I was so glad when the day finally ended. I was mentally and physically spent. I crawled into my simple cot, as happy to see it as an old friend. Though exhausted, I was not as sad as I had been the night before. Though Dad's absence was a hole in my heart that would never be filled, I had made new friends. First Smoke, now Myth. That was two in as many days. It was a new record for me.

I forced my drooping eyes open. I had almost forgotten. I pulled out the Academy manual, flicking on the penlight to examine it in the dark barracks. In seconds I found what I was looking for.

Athena had been right. Just as she had said, I had left out the word "appropriately" from the last sentence of the second paragraph when I had recited that page of the manual to her that morning.

Of course she was right. I should not have been surprised.

CHAPTER FIFTEEN

Hours became days, and days became weeks in a blur of exercise, training, fear, and exhaustion. Trainees dropped out of the Academy like flies. Of these, most left voluntarily. Others were thrown out, mostly for disobeying an instructor or for being lazy. A handful got seriously hurt and were medically discharged. "The scaredy-cats never showed up and the weak bitches are revealing themselves," Athena said dismissively one morning when she noted our numbers had dropped by almost two-thirds. Happily, neither Myth nor Smoke had dropped or washed out. I had come to be good friends with them and would have missed them if they were gone. Except for Myth, everybody still called me Carolina. Even Smoke.

I rarely saw Amazing Man during this period. Every now and then he would show up at a powers training session or while we lifted weights. He did not say anything to anyone. He just watched for a while and then left, like the principal of a school who took a decidedly hands-off approach. All the trainees had heard of his Heroic exploits over the years, so we all viewed him with awe. When it got out that Amazing Man had personally recruited me to enter the Academy—I had made the mistake of telling Myth, who was only capable of keeping his mouth shut if his lips were stapled together—the trainees started looking at me with awe, too. Except for Smoke, that is. It's likely not even Jesus' Second Coming would have awed her.

The drill instructors—Athena, Carbon Copy, Sprint, plus several others—when they talked about Amazing Man at all, referred to him as "the Old Man." The nickname was partly a recognition of the fact that Amazing Man had been a Hero longer than most of the drill instructors had been alive. Even more than that, though, it seemed mostly a term of endearment, a nickname born out of affection and respect. Following the drill instructors' lead, we trainees had started calling Amazing Man "the Old Man" too. Never to his face, though. Nobody had that kind of chutzpah. Not even Smoke, who did not seem scared of or intimidated by anybody.

Though I did not drop out during this period, there were more than a few times I wanted to. I felt like the dog who caught the car he had been chasing: now that the bumper was between my teeth, I did not know what to do other than hold on for dear life.

As far as I knew, I was the only Omega-level Meta going through the Academy. The drill instructors must have known I was Omega-level. In addition to the Old Man knowing, I learned that my records from when I registered as a Metahuman had been transmitted to Camp Avatar for review by the drill instructors before I had even arrived here, as had the records of all the other trainees. It confirmed that Athena and the other instructors had known more about us when we first arrived than they had initially let on. Despite the fact I was supposedly a once-in-a-generation Metahuman, the drill instructors treated me like they did everybody else: namely, harshly. But, Smoke, Myth and I had a hypothesis as to why the instructors treated us this way and pushed us so hard: they were culling from the herd the people who could not stand up under pressure. As Athena kept telling us, being a Hero was not for the meek or for someone who would turn tail and run at the first sign of trouble. Heroes ran towards trouble, not away from it. The instructors were hardening us, tempering us for the adversities we would surely face if we became licensed Heroes, like steel is hardened in the heat of a forge.

Besides, once over half of the trainees dropped out, the drill instructors' attitudes towards those of us who remained shifted subtly. They certainly did not start to treat us like we were their equals. They were Heroes and we were not, after all. But, they did go from treating us like stray dogs they were trying to scare away to treating us like puppies who were not housebroken yet—ignorant, and liable to pee on the carpet from time to time, but trainable.

Even though I started to understand why the drill instructors were so tough on us, that did not mean that I enjoyed this hardening process. I did not. Whoever said "To understand all is to forgive all" clearly had never gone to the Academy. For one thing, we ran constantly. The drill instructors' philosophy about moving from place to place seemed to be that if you were going to go somewhere—whether it was simply to the latrine or through the surrounding woods—you should do it while running as fast as humanly possible. I got to the point where I started praying God would put wheels on my feet. He did not. As I knew all too well, not all prayers were answered.

In addition to seemingly running the circumference of the Earth several times over, we trainees also extensively weight trained. Initially it was every day, then it was reduced to every other day. I did countless deadlifts, squats, bench presses, chin-ups, dips, and a bunch of other exercises I had never heard of until coming to Camp Avatar. It got to the point I started dreaming about working out. I used to dream about girls before coming here. A barbell was a poor substitute for a girl.

Weight training was reduced to every other day because we started combat training a couple of weeks after arriving. I had expected to learn to use my powers to fight. That was why I had come here, after all. What I had not expected was to learn to fight without them. We studied karate, judo, savate, boxing, Muay Thai, jiu-jitsu, wrestling, and hapkido, among other martial arts disciplines. Sprint was our principal instructor for the unarmed martial arts. Sparring with him was no fun. Even when he was trying to not use his super speed, his heightened reflexes made it nearly impossible for those of us who did not also have such reflexes—which was most of us—to lay a hand on him.

Not only did we train in unarmed martial arts, we also trained in the use of so many weapons I cannot even remember them all. Knives, swords, guns, blowguns, darts, slingshots—it did not matter what it was. If someone had figured out an implement to kill or injure another human, we trained in its use. Even sticks. Yes, sticks.

One day I was sparring in a large clearing with Nightshade. A fellow trainee, Nightshade was a big muscular guy who moved like a panther despite his size. We were armed with sticks the size of my wrist and the length of a broomstick. We whacked each other like piñatas, or at least we did when one of us could penetrate the other's guard. I was so slick with sweat thanks to both exertion and the hot day that it was as if I was taking a bath.

We were not allowed to use our powers while sparring with weapons, otherwise I would have telekinetically ripped Nightshade's stick away from him and beat him over the head with it. The rest of the remaining trainees sparred with partners around me and Nightshade under Athena's watchful and critical eye. Athena, her powers being what they were, was of course our principal instructor in the use of weapons.

Nightshade had gotten the better of me in our sparring

session so far. The special fabric our uniforms were made of dissipated the force of Nightshade's blows somewhat, but not entirely. The fabric was formulated out of the same chemicals that composed spider silk. It was therefore incredibly strong and durable. Even with my uniform giving me some measure of protection from Nightshade's blows, I felt like a giant, aching welt.

I said before Nightshade and I were whacking each other like piñatas. That was actually not quite accurate. Nightshade was whacking me like I was a piñata; I was busy trying to not split open at the seams like a piñata. Part of the reason I was getting hit so much was Nightshade's size and quickness. The other part was strategy. The Academy had taught me that guys like Nightshade, because of their size, tended to not have the best endurance. It took a lot of energy to fuel his big muscles and move them around. I was letting Nightshade whack away at me while I played mostly defense. It was a rope-a-dope strategy. If I could keep myself from getting pounded to a pulp or knocked out long enough, Nightshade would tire himself out. Then, perhaps an opportunity would present itself that I could capitalize on.

There! Nightshade dropped his guard a little, obviously tired. Striking like a cobra, I hit his left wrist with my stick so hard that the impact made my forearms shudder. Nightshade cried out in pain. His left hand let go of his stick. I took advantage of the opening. I shoved my own weapon inside of the space between Nightshade's arms, pulled back, and twisted. Nightshade's stick went flying out of his hand, sailing through the air before hitting the ground. Getting disarmed meant the sparring session was over.

Despite the fact I had won, I slammed my own stick to the ground in anger and frustration. I was overworked, in pain, and exhausted. I felt like I was at my breaking point. How was swinging a stick like a monkey on crack getting me any closer to defeating the Meta who had killed my

Dad?

"I'm so freakin' sick of playing with sticks and stones," I fumed to Athena. She was standing nearby. "Are we learning to be superheroes or cavemen?" When I first came to Camp Avatar I never would have dreamed of talking to Athena that way. I had since learned you could talk to her or the other instructors any way you wanted, especially now that the numbers of us trainees had been thinned out considerably. I had once overheard Athena say approvingly to Carbon Copy that a trainee "had spirit" after he had sassed her. As long as you did not cross the line into being disrespectful and as long as you did what the instructors said—preferably while at a dead run—you could talk to them the way you wanted to. I rather liked that fact. It made me feel like a grown-up.

"You've got some sort of problem Carolina?" Athena asked. The look on her face was that of smug amusement. It was the expression that was normally on her face. I wanted to pick my stick back up and use it to wipe the smugness off. I knew it was more likely that Athena would disarm me and use my own stick to cave my skull in. I had sparred with her before. It had been like fighting a ghost.

"Yes I do have a problem," I said. "Why in the world are we learning to fight with guns and knives and sticks? We have superpowers. Shouldn't we be focusing exclusively on those?"

"Gather around infants," Athena said in a raised voice, calling out to the rest of the sparring trainees. The other trainees lowered their sticks and formed around where Athena, Nightshade and I stood. "Carolina here poses a good question, namely why are you all learning to fight with weapons other than your superpowers. Suppose a supervillain somehow neutralizes your powers? What are you supposed to do, stomp your foot like an angry child and accuse the villain of not fighting fair? Take your ball and run home to tell your mommy? No. You pick up a rock or a stick or a gun or whatever else is handy and defeat the supervillain anyway."

"What good will a rock or a stick or even a gun do against someone with superpowers?" someone asked. "If you threatened someone like Mister Sinister with a stick, he'd laugh at you while making your head explode. Rogues like him are too powerful to tackle without superpowers."

"In the hands of the right Hero, any weapon will serve to defeat many supervillains," Athena said. "Or no weapon at all. What you have to understand is that there's no such things as an inherently powerful weapon or superpower. There are only powerful people. And what makes you powerful is in here," she said, tapping the center of her chest. "The cliché 'It's not the size of the dog in the fight, it's the size of the fight in the dog,' is a cliché for a reason—because it's true. Our goal at the Academy is to turn you infants into powerful people who can face anything with confidence, weapon or no weapon, superpower or no superpower. Or at least not wet your pants and run in the other direction. Why will you be able to face anything with confidence? Because you'll have been in tight spots before here at the Academy, and you managed to get out of them. Part of our job is to give you the skills to be a Hero. To teach you how to be a Hero. But perhaps even more importantly, our job is to teach you to think like a Hero, to teach you to approach every situation like there is nothing you can't handle."

"But—" someone interjected. Athena waved them quiet.

"Don't interrupt Grandma while she's pontificating," she said. "The motto of this place is 'Society before self.' It's written over every door here. Why? Because we want you to internalize what it means. It means that you think of the rest of society before you think of yourself. It means that when everyone else is running away from danger, you are the ones who will run towards it. It means that if someone fires a gun at a civilian, you step in front of the bullet. And, it means that you not only know how to use your superpowers, but any other weapon you might need to subdue that guy who shot at the civilian. You have to be ready for anything at any time."

Two shuriken—Japanese throwing stars—materialized in her hands. Without warning, she threw them at me with sharp flicks of her wrists. The shuriken zoomed towards my head.

Lifting my hands a bit, I altered the trajectory of the shuriken with my powers. The shuriken whizzed past my ears, curved around my head like satellites orbiting the Earth. They spun back towards Athena, a slight push from my powers adding to the momentum they already had. Athena raised her forearm in front of her face. A small wooden shield materialized on her arm. The two throwing stars hit the shield, embedding deeply into it with loud thunks.

Athena lowered her shield. She looked down at the shuriken. They were embedded into the shield about eye-width apart. They would have hit her eyes had she not stopped them.

Athena looked up at me.

"Not bad," she said. "And I see you're not even complaining about an unfair sneak attack. Take note, everyone: there's no fair or unfair in a fight, no Marquess of Queensbury rules. There are only winners, and losers. If you don't learn to be a winner, you won't be able to get a Hero's license. Even if you somehow slip through the cracks and become a Hero anyway, if you're not a winner, you won't be a Hero for long. Not a live one, anyway. Some Rogue who is faster, stronger, tougher, smarter, or simply better prepared than you will come along and put you of your misery. The world is what it is, whether you're ready to deal with it or not. You'd best be ready."

Athena turned her attention back to me. "You're learning, Carolina," she said, pointing at the throwing stars. "There's hope for you yet. Though I see I still haven't been able to break you of the habit of moving your hands to focus your powers. We'll work on that some more later." The shield and the shuriken disappeared. Athena clapped her hands together. "Okay, let's get back to work. If you infants think you can trick me into letting you goof off by getting me to shoot the breeze, you've got another thing coming." We all retrieved our sticks. We resumed sparring.

Athena was right: I was learning. I had used my powers to evade the throwing stars and send them back at Athena as instinctively and automatically as one might swat at a biting mosquito. I had not even consciously thought about it. I had just done it. It was my first clue I was no longer the innocent farm boy who had fearfully stepped foot into Camp Avatar weeks before.

There would be other clues.

CHAPTER SIXTEEN

Weeks became months. Trainees continued to either quit or be thrown out, but not nearly at the rate they had left at the beginning. What had started as a torrent of trainees leaving was now reduced to a trickle. Those of us who were left were either too tough to leave, or too stubborn. Or, just too stupid. Maybe all of the above. I was not sure. I was too busy working like a dog and running from place to place and from assignment to assignment like a squirrel on a busy highway to give it much thought. The expression "idle hands are the Devil's workshop" may not have been invented by Academy instructors, but it may as well have been. If we trainees were not asleep or eating, we were busy.

Once we had dropped to where only a fourth of us who had started as trainees remained, it was as if a switch was flipped. All of the trainees moved out of the men's and women's barracks, which were essentially huge open rooms that afforded all the privacy of a cow pasture. We instead moved into another building on the camp's grounds, one with apartments for the trainees. Actually, the word "apartments" overstates the matter. Each apartment was nothing more than a single room with cinder block walls containing two beds, a plain desk and a chair, and a desktop computer. The bathrooms were communal. The women were on the first floor of the apartment building; men were on the second. There was no prohibition against us trainees fraternizing, but if anyone ever hooked up, I did not see it or hear about it. Everybody was likely too tired. I knew I was. If you had told me back when I was at USCA I would soon be too tired to care much about girls, I would have laughed in your face. Assuming I even heard you. I might have been too busy watching that cute girl from English 101 walk away.

We got to choose our roommates when we moved into the apartment building. Myth and I of course roomed together. Smoke roomed with a woman named Warpspeed. Warpspeed was a bit of a loner and no one else was anxious to room with her. Myth and I tried repeatedly to befriend Warpspeed until she pointedly told us to stop. So we did. Some people preferred to be alone. Smoke wound up with Warpspeed because she was still a bit of an outcast among us trainees due to her early admission she had been trained by a supervillain. People tended to be tribal. Even in the Academy where your race, gender, color, appearance, and ethnicity were irrelevant and the only thing that mattered was your performance, there was still an us versus them attitude. Here, the us were Heroes and the them were Rogues. Though trainees respected Smoke's abilities, skills, and work ethic, they were still wary of her. She was guilty by association.

In addition to the trainees moving out of the barracks and into apartments, we also started taking classes and doing all the reading and homework that entailed. For many of those classes, new Hero instructors were brought in to teach us, all of whom were experts in their fields. Our daily exercises and combat training were cut back on to accommodate our academics. They were not cut back much, though. I would not have thought it possible to squeeze more out of a day, but the combination of our physical and academic workloads demanded it. Sleep became an even more prized and rare commodity. Even sleep did not give us an escape from work, though. Most nights we listened to audiobooks on various subjects as we slept. One of our new professors assured us our unconscious minds were absorbing the information like sponges, especially since a Hero named Hypnotist was brought in one day to prime our minds to assimilate all that information while we were asleep. I was skeptical about how much good that alleged nighttime learning was doing until one day in class I effortlessly and perfectly recited the opening lines of *Canterbury Tales* in its original Middle English. I had never in my life read *Canterbury Tales*, much less in Middle English. I had listened to it when I was asleep, though.

We all were required to take certain core classes: Hero Law; English and Literature; World History; the Science of Superheroes; Hero Psychology, Strategy, and Tactics; Metahuman Math; and Heroic Feats, Ethics, and Theory. It was like being in college again, only a lot more demanding. In addition to those classes we all had to take, each trainee had specialized tutelage. Myth, for example, was tutored in mythology (duh!) and art. He studied art because drawing and painting various mythological creatures helped him visualize and internalize them so he could transform into them later. The better he was able to conceptualize a mythological creature, the more powerful he was as that creature. His drawings and paintings of griffins, pegasuses, ghosts, angels, dragons, manticores, and other creatures I did not even know the names of soon filled the walls of our tiny room.

As for me, I was tutored in advanced physics. Studying physics helped me understand the potential I had as an Omega-level Metahuman. Myth could turn into dragons and breathe fire; Smoke could turn into gases that could do anything from knock a crowd of people out to burning a hole through steel; Brute could pick up a small airplane like it was a baseball bat and smash it over your head. There were lots of trainees who had powers that would make your jaw drop. All I could do was pick stuff up and generate force fields. At first, my powers seemed less than awesome in comparison to some of the other trainees. But, my studies at the Academy soon taught me the potential of my powers. I started to understand that what I did when I moved stuff around was manipulating its atoms. I could do it on a macro-scale, like when I had moved the mops around in the latrine or changed the vectors of Athena's shuriken. But, I was learning I could manipulate atoms on a micro-scale as well.

Late one night as I lay in bed, I literally could feel the swirling atoms of everything around me, from the atoms that composed the air, to the atoms that composed the sleeping bodies of the trainees in the building, to the atoms of the building itself. The atoms in the building in particular resonated with me, almost like they were calling to me. The energy that bound them together seem to cry for release. Half-asleep, I almost unleashed that energy, just to see what would happen.

Fortunately, I resisted the temptation. The next morning, before heading to the gym for my morning workout, I sat down to figure out what would have happened had I done what my sleepy self had been thinking about the night before. $E=mc^2$. In plain English, that equation meant energy equaled mass times the square of the speed of light. Einstein had taught us all that long ago. In other words, energy was but another version of mass, and vice versa. The speed of light was 186,000 miles per second. Multiply that by itself, and you had a huge number. Armed with all the new information I had been taught in various classes, I did a rough estimate of the mass of the building I was in. I then multiplied that by the square of the speed of light.

Wow! The result had so many zeroes at the end of it, it shocked me. The energy I would have generated had I broken up the atoms of the building would have been massive. In essence, I would have converted the building into a massive nuclear bomb. My hands shook a little as that realization sank in. It was no wonder Amazing Man had urged me to train in the use of my powers. Without training, I was an unwitting danger not only to myself, but to everyone around me. It scared me a little to think about the things I could already probably do and the things I would one day be capable of if I kept training and studying.

Speaking of the Old Man, he stopped being an ivory tower figure whom we trainees rarely saw. Once classes started, we started seeing him every day. He was our professor for Heroic Feats, Ethics, and Theory, or simply Feats as the full name was a mouthful. Feats was my favorite class. In it, we dissected the provisions of the Hero Act of 1945, analyzed how the Sentinels stopped the V'Loth alien invasion in the 1960s, mulled over why female Heroes tended to wear form-fitting and otherwise revealing outfits and whether that was sexist, debated the merits and demerits of a secret identity, argued about whether President Theodore Roosevelt had been a closeted Meta, and any and everything in between. It was interesting.

"All right," the Old Man said one day in Feats, "let's find out who actually digested yesterday's reading assignment and who merely moved their lips as they read the words. Supernova, thanks so much for volunteering." Supernova jumped a little at the sound of his name. He straightening up in his seat. He had been dozing. I could sympathize. I was half-asleep myself. I could not remember the last time I had gotten what I used to consider a full night's rest. The concept of not always being tired now seemed as mythological as the creatures Myth turned into. "Can you tell us what the advantages of becoming a licensed Hero are?" the Old Man asked Supernova.

"A Meta has to become a licensed Hero in order to legally use his powers under the Hero Act," Supernova said. The redhead visibly suppressed a yawn. "If you use your powers without being licensed, you are deemed a Rogue under the Act. Or, a supervillain as most people call them."

"Yes, that's true as far as it goes," the Old Man said, "but that is stuff they tell you when you register as a Meta. I'm looking for something a little more specific. Go back to sleep. Perhaps the answer I'm looking for will come to you in a dream. Yes, Myth?"

Myth lowered his hand. "There are five advantages to being a licensed Hero." He ticked them off on his fingers. "One, a Hero is protected from legal liability for property destruction and bodily injury if he acts in a reasonable manner and in pursuit of the public welfare. Two, a Hero has limited police powers. Those include the ability to arrest someone who is in the middle of committing a criminal act, as well as someone who has committed certain serious crimes in the past and has not yet been brought to justice. Three, a Hero who maintains a secret identity can seek compensatory and punitive damages from someone who outs him. Four, a Hero with a secret identity can file taxes, testify in court, and perform other duties and tasks as a citizen under that alias without being forced to reveal his true identity. Five, a Hero is authorized to use deadly force to protect himself or others from serious bodily harm." I was not surprised Myth was able to rattle all that off. Despite his sometimes goofy sense of humor, I had learned that Myth took his studies seriously.

"Correct," the Old Man said. "Somebody give that man a cigar. But you'll have to smoke it in the Arctic Circle with the penguins if you raise your hand in my class again, as that's where I'll fly you and leave you. How many times do I have to tell you you don't have to raise your bloody hand? Just speak up. You don't have to ask 'Mother may I?' every time you want to say something. You're a Hero trainee, not a kindergartener. Don't be so damned respectful all the time. Maybe slouch in your chair a little while you're at it. Being so on point all the time makes you look like you lack confidence. If there's one thing a Hero has to be, it's confident."

Myth grinned. "You'll have to bring some penguins to the Arctic Circle along with me then. Penguins are only in the Southern Hemisphere. There aren't any in the Arctic Circle."

"I tell you to be less respectful, and two seconds later you correct me. Uppity. I've created a monster." The Old Man grinned back at Myth. "Let's focus for a few moments on the topic of secret identities. You all are masked to conceal your real identities from one another. If you graduate from the Academy, you are permitted to continue to wear a mask for the purpose of continuing your training. You are not allowed to wear a full Hero's costume, though. Only licensed Heroes are legally permitted to wear full costumes. Can anyone tell me why most Heroes take advantage of their ability to legally wear costumes? Other than to conceal their true identities, I mean. No, not you this time Myth. Give someone else a chance to embarrass themselves. How about you Carolina?" My eyelids slammed open at the sound of my name. Like I said, I had been half-asleep.

"Why do Heroes wear costumes?" I repeated, my mind groping for the answer. It came up empty. "Uh, because they look cool?" The class laughed.

"You're not entirely wrong," the Old Man said once the laughter died down. He glanced down admiringly at himself. "I for one am so cool in my costume that I piss ice cubes. Unfortunately, due to my age, I have to get up several times in the middle of the night to piss them too." The class laughed again. He could joke if he wanted to but I knew that, despite his age, the Old Man was capable of doing things like moving intercontinental ballistic missiles out of their flight paths and redirecting them into space. I saw him do it on television once.

The Old Man spoke again. "But no, looking cool is not the main reason why Heroes wear a costume. Anyone else?"

Silence.

"Because they're a symbol," Smoke finally said. She sat on my right.

"Ding-ding-ding," the Old Man said. "That's right—they are a symbol. They're a symbol the same way a cop's badge is, or a doctor's white coat is, or a businessman's expensive dark suit is. A Hero's costume signifies to the public what you are. But not only that, what you stand for. There's something about humans' monkey minds that makes us look for leaders, that makes us want to identify and follow the alpha. A Hero's costume, especially his cape, marks you as that alpha. The Heroes' Guild has done studies on it. Almost one hundred percent of the world's population associates capes with Heroes. Almost one hundred percent! It's why most of us Heroes who wear costumes also wear capes. You'll notice all of the instructors here at Camp Avatar do, including myself. When the average person sees a costume and a cape, he is inclined to do what we tell him to do. That is of critical importance to us Heroes in a crisis sometimes. Say, for example, a Hero knows a building is about to collapse. If he warns the occupants of that building about the danger while in civilian clothes, he will almost certainly be ignored. If he makes the same warning while dressed in his costume and cape, though, people will take notice and tend to obey that Hero even though they have no legal obligation to do so. The costume and cape is a symbol of authority. Code names are too. That is why they should be chosen with care. They should be something that engenders trust and respect." The Old Man smiled slightly. "I'm talking to you, Honey Buzzard." The guy who had picked that unlikely name flushed. Fortunately for him, the names we had chosen for use at the Academy were not the names we had to keep forever. Thank goodness. I had no intention of going by Carolina for the rest of my life.

"Wait a minute," I said. I was incredulous. "You're telling us that the public will tend to do what we tell them just because of a code name, costume, and cape?"

"That's exactly what I'm telling you," the Old Man said. "I'll give you an example from another field to show you the power of authority and symbols. A few years back as part of a psychological study, someone called nurses' stations at various hospital wards. That person told the answering nurses that he was a doctor. He wasn't. He instructed the nurses to administer a certain drug to patients under their care. Bear in mind that calling in a drug prescription like that was in violation of each hospital's policy, the drug prescribed by the man on the phone was not authorized for use in the wards, the dose he called for was obviously excessive and dangerous, and the so-called doctor giving the order over the phone had never been seen before by the nurses. He hadn't even spoken to those nurses on the phone before. Take a guess as to what percentage of the nurses did what the alleged doctor told them to do."

"Five percent," I guessed. I had been tempted to say zero, but there's a small percentage of any group that's too dumb to even tie its shoes properly. Other trainees in class ventured other guesses. All their guesses were less than ten percent.

"Ninety-five percent," Smoke said. She said it with quiet confidence.

"Right on the nose," the Old Man. "I see someone has been doing some extracurricular reading." If so, I did not know how in the world she found the time. Maybe she did not need sleep. Maybe she just sat in the corner at night and did crunches while boning up on ways to show the rest of us up. "Ninety-five percent of the nurses did as the alleged doctor told them. Why is that? It's because nurses have been trained to obey doctors, almost without question. The white lab coat, the title doctor, all of that goes into vesting a doctor with authority that most nurses leap to obey. It's the same with Heroes. Unfortunately, it's also the same with Rogues. It's why so many supervillains wear costumes just like Heroes do. It's much easier to commit crimes when your outfit subconsciously triggers people to do as you tell them instead of fighting back. Remember, your names, costumes, and capes are all symbols of your Heroic authority. If you keep that in mind, your job as Heroes will be made a lot easier.

"Enough of costumes and masks for now," the Old Man said. "Let's change topics a bit and go back to what Myth correctly stated earlier, namely that Heroes are not supposed to kill unless it is in self-defense or in the defense of others. Can anyone tell me why?" Silence. "Come now, you're not tenderfeet any more. By now the answer should be as obvious as the nose on your face."

"Because killing is illegal?" Sledgehammer said in her soft voice. Her tone indicated she was not sure her answer was correct. Despite her name, she was a mere slip of a girl. Judging from her appearance, she was the youngest of all the remaining trainees. Regardless of how she looked, she could punch a hole through a cinder block building like it was made out of cardboard.

The Old Man shook his head at Sledgehammer. "Your answer is correct, but your delivery is all wrong. If you're going to be a Hero, you've got to command respect and obedience. As we just discussed, your costume and cape are part of that. The rest is how you carry yourself and sound. The way you just answered my question, you sounded like you were apologizing for troubling me by speaking. A Hero is a lion, not a field mouse. Try to sound cockier next time."

"I'll try," Sledgehammer said, again with the same soft-spoken voice. She sounded more like the Cowardly Lion than any other kind of lion.

"Try harder. You should be aiming for a tone of amused mastery, not the meek diffidence you're hitting." He shook his head again. "Regardless of her delivery, Sledgehammer is right. Heroes do not kill because killing is illegal. Unless, of course, it's in self-defense or in the defense of others. We Heroes are not above the law. The use of our powers is sanctioned and regulated by the law. As a result, we are an extension of the law and act in support of it. Never forget that. The moment you do forget, the moment you start to think your powers entitle you to act as a one-person judge, jury, and executioner, the whole system breaks down." The Old Man looked at me as he said that. I shifted in my seat uncomfortably. Had he somehow guessed what I had in mind for the Meta who had killed Dad? The Old Man's gaze shifted away from me. Perhaps him looking at me had been mere coincidence. "People like us are too powerful to do as we please unchecked. The Academy's motto is 'Society before self.' One of the many things that means is that we put the will of society—which is really what laws are, the codified will of society—ahead of our own desires. There may come a time when you are tempted to disobey the law simply because you can or because you think doing so would be for the best. Don't. When you start putting your own personal judgments ahead of that of society's, you are putting yourself on a road that leads to ruin—for both yourself and the rest of us. That's what Rogues do, and we're not Rogues. We must constantly guard against the temptation to do as we will because we can. Remember, as Lord Acton said, 'Power corrupts, and absolute power corrupts absolutely.' We Heroes are some of the most powerful people on the planet. The temptation to let that power corrupt us is always there and we must always be vigilant against it."

Myth interjected, "On the other hand, power corrupts, but absolute power gets all the girls." Everyone laughed, including the Old Man. Everyone, that is, except me. I was too busy thinking about what the Old Man had said. Maybe he was right that Heroes should not kill because that would put them above the law. On the other hand, I could not help but to think of an older law as I thought about the man who killed Dad. That law predated Amazing Man, the Hero Act, and even the United States itself. That law said an eye for an eye and a tooth for a tooth.

"Remember this," the Old Man said once the laughter from Myth's comment had died off. "The fundamental reason why a Hero must be licensed in order to use his powers is because the law says so. A Hero must follow the law. If he doesn't, he's no better than the criminals and Rogues he fights. He's no better than the mugger who takes an old lady's purse simply because he can."

The Old Man came around to the front of his desk. He perched on the edge of it and looked at the class intently. "There are two things I want to make sure everyone in this class learns, and that's one of them. Every Metahuman possesses abilities that ordinary men can only dream of. Some of us Metas are powerful enough to take over the world." He smiled ruefully. "Some of us have tried. The only thing that stops that from happening, the only thing that keeps this world from devolving into a place run by the biggest guy with the biggest stick is the law." The Old Man grinned suddenly. "Or gal, Smoke, as I wouldn't put world conquest past you."

"Uhn-uhn," Smoke said, shaking her head. "The world would be too much of a headache to run. I'd settle for a continent. South America, maybe. They have nice beaches."

"What's the other thing you want us to learn from you?" I asked.

The Old Man suddenly looked somber. "The second thing is the definition of the word 'hero.' No, I don't mean the dictionary definition before one of you eager beavers quotes it to me. Nor do I mean how the Hero Act defines a Hero, namely a Metahuman who is licensed and legally able to use his powers. I mean what the word 'hero' means from a practical standpoint. The Academy is teaching you how to fight, but teaching you why to fight is even more important. Trying to get you all to understand the 'why' of fighting is why we have you read so much history, literature, and philosophy. We want to get you to absorb the lessons of the heroes—both Meta and non-Meta—who have gone before you.

"For my money, the meaning of the word hero can be summed up in one simple sentence: A hero is someone who sees what must be done, and he or she tries to do it regardless of the personal cost. It doesn't sound very profound or important, does it? But it is. The man who works two jobs, deprives himself of sleep and ruins his health all to make sure his family has food to eat and a roof over their heads is a hero. The woman who sees a house on fire and runs in to save a child inside even though she will get burned herself, that woman is a hero. The man who sees another man getting beaten up by a group of people and intervenes at the risk of his own life and limb, that man is a hero."

The Old Man looked each of us in the eye intently. "It's so important that I'll say it again: a hero is someone who sees what must be done, and tries to do it regardless of the personal cost. And, because everyone in this room is a Meta with a greater capacity than the average person to do things, we each have a correspondingly larger responsibility to do the things that must be done."

Myth's arm twitched. I just knew he was about to raise his hand again, but had stopped himself in time.

"So basically you're saying with great power comes great responsibility," Myth said. The Old Man grinned and winked at Myth.

"That's exactly what I'm saying. But, I was trying to avoid plagiarizing from a *Spiderman* comic in order to say it. A real-life Hero ought not quote a comic book. It's undignified."

"The concept is actually much older than Spiderman," Myth said. "In the Bible, Luke 12:48 reads 'When someone has been given much, much will be required in return; and when someone has been entrusted with much, even more will be required.'"

"Okay, now you're just showing off," the Old Man said. "I hereby take back the cigar I was going to give you."

Something was bothering me. It had been bothering me ever since the Academy had been telling us a Hero does not kill. "What if they conflict?" I asked.

"What if what conflict?" the Old Man said.

"What if the law says to do one thing—not kill, for example—and what the Hero thinks needs to be done is the opposite of that thing. What does the Hero do?"

The Old Man looked somber.

"If you stay in this business long enough, you're going to be confronted with that situation many times," he said. "Lord knows I have. All you can do is what you think is best, and pray to hell that you made the right decision."

CHAPTER SEVENTEEN

The first clue that I was no longer the same simple country boy who had arrived at Camp Avatar was when I redirected Athena's throwing stars back at her. The second clue was revealed when I got into a fight on my eighteenth birthday.

Once classes were introduced into the Academy, all the trainees were given a couple of days of leave to use as we wished. Before then, barring an emergency or unless we were under the orders of one of the instructors, trainees were not allowed to leave Camp Avatar. Or its airspace, in the case of those of us who could fly. Myth and Smoke convinced me to use one of my leave days to go into Portland with them to celebrate my eighteenth birthday. Since the drinking age in Oregon had been lowered from twenty-one to eighteen a few years back, they planned to end our day on the town by taking me to a bar for the first time.

The three of us piled into one of the Academy-owned cars that were available for trainees to use. Myth was behind the wheel, I was in the front with him, and Smoke sat in the back. I shifted uncomfortably in my seat. This was the first time in months I had worn anything other than the Academy's red and black uniform. The jeans and polo shirt I had brought to camp with me and that had been packed away until now felt tight on me. Could they have shrunk?

Myth started the car. Smoke said, "Aren't you two forgetting something?" right as Myth was about to put the car into gear. Myth and I looked at each other, puzzled.

"What did we forget?" I asked.

"Our masks," Smoke said. "Don't you think we'll draw attention to ourselves if we drive and walk around with masks on? The camp's guidelines are quite clear—trainees on leave are to not draw attention to themselves, to not use their powers, and to not let the civilian population know they are Hero trainees."

Myth and I looked at each other again.

"I completely forgot I had the darned thing on, I'm so used to wearing it," Myth said. He hesitated. "But if we take the masks off, we'll all know what each other looks like. No offense, but I don't know if I want to reveal my secret identity. I'm used to you all not knowing the real me."

"Me too," I said. Though I certainly did not have anything to hide and I had come to think of Myth and Smoke as my best friends, I did not know if I was willing to reveal my true face either. The importance of maintaining our secret identity had been pounded into us by our instructors. The fewer people who knew who was behind the mask, the less of a chance that information would fall into the wrong hands and be used against you.

"Well, the guidelines are clear," Smoke said. "We either take the masks off or we can't go." Myth and I still hesitated. Smoke rolled her eyes at us. She reached up and peeled her mask away from her face. Her face changed subtly now that the mask's technology was no longer obscuring how she really looked. Her true face was a bit rounder and more feminine than the face I had gotten used to seeing. I had always thought of her as pretty. I mentally upgraded her to hot.

"My name is Neha Thakore. I'm nineteen. I was born in Gujarat, India and raised mostly in Wilmington, Delaware." She pointed at me. "Your name is Theodore Conley, born and raised right outside of Aiken, South Carolina." She pointed at Myth. "You're Isaac Geere, twenty-years-old, born and raised in Los Angeles, California."

There was stunned silence. The shocked look Myth gave Smoke told me she was right about who he was. It was no doubt the same shocked look I had on my face.

"How in the world do you know that?" I demanded of her once I recovered enough to speak.

"Do you really think I would spend as much time around you guys as I do without knowing something about you?"

"That tells us why, but it doesn't answer Theo's question of how," Myth said, pressing her.

Smoke shrugged. "I can transform into smoke. There aren't too many rooms I can't get into. That includes the camp's records' room. I'm speaking hypothetically, of course, since trainees aren't supposed to go into restricted areas. If the camp wants to make sure its records stay confidential, they should make sure the records' room is airtight. That's all I'll say. I don't want to make you two into accessories after the fact." Smoke paused. "I mean hypothetical accessories after the fact."

Myth and I looked at each other.

"I'm glad she's on our side," I said.

"I hope she's on our side," Myth said. He shook his head, and took a long breath. He reached up to peel his mask off. I did the same. We looked at each other. It was weird to truly see your best friend for the first time. Myth—I was having a hard time thinking of him as Isaac—looked similar to how he did before, but there were subtle differences. His eyes were wider, his nose was

139

broader and flatter, and his cheekbones were more prominent now. If I had seen Myth without his mask on before knowing this was what he looked like, I would have walked right by him on the street with the fleeting thought that the guy reminded me vaguely of Myth.

"So, what do you think?" Myth asked me. "Am I as beautiful as all the girls say?"

"Blind girls, maybe," I said, grinning.

"You joke, but I would be totally down with a blind girl. I hear they're good with their hands, what with all the braille reading. I'd let her fingers work my body like she was reading the *Kama Sutra*." Smoke made vomiting sounds from the backseat. "Hey cargo, pipe down back there! The co-pilot and I are trying to have a high-minded conversation about people with disabilities." Myth shook his head in dismay. "Some people just don't have any sympathy for the less fortunate."

Myth—no, Isaac—put the car into gear and drove off.

***

"How about Movement Man?" I asked. Both Isaac and Neha made a face.

"Too close to Bowel Movement Man," Neha said.

"Yeah, what are your powers, throwing feces?" Isaac asked. "What are you, a superpowered monkey?"

"Well I need to come up with a code name at some point. I can't go by Carolina forever. Remember how the Old Man said code names were important?"

"You need to go back to the drawing board," Isaac said. "Movement Man stinks to high heaven. Pun intended."

We were sitting in a corner table at Donnegan's Pub, a bar in downtown Portland. We had spent the day touring the city. It was now evening. The pub was our last stop before we returned to Camp Avatar. Smoke and Myth had made a big production out of buying me the beer I now sipped. I did not have the heart to tell them it was not the first one I had ever had. Dad had made a point of letting me sample various drinks at the house once I became a teenager. "If alcohol is not built up in your mind as something special and forbidden, you won't go nuts over it when you're an adult," he had said.

Isaac had already finished a beer and was now drinking water since he was going to drive us back. Neha and I both nursed our single beers as we did not plan on getting more. If there was one thing we had learned at Camp Avatar, it was that the effective and responsible use of our powers required emotional control. Getting drunk, or even buzzed, was not something to mix with having superpowers. At least not if you did not want to wind up flying headfirst into the side of building.

Drinking beer made me think of Dad since he had been the one to first introduce me to it. "Did I ever tell you guys why I decided to enroll in the Academy?" I asked. Isaac and Neha shook their heads no. It was really more of a rhetorical question; I knew I had not told them. I had already told them the Old Man had recruited me to enter the Academy, but I had not told them why or what had happened after Amazing Man had visited me on the farm. I did not like to talk about Dad's death. Suddenly, I felt a compelling need to do so. I did not know why. Maybe the beer was affecting me. Or, maybe I simply missed him. This was the first birthday I had ever celebrated without him.

After first swearing them to secrecy—I did not want the other trainees all up in my business—I told Isaac and Neha everything that had happened to me, starting with my encounter with the Three Horsemen in the USCA bathroom. It seemed like it had happened an eternity ago, and to a different person. I even told them I was an Omega-level Meta. The only thing I left out was what I planned to do to the Meta who killed Dad once I found him. I did not want them to try to talk me out of it.

"I'm so sorry that happened man," Isaac said, putting his hand on my shoulder. "I can't believe you didn't tell us you're Omega-level before now, though. There are only a handful of Metas like you alive. You're like Metahuman royalty or something."

"They can take my crown back if I can have my dad back."

Neha leaned forward. "Tell me again exactly what the Meta looked like who killed your father and attacked you." I repeated what I had already told them, adding in a few other details about the Meta I had left out before. She nodded when I finished.

"I thought so. The guy you're looking for is named Iceburn. I recognized him from your description."

"Wait, you know this guy?" I asked, excited.

Neha shook her head. "I don't know him personally. Well, I did see him once, but it's not like we had a conversation or anything. It's really more along the lines of I know of him. He's a high-priced Metahuman contract killer. He's said to be very good at what he does and completely ruthless. Does a lot of work for Rogues. They hire him when they don't want their own fingerprints all over someone's death." Neha's eyes were a bit wide. "Iceburn's a real heavy-hitter. Somebody big is out to get you if they sent Iceburn after you. It's not as though guys like Iceburn are listed in the phone book where anyone can get a hold of them. Iceburn's very selective about his clientele. He doesn't work for just anybody."

"Do you know how to find him?" I sounded as eager as I felt. Birthday or no birthday, I would go find this Iceburn character right now.

"No," Neha said. "Everything I know about him I just told you." I sank back in my chair, deflated. Though I had not initially planned on tracking Iceburn down until I had gone further in my Hero studies as I did not know if I was yet ready to face him from a skills and ability standpoint, I was willing to chance it and find out.

"If Iceburn is this high level Metahuman assassin like you say who only works for elite bad guys, that begs the question of who hired him to target Theo and why," Isaac said.

"Amazing Man's guess is it's because I'm an Omega. He says some people find my mere existence threatening. Maybe it's one of them."

"Yeah, but who?" Isaac said. I shrugged.

"When I find Iceburn, I'll ask him." Asking him questions was not the only thing I planned to do to him.

"You're not ready to go up against a guy like Iceburn alone," Neha said, as if she could read my mind. I guess it was not too hard to read the expression on my face. She put her hand on my forearm. My arm tingled a little where she touched me. Neha was a very pretty woman, and even prettier with her mask off. I suddenly had very more-than-just-friends thoughts about her. Neha looked at me with deep concern in her beautiful hazel eyes. "If you do manage to find Iceburn, let me know. I'll help you."

"Let us know," Isaac immediately corrected her. He flicked a peanut at her. "He's my roommate. I've got dibs on helping him."

"I appreciate the offer guys, but this is my fight, not yours."

"You're one of the few friends I've got," Neha said. "I don't plan on losing you. Besides, you've already helped me. Returning the favor is the least I can do."

"Helped you? You're one of the best trainees at camp, if not the best. How have I helped you?"

"You've helped me not be a complete social pariah. If it weren't for you and Isaac, the trainees at camp would barely speak to me. I don't care too much about what people think about me, but it's still no fun to be alone and isolated."

"You can say that again. I've spent my fair share of time alone and isolated," I said.

"So promise us you won't try to take Iceburn down alone," Neha pressed.

"I'll try," I said noncommittally.

Isaac shook his head. "Don't give us that 'I'll try,' nonsense. You think we're idiots? You're just trying to get us off your back without committing to calling on us for help. Give us your word you won't try to take Iceburn down alone. If you don't promise us right now, I'll nag you day and night until you do. My mother has an Olympic gold medal in nagging. I've learned from the best."

I sighed. He was right, I was trying to avoid committing myself. Besides, based on my less than successful first encounter with Iceburn and what Neha had told us about him, maybe I needed all the help I could get to take him down. What kind of justice would it be for Dad if Iceburn killed me instead of vice versa? Regardless, having Neha and Isaac around would not change what I planned to do to Iceburn. So what if there were witnesses? I planned on turning myself in to the authorities after I killed Iceburn anyway. I had learned in the Academy the importance of Metas complying with the law. If I could not do that when I killed Iceburn, at least I could do it after the fact.

I made up my mind. "Okay, you win. I promise I'll contact you guys when I find Iceburn." Isaac clapped me on the shoulder.

"Good man," he said. "If he was smart, Iceburn would just turn himself in now. Against the three of us, he doesn't stand a chance. Like I always say, 'All for one, and one for all.' I invented that expression, you know."

"No you didn't," Neha said. "Dumas wrote that as the motto of the *Three Musketeers*."

"Dumas stole it from me."

"How did he steal it from you when he wrote the book in the 1800s, long before you were born?"

"Time travel. He said he'd credit me, but didn't," Isaac said. He shook his head in mock sorrow. "That thieving, time-traveling bastard. You can't trust anybody these days.

Or those days, for that matter." He frowned a little as he looked at Neha. "Wait, a minute—if this Iceburn guy is such an elite badass, how do you know about him?"

Neha took a long pull of her beer. Her eyes were thoughtful, her face conflicted. It looked like she was wrestling about whether to answer. Finally, she sighed.

"I already told you I was trained by the Rogue Doctor Alchemy. He was not just my trainer though. He's also my father. That's how I know about Iceburn."

Isaac and I looked at each other, then back at Neha. Isaac's mouth was open as wide as mine was.

"Why is the daughter of Doctor Alchemy, one of the most infamous Rogues in the world, in training to become a Hero?" I asked.

"My father is insane," she said flatly. "He wasn't always that way. When my mom was murdered by one of dad's rivals a few years back, it's like something in him snapped. He used to just use his powers to make a living. I'm not excusing that or apologizing for it because he still was doing illegal stuff. But before my mother died, he made it a point to avoid hurting people. Now that mom's gone, he's different. He's gotten it into his head that he is destined to rule the world so he can prevent deaths like mom's from happening. To achieve that goal, he'll stop at nothing. He's already murdered a bunch of people that I know of." She shook her head. "Now, how crazy does that sound? 'I must kill all these people to gain power so I can stop people from killing people.' I'm telling you he's gone nuts. I ran away from home a few years ago after Mom passed away. I've been living on my own since. I hope to get my Hero's license to help prevent my father from achieving his goals."

Our table was quiet for a bit as Isaac and I digested that.

"Holy Moses!" Isaac said. "Theo is an Omega-level Meta whose father was killed by the Metahuman assassin to the stars, and your dad is Doctor Alchemy who is bent on world conquest? Any more bombshells you two need to drop? Is one of you having a torrid love affair with Athena? Is the Old Man an alien invader in disguise? My heart can't take too much more of this."

Neha looked uncomfortable talking about her father, so I decided to change the subject. "Both Neha and I have told you why we decided to try to become Heroes. What's your story?" I asked Isaac.

"The story of my origin is not particularly interesting," Isaac said with a shrug. He grinned. "Like your average man of destiny, I was born in a manger. Three wise men showed up shortly thereafter to honor me with gifts. I decided to become a licensed Hero to give all you little people something to look up to. I think that's quite big of me. You're welcome."

"Stop kidding around. I'm serious," I said. "We shared. It's your turn."

Now Isaac looked uncomfortable. It was not an expression I was used to seeing on his face.

"Look, I realize we're playing show and tell, but I'm going to have to take a pass on sharing. For now, at least." He pushed his chair back and stood up. "I've got to go to the bathroom." Isaac looked so discomfited I decided to let the matter drop. I stood up also.

"I'll go with you. I've got to go too," I said.

"I thought only women went to the bathroom together," Neha said.

"When you're packing the kind of equipment I am, holding it up is a two-man operation. Theo's going to help."

"Sure I'll help," I said. I grinned at Isaac. "You got a pair of tweezers I can use?" He looked pained.

"If I weren't a Hero-to-be with ironclad self-esteem, that would hurt my feelings."

"If you survived being born in a manger, you'll survive this. Come on Fire Hose Man, let's go," I said. Since our waitress was nowhere to be seen, Neha said she would settle our tab with the bartender. Isaac and I went to the bathroom in the rear of the bar. I finished before he did, and went back to our table.

Neha was not here anymore. After looking around for a bit in the crowded place, I spotted her by the bar. Neha was talking to a group of guys who had been sitting and drinking at the bar in the middle of the pub ever since the three of us had come in. Rather, the guys were talking to her. Neha clearly was trying to ignore them while she settled up with the bartender. As I watched, the guy seated closest to where she stood kept touching her shoulder, and she kept brushing him off. I knew Neha could handle herself, so I stayed at the table. When that guy reached down and cupped her butt, though, I was moving towards them before I even consciously realized it.

Neha smacked the guy's hand away. I got to her side in time to hear the guy slur to her, "What, you think you're too good for me?"

"Yes," Neha said. The guy was white, bearded, big and burly, and obviously drunk. He and his four friends looked to be all about the same age, maybe in their mid-twenties.

"There a problem here?" I asked Neha.

"Nothing I can't handle," she said. The guy who had touched her blinked his bloodshot eyes repeatedly as he tried to focus on me.

"Who are you, Captain Save-A-Ho?" the guy said, his breath smelling like a distillery. His friends laughed.

"Something like that. Come on, let's go back to our table," I said to Neha.

"Not so fast Pocahontas, I'm not done talking to you," the guy said to Neha. He grabbed at her again. Neha pushed his hands away.

"I'm not that kind of Indian," Neha said. She did not call him a jackass, but her tone implied it. The beefy guy reached for her again, this time grabbing her forearm. Neha twisted out of his grasp. Acting on instinct, I grabbed the guy's arm, digging my thumb hard into the crease of his forearm opposite his elbow. The guy yelped in pain. I was poking my thumb into one of his body's pressure points. The guy tried to stand up. I kept him seated by pulling down on his arm where I was still applying pressure, making him cry out in pain again.

"Didn't your parents ever teach you to keep your hands to yourself?" I asked the guy, still holding onto his arm and exerting pressure on it with my thumb. His friends got up from their barstools and moved towards me. They were all bigger than both Neha and I. This was about to get ugly fast.

"Oh look, a party no one invited me to," came Isaac's voice. Unnoticed, he had come up to stand behind the four now standing guys. "What game are you all playing? I hope it's charades. I love charades."

The four guys twisted to look at Isaac.

"Why don't you mind your own business, sambo?" one of them said.

"Oh, so it's Jim Crow you're playing?" Isaac said. "Can't say I like that game as much as charades, but it's not my party, so who am I to judge? Tell you what fellas, why don't you have a seat and we'll all be friends? I'll even buy you a drink. We'll tell our kids one day the funny story of how we all met."

"Fuck your drink," another of the four said. "And fuck you. I ain't drinkin' with the likes of you." He stepped towards Isaac. The other three stepped towards me and Neha. I was about to incapacitate the guy whose arm I was still holding so I could deal with his friends when there was a sudden crash from the bar. Startled, everyone looked over.

The bartender stood there behind the bar, holding the baseball bat he obviously had just whacked against the top of the bar. He was a bear of a guy, with a big belly and thick arms corded with muscle.

"There's no fighting in here," he said. "Get out." I let go of the arm I was holding. I stepped back from the guy I released in case he planned on taking a swing at me. He squeezed his no doubt numb arm against his body. He rubbed his arm with his working hand, staring daggers at me.

"Vic, these guys started it," one of the standing four said.

I said, "That's a lie! We didn't start any—" The bartender interrupted me by whacking the baseball bat against the bar top again.

"I don't care who started what. Get out. All of you," he ordered.

Neha, Isaac and I left the bar. We were followed by the five men. I hoped they would let this thing go, but they followed behind us as we walked in the direction of where we had left the Academy car. We kept an eye on them, expecting trouble.

When we got to an area that was away from everyone else and shrouded in shadows, the five men rushed us.

It all happened so fast. I hit one of the guys, the one who had grabbed Neha, in the side of his neck right under his jaw. He went down like a puppet with its strings cut. A second one I kicked in the stomach. The air whooshed out of him like a slashed tire. He bent over, holding his stomach. I followed the kick up with a quick knee to his jaw. He jerked backwards. He hit the ground, joining his friend there. Neither of them moved.

I turned to help Neha and Isaac. I need not have bothered. Neha stood over two of the guys. One was facedown on the ground, the other was faceup. Neither moved.

I looked over at Isaac. He was moving slightly behind the sole remaining guy, the one who had called Isaac sambo. The guy's face was bloody. A knife flashed in his right hand. Isaac kicked him behind his knee. With a cry, the guy dropped to that knee. He dropped the knife. Isaac wrapped his right arm around the kneeling guy's neck, grabbed his own left bicep with his right hand, and pushed the guy's head forward a bit with his left forearm. Isaac squeezed. In seconds the guy's eyes fluttered and then closed thanks to Isaac's rear naked choke. Isaac let him slump to the ground.

The entire fight lasted less than a minute. Actually, it was not a fight. It was a slaughter.

"Carolina and I knocked two guys out in the time it took you to deal with just one," Neha pointed out to Isaac. He got a defensive look on his face.

"I was pacing myself," he said. He breathed hard. "Besides, my guy had a knife. It's harder when they're armed." Isaac went over to where the knife had fallen. He pulled a handkerchief out of his pocket, and carefully picked up the knife with it. He pressed the knife back into the hand of the man he had just knocked out. Then, he quickly frisked the unconscious man.

"What in the world are you doing?" Neha asked. She glanced around to see if anyone was watching us. "We should get out of here. The Academy said we're not to draw attention to ourselves. Standing over the bodies of five unconscious guys we just knocked out is the opposite of not drawing attention to ourselves."

Isaac waved at her dismissively. He had already moved on to frisk another of the five men. "I'm doing my civic duty," he said. Again using his handkerchief, he pulled a small bag of white powder out of the pocket of the guy he was frisking. Isaac made a *tsking* sound. He held it up so we could see it.

"I'm guessing this isn't baby powder," Isaac said. He put the bag back into the man's pocket. He moved on to frisk the other guys. In addition to the bag of white powder, he found several joints and another knife, all of which Isaac put back where he had found them.

Isaac stood back up straight. One of the guys' cell phones was now in his hand. He said, "We can't get these guys thrown in jail for assault. That would require us to file charges. Like you said Neha, we're not supposed to draw attention to ourselves. But maybe we can get these knuckleheads locked up for drug and weapon possession."

Isaac dialed a number on the phone. "Hello, police?" he said into the phone. His voice was frantic and panicked. "Five guys just jumped me! One of them had a knife. A Hero intervened and started to fight them. A really handsome black guy. He was amazing." Isaac winked at us. "I managed to run away. Send help right away!" He gave the person on the other end of the line the address we were at, and hung up. He looked down at the unconscious guys.

"Sambo? Really?" Isaac said in amazement in his normal voice. He shook his head and looked back up at us. "Maybe these guys are time travelers from the 1800s like Dumas. Let's get out of here before the cops show."

We left. On the way back to the car, Isaac wiped the cell he had called the police with clean of his fingerprints. He dropped it into a trash bin.

We got into the car, and started the drive back to the camp. It wasn't until I had settled back into the front seat that the significance of what had just happened sank in. Not only had I confronted and defeated those guys, but I had done it easily and reflexively, without using my powers and without being scared out of my wits. It was a far cry from how I had felt months ago when I had that run-in with the Three Horsemen. Back then, I had nearly pooped my pants in fear, and the Three Horsemen had manhandled me as easily as if I was a child before my powers had kicked in. Facing those five guys back there, I had not been afraid. I certainly had not felt like a child.

"Hello! Earth to Theo," Isaac said. "Is something wrong? Did you hurt your hands back there?"

His words startled me out of my reverie. I realized he had been talking for a while. I had missed what he had said. Lost in thought, I had been staring at my hands as if I had never seen them before. They seemed bigger. Stronger. Different. As was I, I now realized.

"I'm kind of a badass," I said. My voice was filled with wonder.

My revelation was met with silence for a few seconds.

"You're studying to be a Hero," Neha then said. "Duh!"

CHAPTER EIGHTEEN

Standing shirtless in front of the bathroom mirror in my apartment building at Camp Avatar, I looked at the nude full-body photo that had been taken of me when I had first entered the Academy. It was later the same night Isaac, Neha and I had the run-in with those five guys in Portland.

At the time the photo had been taken, I had not understood why the Academy had mandated that the picture be taken and a copy given to me. Much later it had occurred to me that maybe it was another way to humiliate us trainees, a tactic to psychologically break us down with the intention of later building us back up with a different, more Heroic, mentality. And, maybe that had been part of the reason the photo was taken. But now I thought there was a different reason: to give us trainees who made it this far a basis for comparison, to show us how far we had come.

A picture told a thousand words. What the naked picture was now telling me was that I had changed in the months I had been at Camp Avatar. I was no longer skin and bones like I was in the photo. While I hardly looked like Mr. Olympia now, I definitely was bigger and more muscular. Training as hard as I did and eating as much as I did clearly were having an effect. How much bigger and stronger would I be if I continued on the path I was on? Would I one day look like Amazing Man, who despite his age had the body of an underwear model? Also, in the picture my face was boyish. Now, my face was more rugged, more masculine.

Not only was I different looks-wise, I also had a different mentality and was capable of handling myself in a scrap. Our fight with those guys from the bar in Portland had proven that to me. I did not know if I was yet ready to tackle Iceburn. There was no doubt, though, that I was readier than I had been months ago.

I put my mask back on in case I encountered another trainee on the way back to my room. I walked back to the room I shared with Isaac. He was off chewing the fat with some of the other trainees. I put the picture of myself back into the envelope it had been in, and put the envelope into the chest containing my few possessions.

Though it was late, I was too keyed up to sleep. Still shirtless, I pulled out one of my history books. World history was by far my worst subject, mainly because I did not have much of a grounding in it. In the small-town schools I had gone to in South Carolina, if an American hadn't done it or Jesus Christ hadn't said it, then it wasn't considered important. I settled in at the desk to start reading about China's Taiping Civil War in the mid-1800s. It was fought by the Chinese government against a Christian sect led by a Chinese man who believed himself to be the younger brother of Jesus, which was certainly news to me. Jesus having a Chinese brother had been left out of all of the versions of the Bible I had read.

I had been studying for about half an hour when a knock came at the door.

"Come in," I said. The door was not locked. It did not even have a lock. Even if someone had something in his room worth stealing, we trainees lived under a strict honor code. No one wanted to wash out of the Academy by violating it after having come this far.

Neha opened the door and walked in. She closed the door behind herself. Though she now had her mask on so she would not reveal her true appearance to the other trainees, she still wore the skirt and blouse she had on when we had driven to Portland. Her long, shiny black hair was still down. When she was training, she always wore it up in a bun to keep it out of her eyes and to make it harder for opponents to grab her. Her shirt was unbuttoned enough that there was a hint of cleavage. I was suddenly even more aware than usual of the swell of her breasts and the curve of her hips, not to mention the fact I did not have a shirt on. Though Neha had been in my room countless times, Isaac had almost always been present when she had been here. For some reason, being alone here with her was making my chest tighten.

"Isaac is not here," I said, though she had not asked. I was inexplicably very nervous.

"I know. I just left him. He's telling everyone who'll listen about our fight with those guys in Portland. According to him, there were ten guys, not just five." Neha shook her head. "By the time the night is over, he'll have us fighting off hordes of Hells Angels and Klansmen."

I grinned. "Isaac has a flair for exaggeration," I said.

"Isaac is a liar." Neha smiled, taking the sting out of her words. "But, he's our liar." It was weird hearing Myth being called Isaac and calling him that myself, especially now that we were back on the grounds of the Academy. Even so, I liked the fact I now knew Smoke's and Myth's real names. Using their real names here at camp made it like we were a part of a special club that only the three of us belonged to.

"So, can I help you with something?" I asked. I was still nervous. Oddly, Neha looked nervous too. She usually never looked nervous. She normally looked calm, cool, and collected, like there was nothing that could happen she was not capable of dealing with.

"I just wanted to thank you." She said it almost shyly.

"Thank me? For what?"

"For standing up for me."

"Oh. Not a problem. Though I think you and I both know that if Isaac and I had not been with you tonight, you could have handled those guys all by yourself."

"Of course I could have." False modesty was not one of Neha's vices. "Even so, it's nice to have someone stand up for me for a change. I'm so used to having to always do it myself. And, I'm not thanking you for just standing up for me tonight, but also here at camp. I know you stick up for me when people around here start talking crap about me. I just want to let you know how much I appreciate it."

Neha seemed vulnerable, more open than usual. With a flash of sympathetic insight, I realized how hard it must have been for her, with her mother having been murdered and her father a noted supervillain. Plus, she had to fend for herself these past few years. Maybe it was that vulnerability that made me do it. Maybe it was the fact I felt more confident than I ever had before. Maybe it was the fact I was more aware than usual of just how pretty Neha was. All of the above, maybe.

Regardless of why, I stood up. I stepped up to her and took her in my arms. I lowered my head and kissed her. For one frightening and agonizing moment, Neha tensed up against me. Then, she relaxed. She kissed me back. Her mouth opened hungrily to mine. We kissed for what felt like both an eternity and just an instant.

Neha broke our kiss. She stepped back. I was afraid she was about to leave. She did not. Looking at me the way Delilah must have looked at Sampson, she reached down. She unbuttoned her shirt. A black lacy bra was revealed. She pulled her shirt off and dropped it to the floor. I watched her intently, transfixed. Neha unhooked and shrugged out of her bra. Blood roared in my ears, pounding like a jungle drum. Outside of movies and the Internet, I had never seen a woman topless before. I shook a little. I pulled Neha to me. Her bare skin pressed against mine, soft and hot.

We fell together into my bed. At some point, I'm not sure when, we pulled each other's masks off. We saw each other clearly and intimately. At first slowly and then more frantically, we explored each other. A new sensual world of sights and sensations opened before me.

Much later, after it was over, Neha curled up against me. Her soft flesh pressed against me. "Happy birthday, Theo," she murmured into my ear.

It was the first time she had ever called me anything other than Carolina. Though I did not know it at the time, she would never call me Carolina again.

It was the best birthday ever.

CHAPTER NINETEEN

Soaring above the flames and trying to avoid breathing in the rising plumes of smoke, I generated as large of an air-impermeable force field as I could around part of the edge of the raging wildfire. The field was not as big as I wished it was, though it was as big as the current state of my powers was capable of making it. The field was maybe the length of an eighteen wheeler, and twice as wide. It shimmered slightly in my eyes, though I knew it was invisible to everyone else. Even though it was not as big as I would like, I had come a long way thanks to my Academy training from the days where I could only generate a force field around my own person. My powers seemed to be like my muscles—the more I used them and the harder I pushed them, the stronger they got.

The part of the fire contained in my force field died in intensity and then went out, having consumed all of the oxygen within the field. I released my hold on the field, and generated another one around the fire right next to where I had just extinguished the flames. I had been at this for well over an hour. I felt like an invisible giant putting out a fire by stamping it with his huge feet. Though it was slow going, it was working. I had already created a firebreak over a large area on the perimeter of the wildfire. There was so much more to be done though. I felt like Sisyphus pushing his boulder up a hill, only for it to roll back down to the bottom so he had to start all over again.

Sisyphus? Huh. Hanging out with Myth so much clearly had rubbed off on me. With Neha, more than just mythological knowledge had rubbed off on me. I smiled to myself at the thought.

I was not working alone in fighting the fire. All of the trainees and instructors at the Academy were spread around the perimeter of the wildfire, doing our best to contain and extinguish it. The fire had started early yesterday, and had spread rapidly thanks to the unusually dry weather Oregon suffered from lately. The fire had quickly overwhelmed the efforts of firefighters, and had burned well over 200,000 acres since it had started. Many homes had been destroyed, and several people had lost their lives. When it had become clear the state and local authorities needed help, Oregon Governor Adrian Patterson had called Amazing Man. The Old Man had volunteered the assistance of all of the Hero instructors and the trainees. All of us from the Academy were split into various sectors of the wildfire. Each of us trainees was in charge of fighting the wildfire in our own sector. Since we were under the supervision of the Hero instructors who were fighting the massive blaze with us, we were authorized to use our powers here outside the confines of Camp Avatar.

There were some boulders below. With effort, I moved the massive rocks one by one until they formed a short line in front of the encroaching fire. The line of boulders should stop the fire from spreading further, at least in that small area. Months ago I would not have been strong enough to budge a single one of these rocks. I wondered what else I would be able to do in the future as my powers and I grew stronger.

As I moved the boulders into place, I heard the Old Man in my ear through the earbud there, coordinating the firefighting efforts of the trainees and Heroes. On my wrists were devices that looked like thick silver wristwatches. One was a miniature computer that also monitored each trainee's vital signs so the Academy Heroes would know if one of us trainees got into trouble fighting the blaze. The other was a communicator so I could speak to my comrades had I the need. I had not used it since I had been fighting the blaze, nor had I seen anyone from the Academy. The blaze was too massive and those of us from the camp were spread too far apart for me to have run across anyone.

No, wait. There was someone now, flying in the air at the same altitude I was at. I could not see him or her clearly due to the smoke billowing up from the blaze below. I squinted. The figure slowly came closer towards me in the air. His form became clearer.

No.

It couldn't be.

Yes! It was!

The figure approaching me was not a figment of my imagination, not a mirage created by heat and wishful thinking.

It was Iceburn.

He looked just the way I remembered him, just the way I saw him almost every night when I confronted him over and over again in my nightmares. He wore a pitch black costume that covered him from head to toe. Glowing lines riddled his costume like weird varicose veins. Half of his body glowed orange-red; the other half glowed light blue.

An odd combination of rage and excitement filled me. I had waited for this moment for what seemed like forever. I had rehearsed over and over in my mind what I could have done differently when I had first encountered Iceburn, and what I would do in the future once I was better trained in the use of my powers.

The future was unexpectedly now.

I immediately forgot all about the wildfire. I raised my hands up towards Iceburn. I exerting my will to attempt to form a spherical force field around him and trap him like a bug in a jar. Once formed, I would tighten the force bubble around Iceburn, squashing him like a cockroach. I would do it slowly, though. I wanted him to die agonizingly. He deserved no less.

As usual, my hands burned as I used my powers. Despite the fact my powers had been triggered, the visible-to-me-only force field I expected to form around Iceburn did not do so. I redoubled my efforts, concentrating mightily to encage Iceburn. It was not working. Iceburn continued to move towards me, slowly and upright, like he was standing on an invisible conveyor belt.

Iceburn came to a halt. Though he was still pretty far from me, I could see him shaking his black-clad head.

"You can put your hands down, kid," he said in his gravelly voice. "Your powers won't work on me. It's the suit. It nullifies Meta's powers so they can't affect me directly." Though I normally would not believe this murderer if he told me the sky was blue, he clearly was right about this at least: my powers were not working on him. I kept trying anyway. I scowled with concentration. My hands felt like they were going to explode with the intensity of my effort. Iceburn shook his head at me again. Though I could not see his face due to his costume, I could sense his disgust at my futile effort.

"I see you're still not the brightest bulb in the store," Iceburn said. He glanced down at the partially extinguished crackling fire below. "Even so, your ability to use your powers has come a long way since I last saw you. I've been watching you fight the fire the past few minutes. Actually, I've been watching you from afar ever since you enrolled in Hero Academy. Your face looking different than before threw me at first—you trainees use some sort of face masking technology apparently—but your powers make you easy to recognize. I thought about trying to take you out there, but not even I felt comfortable going up against a truckload of self-righteous Metas to get to you. Besides, I'm supposed to make your death look like an accident. It's why I didn't make a move against you when you were out with your friends in Portland last week. Too many witnesses. Then I hit upon the idea of setting this fire. I figured if I made it big enough, the state would ask the Metas in the Academy for help in putting it out. I just knew you all would jump at the chance to lend a hand." Iceburn shook his head. "You Hero types are too predictable. It's a weakness. And here you are, practically gift-wrapped for me. Now when you die, it'll look like you got overwhelmed by the fire. So tragic." The bastard sounded smug.

"You set this fire? All to lure me out of camp?" I asked. I was in disbelief. I guess I should not have been. A murderer like Iceburn would not hesitate to commit arson. "Do you have any idea how much damage you've caused with this fire? How many people you've killed?"

"Non-Metas are little more than ants. They don't matter. Besides, if they're dumb enough to let themselves burn to death, they deserve to die. It's natural selection." Iceburn shrugged. "If it makes you feel better, think of their deaths as a compliment to how important you are to my employers. I hope you enjoyed it. It's the last compliment you'll ever get." He raised his arm on the side of his body that glowed orange-red. The glow of his palm grew brighter, like the lights of an oncoming train.

The small boulder I had been stealthily raising into the air behind Iceburn slammed into his back at my mental command. He cried out in pain, flailing in the air. I shifted the boulder slightly so it was on top of him. Maybe I could not act on Iceburn's body directly thanks to his suit. That did not mean I could not use other items as weapons against him. The power lines I had wrapped around his body the night of Dad's death had shown me that.

CAPED

Still exerting my powers on the boulder, I sent it plummeting towards the ground with Iceburn underneath it. If I could not squeeze Iceburn to death directly with my powers, I would kill him this way. There was more than one way to step on a bug. I too dropped in the air as the boulder dropped, keeping pace with it. The wind whistled in my ears. My heart sang with anticipation, though doubt nagged at the edge of my conscience. No, there was no time for doubts now. I had waited too long for this moment. I had to focus.

Iceburn tried repeatedly to fly away from the boulder. I shifted the boulder as he shifted, keeping it on top of him. Iceburn twisted around. He touched the boulder with his hand that glowed blue. Almost instantly, the boulder was covered in a thick sheath of ice. Now the boulder was too heavy for me to handle. It had taken every bit of will I had to lift the small boulder into the air and shift it around when it had not been encased in ice.

Iceburn flew from under the boulder now that I could not properly adjust it. I released my hold on the boulder, letting it fall unfettered to the ground. It was now too heavy for me to use it as a weapon.

I rocketed towards Iceburn with my force field around me. I intended to pummel him to death with my bare hands. Right as I was about to slam into him, Iceburn moved out of the way at the last moment. My momentum made me sail past him. I brought myself to a stop as quickly as I could. I gathered myself and reoriented, spotting again where Iceburn hung in the air. I launched myself at him again like a guided missile. He dropped out of the way right as I was about to hit him. I again sailed past him, twisting in midair to keep him in sight as I decelerated. My last attack had just been a feint, anyway. The partially burnt tree I had already ripped from the ground shot towards Iceburn like a thrown spear. A red-orange beam burst from his hand. Even from this far

163

away, I felt the heat of the blast. The tree burnt to literal ash before it hit him.

Iceburn twisted in the air to face me. He shouted, "I was right before, kid: you have been learning. You're not the easy target you were when I first met you. I wonder if you're as fast as me, though."

With that, he turned, and shot off towards the horizon. Without hesitation, I took off after him before I lost sight of him. He was not going to get away. Not this time.

Iceburn zigged and zagged in the air. I mimicked his movements, following him like the tail on a rabid dog. Flying as fast as I could, I started to close the gap with him a bit. My stomach tightened in anticipation. Then, suddenly, I could close the gap between us no further. This was despite the fact I strained with effort, flying faster than I ever had before. What I needed was something to stop Iceburn with, or at least slow him down. We were high up in the air, flying in and out of the clouds. There was nothing up here I could use as a weapon. I hazarded a quick glance down. Everything below was a blur as we zoomed over the earth. I would have to slow down to see well enough to pick something up to use against Iceburn. At the speed Iceburn flew, I knew if I slowed down, I would lose him.

The fact I initially closed the gap with Iceburn and then could get no closer to him made me suspicious. That, plus the fact I had not been able to get ahold of him in our brief aerial dogfight made me think he was a faster flyer than I was. Was Iceburn deliberately not losing me? Was he leading me somewhere? But where? And why?

I soon had my answer. Iceburn dropped sharply towards the ground at a forty-five degree angle. I slowed as I approached where Iceburn had dropped, alert for a trap. I arrived above where Iceburn had descended in time to see him land in front of a multi-story building. It was in a cluster of smaller buildings. The buildings were in a small clearing surrounded by trees. I had no idea where we were.

I had been chasing Iceburn for several minutes at top speed. There were no landmarks I recognized. I was completely disoriented.

As I watched, Iceburn looked up at me. He gave me a cheery wave. He opened a door to the tall building. He stepped inside and out of my view.

Hyperalert to any sign of danger, I landed as far as I could from where Iceburn had entered the tall building while still keeping the entrance in site. Signage around the building indicated it and the surrounding smaller buildings were a vacant office complex scheduled for demolition in a few weeks. Part of me want to charge into the building after Iceburn and end this once and for all. The other part of me knew better. "Never let the enemy pick the battle site," came the words of General George S. Patton into my mind. I had learned them in my Hero Psychology, Strategy, and Tactics class. Iceburn wanted me to follow him into that building. It was as clear as the nose on my face.

Going into the building alone would play into Iceburn's hands. I was sure of it.

It was time to call for backup.

CHAPTER TWENTY

Perhaps Iceburn had not planned on me having help. Besides, I had promised Isaac and Neha. My promise to them had flashed through my mind when I had first seen Iceburn, but I had been too busy fighting him to get into touch with them before now.

I punched the code for Isaac's communicator into my wristband so I could speak to him without everyone else from camp hearing.

"Why are you bothering me Theo?" came Isaac's voice into my earbud in a few seconds. "I'm busy toasting marshmallows over the world's biggest campfire."

"Iceburn confronted me a little while ago," I said without preamble into my communicator. "I've chased him to a building. He went inside. I have it under surveillance right now. I think I need some help."

"I'll pick Smoke up and hone in on the GPS in your wristband," Isaac said. His voice was suddenly all business. "We'll be there as soon as we can."

I launched myself back into the air, moving high and far enough away from the building so I could see if Iceburn flew out of it. Now that I was not so busy chasing Iceburn, I could pay more attention to the details of my surroundings. The building Iceburn had gone into was ten stories tall. It was grayish-white in color, and rectangular in shape. Many of its windows were broken. From my vantage point high in the air, I floated and watched, waiting impatiently for Neha and Isaac.

After a while—it seemed like an eternity but was probably only fifteen minutes or so—I spotted a white dot up in the sky. As I watched, the dot grew bigger and bigger. It was a white horse. No, it was not merely a horse: it was a pegasus. Its broad white wings beat the air rapidly. I had never seen one before in real life of course, but I had seen plenty of Isaac's drawings of them taped up onto the walls of our room. Neha sat astride the pegasus, gripping its long white mane as it flew towards me. In her camp uniform and mask, she looked the way a Valkyrie might have looked when she rode into battle.

The pegasus came up alongside of me. I dropped back down to the ground in front of but far away from where I had seen Iceburn enter the building. The pegasus followed, beating its majestic white wings powerfully. Gusts of air from its wings kicked up dust from the ground when it landed gently next to me. Neha swung her leg over, and hopped off. The pegasus shimmered and glowed, shrinking in on itself. In moments the costumed and masked figure of Isaac stood where the pegasus had been.

"It was your first time riding me," Isaac said to Neha. "Was it as good for you as it was for me?" I doubted he would have made that joke had he known Neha and I had slept together. We had not told him. It was none of his business.

Neha rolled her eyes slightly at Isaac's words, but otherwise ignored him. She turned to me.

"What's the situation?" she asked. I quickly sketched out what had happened in my encounter with Iceburn. Since I had not seen him leave the building while I waited for them to arrive, I told them I assumed Iceburn was still inside. I also told them I assumed Iceburn was lying in wait for me.

"At the risk of being made fun of for being the voice of reason, shouldn't we call for more backup?" Neha said. "There are several fully licensed Heroes nearby, not to mention a bunch of trainees. We could meet Iceburn with overwhelming force, trap or no trap. Shock and awe." I was about to protest calling in others to help when Isaac beat me to it.

"Are you insane?" he said. "That guy in there killed Theo's father. If somebody takes him down, it has to be Theo. And we're going to help him do it." I could not have said it better myself. I nodded firmly in agreement.

"I know we're going to help him," Neha said. She sighed in resignation. "Just like I knew that would be your attitude about calling for reinforcements." Her lips tightened grimly. "I can't say I even disagree with you. I just thought someone ought to point out walking into a fight with a gun is probably not the most sensible move when you can walk in with a nuclear missile instead."

"Come on, let's go," I said. I was tired of all the talking. I was anxious to end this once and for all. With my personal force field up, I started walking towards the door Iceburn had gone into. Isaac stopped me.

"Hold on Theo," he said. "We don't want to have to search the whole building for this guy." As Neha and I watched, Isaac's form glowed as it always did when he underwent a transformation. His form grew taller, though slightly hunched over. His uniform disappeared, replaced with long, coarse black fur that covered his entire body. His ears became long and pointed, and his mouth elongated into a snout full of yellowed, sharp teeth. His eyes were small, beady, and red. The fingernails of his hands stretched out into long black claws. His now bigger body stopped glowing, making the big sinewy muscles he now had become obvious.

Isaac had turned into a werewolf. He looked terrifying, like a nightmare come to life.

"I'll go first," Isaac said. The words came out as a snarl. They were hard to understand. "I can track him like this." We all cautiously approached the door. Isaac opened it, and we went inside. Neha brought up the rear.

It was dim and hushed inside. We could still see adequately thanks to the sunlight coming in through the broken and dirty windows. We were inside what probably was once the welcome area for the old office building. The place was a mess, with debris everywhere. Everything was still and quiet. There was no sign of Iceburn.

Isaac's snout tilted into the air. I heard him sniffing. His big nostrils dilated and contracted over and over. With a slight jerk of his big wolf head, he motioned Neha and me to follow him down a hall to the left. Despite his size, Isaac's werewolf form moved gracefully over and through the debris. He barely made a sound. I could not say the same for Neha and myself. In the stillness of the building, the two of us sounded like stampeding elephants. Iceburn would hear us coming from a mile away like this. I activated my powers, lifting myself into the air to float after Isaac. I glanced back meaningfully at Neha. She nodded in understanding. Her lower body became smoky and translucent. She now glided after Isaac and me as silently as a wisp of smoke.

Isaac led us down one hallway after another. It felt like we were in a maze. Finally, Isaac paused before reaching an open doorway on the right. He looked back at us, pointing repeatedly at the door with his clawed hand. It was obvious he meant Iceburn was in there.

I held up my hand with my fingers extended. I dropped them one at a time. When I reached the count of five, we burst into the room like we had been shot out of a cannon.

Iceburn was inside. He stood in the middle of the room, facing us, unmoving. The room was large and mostly empty except for a heavy-looking wooden desk and some matching empty bookshelves. An executive's old office, maybe.

My friends and I spread out in front of Iceburn so as to not present a single target. Iceburn was on top of something. It was a couple of inches tall, metallic, circular, and maybe two feet or so in diameter. I did not know what it was. As long as it did not keep me from taking Iceburn out, I did not care what it was.

I was close enough to Iceburn to get a look at his eyes behind his mask for the first time. They were a dark brown. They flicked from Isaac, to Neha, to me. I also noticed he wore a thick black belt with big buttons where a buckle would normally be. I had not noticed it on him before because it was the same dark black as his costume.

"I was wondering how long it would take you to come in after me, Theo," he said. I hated the fact he called me Theo. My friends called me Theo. "And you brought your girlfriend and your dog. How cute." He did not seem concerned about the fact he was outnumbered. His lack of concern made me all the more concerned. What was he up to?

"You have two options, Iceburn," Isaac snarled. "Option A is you surrender. Option B is we beat the crap out of you. I for one hope you pick B."

Iceburn tilted his head slightly to the side in surprise.

"So you know my name? That was unexpected. Soon enough, it won't matter," he said. "As for the choices you've presented me with, I don't like either A or B. I choose Option C instead."

Iceburn reached down and hit one of the buttons on his belt. His body flickered like it was a television getting a bad signal. Before any of us could react, Iceburn disappeared.

I glanced around frantically. "Where did he go?" I demanded, confused, frustrated, and angry. "Invisibility?"

Isaac sniffed the air.

"He's nowhere around here," he said.

"He could be anywhere in the world," Neha said. She sounded disgusted. She pointed. "That's a transporter pad he was standing on. I recognize it now. I've seen my dad use one before. As long as another pad elsewhere is programmed to receive you, you can use those pads to teleport just about anywhere."

Dread stabbed me in the heart like a dagger. I had suspected this was a trap. Now I knew it was. Why else would Iceburn lure me into the building, and then teleport away as soon as he confirmed I was inside?

I raised my voice in urgency. "Let's get out of—"

I could not even finish the thought. We heard several loud booms. The floor vibrated and moved like an earthquake was hitting. The walls shook.

We all sprang for the door.

The building collapsed around and on us.

CHAPTER TWENTY-ONE

Darkness. Someone was coughing.

"It's as dark as the inside of a cow. I wish I had a match or a lighter," Isaac's snarling voice said. He wheezed. I heard him spit. I could not see him. I could not see anything. "What a time to realize I should have taken up smoking."

Something started to glow in the darkness. The tiny space we were in slowly lit up enough that I could see. There was so much dust swirling around it was like standing in a thick fog. Breathing it in made my throat and lungs burn. The glow came from Neha. Her forearms and hands glowed a bright yellow. Isaac looked at her like she was a magician.

"Radon gas," she said in explanation of her glowing arms. "Cooled below its freezing point radon glows. Very radioactive, of course." She glanced up at the crush of building rubble less than a foot over her head. "If we don't get out of here soon, radiation exposure will be the least of our problems."

My arms were extended out at ninety degree angles from my side. My powers were going at full blast. My hands burned like they had been plunged into a forge. I was keeping tons of collapsed building off of us using a force field in the shape of a dome. It was barely big enough to protect the three of us. Isaac, the tallest of us in his werewolf form, had to stoop over to avoid banging his head into it. He changed into his normal form as I struggled to maintain the force field.

I had never supported this kind of weight before. My brain literally throbbed, like it was going to explode. I felt an impossibly heavy weight on the back of my neck, like someone had placed a fully loaded barbell there and was forcing me to squat the weight. Moving many stories of rubble from off of us was out of the question. It was all I could do to hold it up and keep it from killing us.

"Save yourselves," I gasped. Speaking was an effort. Doing anything but focusing on keeping tons of twisted metal and concrete and God knew what else from falling and crushing us was an effort. "Neha, turn into smoke and seep through the rubble and out. Isaac, turn into a ghost and phase through it. I'll hold the rubble up until you both change. Hurry!"

"Don't be ridiculous," Isaac said. "We're not leaving you here to die. All of us get out, or none of us do." Neha nodded in agreement. Both of them were caked with dust and dirt.

"Any idea how?" Neha asked.

"I already came up with the idea of all for one and one for all. I'm fresh out of others."

"No time for jokes," I spat. My teeth were clenched. "I can't hold this much longer." My mind automatically started to estimate how much weight I must have been holding up based on the height of the building and its size. The more I thought about all that weight, the harder it was to keep it from falling in on us. I shook the thought away like it was an annoying gnat. Sweat dripped into my eyes. My outstretched arms shook with exertion.

"I've got an idea," Isaac said. He sighed with resignation. Even with his face covered with building dust, he looked wan and drawn. "I'm not sure if I can change into something that big as I've never tried before. Plus I'm already exhausted from transforming into so many creatures today. But I'll have to try." He sketched out his idea to us.

Neha shifted position slightly to stand even closer to me than before. She pressed her body tightly against mine except for her glowing arms. She held her arms away from me to avoid touching me with them as they were freezing cold. Isaac began to glow as he always did when he was undergoing a transformation. He began to swell, as if he was a tire being inflated. He got so big that his head started to press against the top of my force field. He bent over, hunching over me and Neha as he continued to grow in size. His body grew to dominate the tiny space we were in, filling it like a balloon being inflated inside a glass jar.

"Now!" he yelled, his voice strained.

Neha stopped glowing. She wrapped her arms around me. I dropped the force field that kept the rubble from collapsing in on us. I simultaneously activated one around myself and Neha. She pressed against me so tightly it was as if she was trying to climb inside of me. Dust and debris fell in on all of us with a deafening roar, bouncing off the force field around me and Neha. Isaac was not so lucky. The weight of the destroyed building bore down on him while he simultaneously grew in size and tried to lift it off of us. He was trying to transform into Atlas, the Titan who supported the entire world on his shoulders in Greek mythology.

For a horrifying instant, Isaac stopped growing. He shrank a little. He was not going to pull it off. This was it. I found Neha's hand and squeezed it tight. Isaac roared in pain and effort. The sound competed with the thunderous noise of falling debris. His primal scream made my bones rattle and my ears hurt. He started to grow again, slowly at first, then faster and faster and faster. He was soon a behemoth that towered over us the way a man towers over an ant.

In his Atlas form, Isaac stood up straight. He shrugged the rubble off of himself like it was crumbs. Rubble crashed and rumbled around us, bouncing off my force field. Isaac reached his massive hands down and swept debris and rubble away from me and Neha like it was dirt. We were free! I blinked at the sudden brightness as the now exposed sun was shining brightly.

Isaac stood up straight again. His giant form loomed over us like the now destroyed building once had. Isaac's massive eyes were bloodshot and unfocused. He took two unsteady steps backward, away from us. Each step made the ground rumble and my teeth rattle. Isaac swayed for a moment, like a cornstalk in the wind. Then, he slowly fell backward. He was so tall, it took him a few seconds to hit the ground. But when he did, he hit the ground so hard, it was like a bomb had gone off. Some of the smaller buildings around us collapsed. Trees on the perimeter of the building complex were crushed under Isaac like they were matchsticks. Birds launched into the air.

Isaac's now supine giant body began to glow. The light was so intense, Neha and I had to look away and shield our eyes. When we finally were able to look again, Isaac's giant form was gone.

It took Neha and I several minutes to find Isaac's body amid all the devastation and debris. He was on his back with his eyes closed. He was covered with cuts and bruises. His uniform was little more than bloody rags.

Neha and I rushed up to him, fearing the worst.

I checked Isaac's neck for a pulse. It was a few seconds before I felt anything. It was some of the worst seconds of my life. He was alive! His pulse was thready and weak, but he was alive.

Isaac stirred a little as I touched him. His eyes slowly opened to slits.

"Are we in Heaven?" he whispered. His voice was weak.

"No," I said. I blinked away tears.

Isaac frowned a little.

"The other place?" he asked.

"No," Neha said. She smiled down at him. "We're very much alive. Thanks to you."

"Good. I'm glad we're not dead. I loaned Theo some money the other day. He never paid me back." He paused, licking his cracked lips. His voice was getting even weaker. "We survived a massive explosion. An expression springs to mind. If I felt well, I'd say it. Theo, you say it."

"Say what?" I asked, confused. Isaac's eyes flicked over to Neha.

"Surely you know," he said. "You know everything."

"It's not usually my style. But for you, this one time, I'll make an exception." Neha paused for effect. "That explosion was da bomb."

Isaac smiled.

"That's my girl," he said.

And with that, Isaac's eyelids fluttered shut.

CHAPTER TWENTY-TWO

"I've seen people do some stupid, reckless, irresponsible, and foolhardy things in my time," the Old Man said, his voice raised and his steel-grey eyes flashing in anger, "but this takes the absolute cake." He thumped his fist against the top of his heavy wooden desk. The legs of the desk collapsed. The top of the desk cracked with a loud splitting sound. This was the first time I had ever seen the Old Man angry. I hoped it was the last time.

We were back at Camp Avatar. We were in the Old Man's office. It was the day after my fight with Iceburn. The Old Man stood behind his desk wearing, as he always did, his full costume. Neha and I stood at attention on the other side of his now-cracked desk. Isaac was in the camp infirmary, which was where he had been since I had flown him there yesterday. Athena leaned against the wall to the right of me and Neha. Her arms were crossed and her face was impassive as she watched the Old Man rip Neha and me a new one.

"You could have gotten yourselves killed," the Old Man said. "If you had, I would have nominated you three for a Darwin Award. You nearly did get Myth killed. What were you thinking, going up against that Meta by yourselves? All of Camp Avatar was out fighting that wildfire. A passel of Heroes were a simple communicator's call away." Neha and I glanced at each other.

"We thought we could handle it," Neha said.

"Truth be told, Smoke suggested that we call for reinforcements," I added, trying to take the heat off of her. "I vetoed the idea." Isaac had too, but I certainly was not going to throw him under the bus. I already felt incredibly guilty that he was lying in the infirmary, injured because of me. I was also angry and frustrated that I had let Iceburn get away. Again. What was worse, I still did not even have a clue as to how to find him.

"You should have listened to Smoke," the Old Man said, glaring at me. "And Smoke, you should have called for reinforcements despite what those other two knuckleheads told you. Not only are you three guilty of stupidity so egregious it ought to be criminal, but you used your powers without the supervision of a licensed Hero for unauthorized purposes, which actually is a crime. You had authorization only to use them for purpose of fighting the wildfire, not for the purpose of playing cowboy and chasing after a Metahuman murderer. And, not only did you recklessly chase after him, you chased after him unsuccessfully. He killed not only your father, Theo, but eleven people died in that wildfire he set. If he's a killer for hire the way you say he is Smoke, God knows how many other people's deaths he's responsible for. If you had exercised the common sense of a toddler, you would have yelled for help and we would have Iceburn in custody right now. And did I leave out the fact that you abandoned the sectors of the fire you were assigned to fight?" The Old Man shook his head at us in disgust. "I have half a mind to throw you out of the Academy, recommend to the Heroes' Guild that you be forever barred from being licensed, and ask the local prosecutor to charge you with unauthorized use of Metahuman powers." I glanced over at Athena. Her arms were still crossed and her face was still expressionless. I was surprised she was not yelling at us too. Yelling at trainees was what she did best. I guess she figured the Old Man had the situation well in hand. Too many cooks spoiled the broth.

The Old Man sat down heavily in his leather chair. He let out a long breath.

"Once I calm down enough that I'm not tempted to rip your arms off and spank you with them, I'll decide on your punishment. In the meantime, go to your quarters. Confine yourselves there until further notice. Now get out."

"But—" I started, intending to take full responsibility for what had happened. I was not about to let Isaac and Neha take the fall when they were merely being good friends and helping me.

"Get out!" the Old Man roared. My ears rang. My skin rippled backwards, like I had stepped into a wind tunnel. Papers flew off the Old Man's desk and flipped through the air like giant pieces of confetti.

Neha and I turned and quickly left the Old Man's office, closing the door behind us. I had to stop myself from running out.

"Did you know the Old Man had super breath?" Neha asked me a bit later. We were walking down the stairs towards the ground floor of the camp's administration building. The Old Man's office was on the second floor of the building.

"No," I said, distracted. My mind was too busy thinking about this mess, and the fact that Isaac and Neha were in trouble because of me. If they were thrown out of the Academy because of me, I would never forgive myself. Graduation was so close, less than a month away. I knew how important it was to them for them to graduate and go on to get their licenses. "Did you?"

"No. I wonder what else he can do we don't know about."

"I don't know." I stopped in the middle of the stairwell. "I left something in the Old Man's office. I need to go back."

"Just leave it there. He said to go right to our rooms. He's mad enough as it is."

"It'll just take a second," I said. "You go ahead to your apartment."

"Okay," Neha said dubiously. She smiled grimly. "But if the Old Man's actually does rip your arm off and beat you to death with it, I hope your ghost remembers that I warned you." Neha proceeded down the stairs. I turned around and went back up them. I had not left anything behind in the Old Man's office, of course. I was going to go back there and fall on my sword. I would beg the Old Man to just punish me and to leave my friends out of it. I very much wanted to continue training and become a Hero, yet it would not be the end of the world if I was thrown out of the Academy. I did not have to be a Hero to track Iceburn down and take him out. Even though it was illegal, I would figure out a way to continue to train and prepare myself for Iceburn on my own. "Where there is a will, there is a way." Another Jamesism.

I walked back down the hall towards the Old Man's office. Once I arrived at the door, I heard raised voices. Through the thick wooden door, I could not entirely make out what was said, though I did hear my name repeatedly. Curiosity killed the cat. Though I was in enough trouble as it was without adding eavesdropping to my list of offenses, I pressed my ear to the door. I still could not entirely hear what was said. What I needed was a cup, or an ear trumpet like I had seen in old pictures.

That gave me an idea. I triggered my powers. I formed a force field cone, with my ear on one end, and the surface of the door on the other. Now the raised voices were clearer. I could hear what was being said.

"Well what in the hell did you expect them to do, Raymond?" It was Athena. I would know that yell anywhere.

"Like I told them, I expect them to call for help," the Old Man said. I was so startled, I almost let my force field dissipate. The idea of anyone, even Athena, yelling at the Old Man was shocking. Around us trainees, Athena acted like every utterance of the Old Man's was one of the Ten Commandments and like she was Moses delivering it to God's people. And was Raymond the Old Man's real name?

"Oh please," Athena said. "Every day we pound into these kids' heads that there is nothing they can't handle. We have to make them believe it, otherwise they'll turn tail and run the moment some bad guy looks at them hard or speaks to them harshly. We can't indoctrinate them into believing they are capable of handling whatever the world throws at them one day, and then the next day expect them to holler for mommy and daddy when they are faced with a problem."

"They could have gotten themselves killed."

"You keep saying that. But they didn't get themselves killed. They did exactly what they were trained to do: they encountered a Rogue and they confronted him. Sure, they didn't win. And sure, they walked into a trap. But they got themselves out of it. They lived to fight another day, which is sometimes the best you can do. If they had actually managed to subdue this Iceburn guy, we would have given them a medal. Instead, you're talking about throwing them out for trying and for doing exactly what we expect Heroes to do. You and I both know throwing them out is an idle threat anyway. Smoke and Myth are two of the best trainees we've got, if not the best. Theodore is no slouch either. Not to mention the fact he's got the biggest potential of all of them since he's Omega-level. Plus, he's more empathetic than most of the trainees. Look at how he befriended Smoke when no one else would. Empathy is almost as important a trait in a Hero as superpowers are. All three of them are going to make fine Heroes one day if they keep at it." It was the first time I had ever heard Athena call me Theodore. It was also the first time I had heard her talk about us trainees as if we were anything other than unhousebroken puppies who might at any time take a dump in the middle of the living room.

"You know we don't give out medals." The Old Man sounded almost petulant.

"It was a figure of speech. You're right, we don't give out medals. Why? Because awarding a medal implies the person you're giving the medal to has done something exceptional. We expect Heroes and Hero trainees to always be exceptional, not just sometimes. You don't get a medal or a cookie for doing what you're supposed to do. The world can afford no less than exceptional behavior from us. We've got too much power for the world to expect otherwise. I say those three lived up to our expectations. You should be patting them on the back, not punishing them."

There were a few moments of silence.

"Whose side are you on, anyway?" the Old Man asked. He sounded tired.

"The side I'm always on," Athena said. She sounded amused. "That of truth, justice, and the American way."

"You read too many comic books."

"Some girls collect handbags. Others of us collect comic books. So sue me. I can't be a hard-ass all the time."

"You could have fooled me."

The two of them said other stuff, but I could not hear them as they were not shouting anymore. I pulled my ear away from the door. As it did not sound like my friends were going to get thrown out after all, I quietly went back to the stairs. I went down them, out of the administration building, and started back to my apartment. I wanted to go visit Isaac in the infirmary, but the Old Man had confined me to my quarters. I had pushed my luck too much as it was to defy him again. Besides, the doctor had already assured me Isaac would be as good as new in a few days. The doctor was using his Metahuman healing powers on Isaac. Isaac was apparently responding well to the treatment. I still felt guilty about his injuries, though. He would not be in the infirmary at all if it had not been for me.

I entered my room. I plopped down on the bed. A bunch of thoughts swirled in my mind as I lay there. I thought about Athena and how she had defended us to the Old Man. Whenever we trainees dealt with her, she seemed like she could just barely stand us. I knew that the Academy was deliberately hard to weed out the trainees who had no business being Heroes, but Athena's contempt for us had seemed real. She had sounded positively affectionate towards us in the Old Man's office, though. It seemed like the domino mask she sported was not the only mask she wore.

I thought of both Isaac and Neha. I was so grateful for both of them. Never before had I had friends who had my back the way they did. It made me feel doubly guilty about Isaac. What if he or Neha had been killed? The mere thought made me sick to my stomach, as did the fact eleven people had died in the wildfire because of Iceburn trying to get to me.

I thought of how Neha had been in my bed just a week ago. Nothing had happened between the two of us since then, nor had we spoken of it. At some point I imagined we would. Right now, though, we were both too concerned about graduating the Academy and finding an Apprenticeship with an already licensed Hero.

And, of course, I thought of Iceburn. I still did not know who had hired him to kill me. That was not what I was the most concerned about. I was more concerned about the fact Iceburn had bested me yet again. I seethed at the thought of it. At least this time I had acquitted myself better than I had when I had first encountered him.

I had come closer to defeating him this time. But, as Athena was fond of saying, close only counted in horseshoes and hand grenades. It sounded like a Jamesism.

I stared up at the ceiling as those thoughts all swirled in my brain. I resolved to train even harder and to get better at using my powers. To be better. When I encountered Iceburn again, I would be ready to end things once and for all. Next time, only one of us would walk away. I was determined that someone would be me.

I burned with anger and frustration. I repeated the words Iceburn had spoken to me the night he killed my father.

"This is not over," I said aloud.

CHAPTER TWENTY-THREE

Four days after being confined to our quarters by the Old Man, Neha and I were back in his office. Isaac was here too, having been discharged from the infirmary early this morning. Other than a scar across his forehead, Isaac was mostly as good as new thanks to the doctor's Metahuman healing powers. He had been cleared to resume classes and training. Isaac had said earlier he did not mind the scar. He said it made him look dangerous.

"I'm thinking of changing my name to Captain Danger," Isaac had said. "The ladies love a daredevil." He had not even cracked a smile. He might have been serious.

The Old Man had summoned us here to his office. Despite the conversation I had overheard between him and Athena, I was still a little worried about how he might decide to punish us, especially Neha and Isaac. I had not shared what I had overheard with Neha and Isaac. It was bad enough that I had eavesdropped.

Unlike last time, Athena was not here. It was the first time I ever wished Athena was around. Before overhearing her conversation with the Old Man, wishing Athena was around would have been like a slave wishing his overseer was around. It was amazing how one overheard conversation could change my perspective on things.

"Are the three of you planning to seek Apprenticeships once you graduate?" the Old Man asked. The question caught me off guard. I thought he was going to tell us how he had decided to punish us. "If you graduate," the Old Man added wryly. "Maybe you'll get it into your heads to break into MetaHold to fight the supervillain Chaos before then and you'll get yourselves killed."

I nodded in answer to his question, as did Neha and Isaac. Graduation was less than two weeks away. Trainees who managed to graduate from the Academy who wanted to continue on to try to get licensed as Heroes had to find a Hero willing to sponsor them and take them on as Apprentices. The Hero sponsor would continue to train his Apprentices in preparation for the Trials. If you could not find a Hero willing to sponsor you, there was a handful of for-profit superhero schools an Academy graduate could go to instead. I had learned those schools were looked down on in the Hero community. Having a school prepare you for the Trials instead of a Hero sponsor was like getting a degree from a small town community college instead of a degree from an Ivy League university—you still had a degree, but nobody thought it was as good.

"How would you like to become my Apprentices?" the Old Man asked. Neha, Isaac, and I looked at each other in shock. None of us had expected this.

Neha was the first to recover. "After threatening to kick us out, you're now offering to be our Hero sponsor?" she asked incredulously.

"It was pointed out to me that perhaps I overreacted a bit to you all facing Iceburn alone," the Old Man said. "Don't get me wrong—I still think you should have called for help. That's why I let Smoke and Theo stay confined to quarters as punishment the past few days. With that said, the person who told me I was overreacting was right: we instructors have repeated over and over that you have to rely on yourselves when faced with a tough situation. If you become Heroes, God knows people will rely on you to deal with whatever situation you're presented with. Once I calmed down, I realized that after hearing our message of self-reliance repeated over and over, if you had then turned around and immediately hollered for help, that would mean either you were too stupid to absorb what we've been trying to teach you here, or that we instructors are not good at our jobs." He smiled wryly. "Whatever else you three might be—the words headstrong and stubborn spring to mind—you're not stupid. And, we instructors are very good at what we do.

"As for why I'm offering to be your Hero sponsor, the answer is all three of you show a lot of potential. While it's ultimately up to you as to whether you will live up that that potential, I'd like to help. Plus, Iceburn's repeated attempts on Theo's life make it clear he will likely try again. Clearly someone out there is not pleased a new Omega exists." When I had told the Old Man about our confrontation with Iceburn, I had also told him I had shared with Neha and Isaac the fact I was an Omega-level Meta.

"Theo is safe enough here at camp. Not only is he surrounded by several Heroes and other Metas, but there are some security measures in place that you trainees do not even know about. Once he leaves, he will be more vulnerable. Someone needs to keep an eye on him until he can fend for himself. As the head of the Academy, I'm willing to shoulder that responsibility. Also, since he's an Omega, I want to make sure he gets steered in the right direction. Since the three of you like each other and seem to work well together, it would be a shame to split you all up. Think it over, and give me an answer by tomorrow."

"I don't need to think it over. I accept," I said. The Old Man was one of the world's most famous Heroes, and he wanted us to be his Apprentices. Wow!

"Me too," Isaac said.

"At the risk of sounding like a broken record, I accept as well," Neha said.

"Good," the Old Man said. "Now that that's settled, I believe I've made you three late for World History. You've got days of catching up to do. Try not to do something to get yourselves kicked out between now and graduation, like poisoning an instructor or assassinating the President or something."

The three of us trooped out of the Old Man's office, closing his door after us. We walked down the hall towards the stairwell.

"We're going to be Amazing Man's Apprentices," I said excitedly. I did not care I was stating the obvious. My mind was blown. Amazing Man was one of the most famous, well-respected Heroes of all time. Him asking us to be his Apprentices was like being accepted into Harvard or being drafted into the National Football League.

"And the best part is, we get to hang out and train together," Isaac said. He was grinning from ear to ear. He high-fived me. "I was kinda dreading graduation because I knew I was going to miss you Theo. I'd even miss you Neha. You're like a hemorrhoid—a pain in the butt sometimes, but I've gotten used to you." Barely breaking stride, Neha's leg shot out. She swept Isaac's legs out from under him. He landed on his rear end with a thud. Neha kept walking. I paused to help Isaac up.

"Now you know what a real pain in the ass feels like," Neha said, smirking over her shoulder at Isaac.

"Hey, what's the big idea?" Isaac said to Neha's receding back. "I just got out of the infirmary. I'm a sick man." Despite his words, he was grinning.

"A shame your illness hasn't affected your mouth," Neha shot back before disappearing into the stairwell. The door closed behind her. Isaac turned to me.

"I'm pretty sure she's in love with me," he said. His eyes danced. "I sensed it happening before. Now I suspect my new scar pushed her over the top. What do you think?"

"If that's love, I don't want to see what hate looks like," I said. Isaac and Neha bickering like they were brother and sister was now a familiar pattern. It was a pattern I would have missed had we all gone our separate ways upon graduation. Instead, we were all going to be together.

I had a warm feeling in my heart about that as Isaac and I trailed after Neha towards class. Isaac and Neha bickered like brother and sister because that was how they had come to feel about one another. Isaac had said as much once. Neha was far too closed off emotionally to ever say such a thing aloud, but I saw how she looked at Isaac. Sometimes she looked at him with irritation or annoyance when he was trying unsuccessfully to be funny, but even then there was an undercurrent of affection. The rigors of the Academy had forged us into a family. Happiness mingled with sadness as it hit me Isaac and Neha were the only family I had. Sure, technically Uncle Charles was family, but there was more to being a family than sharing some DNA through an accident of fate. Family was about shared history, shared struggle, and being there for each other, in good times and bad. Under that definition of family, Isaac was the brother I never had. And, Neha was my sister. No, scratch that. Brothers and sisters did not do what Neha and I had done together. Unless they were ancient royalty. Cleopatra had been married to her brother, and she herself was the offspring of a brother-sister union. Who would have guessed the incestuous lifestyles of the rich and famous would be something I learned about in Hero Academy? Who would have guessed how much I would learn, period? I had learned so much, and come so far. If Dad was watching, I hoped he was proud of me.

"Hey, are you all right?" Isaac said, shaking me out of my thoughts. He looked at me with concern. I realized I had started to tear up. Feeling like the world's biggest baby, I wiped my eyes with the back of my hands.

"I'm fine," I said. "I just got an eyelash in my eye is all." Isaac looked at me doubtfully. Thankfully, he did not press further. We walked the rest of the way to class in companionable silence.

CHAPTER TWENTY-FOUR

Graduation two weeks later was a simple affair. Even so, it was the best day of my life.

Over a hundred of us Hero trainees had started the Academy. Only twenty-one of us—fifteen males and six females—lined up in the building that used to house the men's barracks to graduate. From what I had gathered from talking to trainees before the ceremony, each of us intended to continue on to attempt to get our Hero's license. Brute, Nimbus, Nightshade, and so many others we had started this journey with were gone. The ones who remained I felt as close to as I did anybody else on the planet except for Isaac and Neha. Our shared struggles had made us into comrades. I had started the Academy and the process of becoming a licensed Hero to learn the skills I needed to take on Iceburn. I of course still intended to take on Iceburn, but my ambitions were now bigger than just him. I wanted to become a Hero so I could continue to be a part of this extended family I had formed. I knew that if—no, when—I killed Iceburn I would be shunned from this family. In the meantime, I would savor the feeling of belonging and camaraderie.

The oldest of us lined up for graduation was twenty-nine. His name was Dreadnought. Most of us affectionately called him Uncle Dreadnought because he was so much older than the rest of us. The youngest was Sledgehammer, who was only fourteen. We were all dressed in the red and black uniforms we always wore. We were so used to wearing them at this point that they felt like a second skin.

Neha was at the front of the line of graduates. To the surprise of absolutely no one, she was class valedictorian. Isaac was right behind her since he was class salutatorian. There had been a murmur of surprise among the trainees when that had been announced. I, however, had not been surprised. I lived with the guy. Despite his often goofy persona, I saw how hard he worked. He was driven. By what, I still had not figured out and he had not been willing to share. It did not matter. I was proud of both him and Neha.

The rest of us were lined up alphabetically by code name behind Neha and Isaac. Isaac's and Neha's standings in the class were the only ones that had been publicly shared. The rest of us had been told privately what our class rank was. I was neither at the top—math had really kicked my butt and had dragged down my overall average—nor at the bottom. It did not matter anyway. The fact I was graduating was the important thing. It was like that old joke: What do you call a guy who graduates last in his medical school class? Doctor.

The Old Man announced Neha's code name. She stepped forward and mounted short stairs to where the Old Man stood on a dais at the front of the large room. Athena stood next to the Old Man. The other Academy instructors were all arrayed behind them. The Old Man draped a vivid red cape around Neha's shoulders, securing it around her neck with a thick silver-colored clasp. The cape hung to her ankles. It complemented her red Academy uniform top. By tradition, Academy graduates got a red cape. It was the equivalent of a diploma. Fully licensed Heroes got a white cape after they passed the Trials.

Once Neha's cape was secure, the Old Man shook her hand and congratulated her. Then Athena handed her a metal cylinder for the purpose of storing her new cape in. Athena then leaned forward and kissed Neha on the cheek. There were audible gasps of shock among the trainees. They would have been less surprised had Athena punched Neha in the throat instead. It would have been more in character. Or, so they thought. The conversation I had overhead between Athena and the Old Man had opened my eyes. There was more to Athena than her being simply a yelling martinet. Not all masks were worn on the face.

Neha walked back off the dais and towards the end of the line of trainees. Isaac's code name was announced. He went through the same process Neha had gone through. Each trainee's code name was announced and that person stepped forward until the Old Man's got to me.

"Kinetic," he intoned. I stepped forward. There were slight murmurs behind me. I suppressed a smile. Kinetic was the new code name I had chosen after giving it much thought. I had not even told Isaac and Neha about my new name, sharing it only with the Old Man so he would call me by that name at graduation. Today seemed to be the right time to shed the name Carolina. I had thought at first about going by the name Kinetic Kid. The alliteration sounded cool. But then I realized I was no longer a kid. I sure as heck did not feel like one.

The Old Man draped my new cape around me. He secured it around my neck. He shook my hand. He did not say he was proud of me, but looking at his eyes, I felt like he was. When I stepped in front of Athena, she handed me a cape storage cylinder and then kissed me on the cheek as she had with the graduates who had gone before me. The kiss felt like a stamp of approval.

I returned to the line of trainees. Neha smiled at me as I passed by. The grin on Isaac's face looked like it was going to split his head open. He winked at me. I too was grinning like a drunk clown. I did not care. I knew Isaac did not either.

I got to the back of the line. In my new cape, I felt like an actual superhero. I felt like I was ten feet tall and could single-handedly conquer the world. I could not wait until I got to a mirror so I could check myself out. I was not an actual Hero yet, of course. I first had to complete my Apprenticeship and then stand for the Hero Trials. The long disclaimer that was in the cape storage cylinder said as much. I read it carefully later, after the graduation ceremony was over. In essence, the disclaimer said that despite the fact I had earned a red cape as a graduate of the Academy, I was still not a licensed Hero and my powers were only to be used under the supervision and guidance of a duly licensed Hero.

I did not care what the disclaimer said. It did not shrink the significance of what I had accomplished. Nor did it make my cape less beautiful. I loved my new cape.

I had never been so proud of something in all my life.

CHAPTER TWENTY-FIVE

"**D**o you think the Old Man has a jet? I'll bet he has a jet," I said excitedly. "One of those cool futuristic ones that's black and has missiles and can take off and land vertically and can fly faster than the speed of sound. Riding in one of those babies, we'll be in D.C. in no time."

"Maybe it's an invisible jet," Isaac said. He was also excited.

"Naw, that's comic book stuff. There's no tech that can make something invisible."

"That you know of. You don't have a PhD in physics. I'll bet you invisibility tech does exist. If it can be imagined, some egghead scientist can create it."

"How about you two Buck Rogers pipe down?" Neha said. "We'll find out soon enough." Isaac and I glance at one another.

"If we really are Buck Rogers, I don't remember the women of the twenty-fifth century being this lippy," Isaac said in a stage whisper to me. If Neha heard him—I did not know how she could not have—she gave no sign.

It was the day after graduation. After saying our farewells to our fellow graduates, we had started our trek towards where the Old Man had told us to meet him in the woods on the outskirts of camp at 0800 hours sharp this morning. He had told us we would fly from there to his home outside of Washington, D.C. It would be our new residence for the duration of our Apprenticeship.

As instructed, the three of us had our Academy masks and uniforms on. The Old Man said we could keep them for the purpose of continuing training during our Apprenticeships. We also had our camp earbuds in and our silver wristbands on. We had stuffed the rest of our meager belongings into a single chest. Using my powers, I had it float behind us as we tromped through the woods that surrounded Camp Avatar towards the location the Old Man had specified.

Soon we stepped into a small clearing in the woods. The Old Man was in the middle of it. As usual, he was fully costumed. He hovered five feet or so in the air. His legs were tucked under him in the lotus position. A large brown leather satchel was on the ground under him. The Old Man's eyes were downcast. He tapped on a computer tablet as we approached. There was no jet, futuristic or otherwise.

"Oh my God!" Neha said to us. She pointed to the empty area around the Old Man. "Myth was right. Amazing Man does have an invisible jet."

"You're not funny," I said. I was disappointed there was no jet.

Neha looked smug. "Apparently your sense of humor is invisible too."

The Old Man looked up when we arrived in front of him. "There you are. And right on time, I see." He tapped on his tablet some more. "I'm sending the coordinates to your new home to your communicators' computers."

"How are we getting there?" I asked. The Old Man looked surprised by the question.

"Flying, of course."

"Yes, but in what?" I asked, confused. There was nothing in sight except the four of us.

"The question is not in what, but with what." The Old Man made a slight flapping motion with his hands. "The answer is with your powers. I would have thought graduating from the Academy would knock silly questions like that out of your head."

"You want us to fly across country with our powers?" Isaac said. He sounded as incredulous as I felt. "We've never done that before. It'll take us forever."

"By my calculations Myth, assuming a moderate pace, you can make the flight in six days. Kinetic is a much faster flyer than you, but I expect the three of you to stay together during the trip. Iceburn is still out there somewhere after all." The Old Man reached down, picked up his satchel, and slung it over his shoulder and across his chest. He began to rise higher in the air. He looked down at us. "I said you are capable of making the flight in six days. I'll expect you all in five. See you then."

With that, the Old Man rose higher in the air, faster and faster, until he was but a large speck in the ocean-blue sky above us. Then, as if he had been fired from a gun, he shot off towards the east. In an instant he was gone from view. We heard a small boom as he broke the sound barrier.

"Myth, you can make the flight in six says, but I'll expect you in five," Isaac said in a deep voice, doing an eerie impersonation of the Old Man. "Is this another test?" he asked, now in his normal voice. "It feels like a test. The day after graduation, and we have to pass another test. Does everything have to be a freaking test?" He looked and sounded disgusted.

"Life is a test," Neha said.

"Well it's certainly no cabaret." Isaac jabbed a finger in her direction. "'Life is a test'? Really? I'm gonna start calling you mini-Athena. Next you'll be telling me the obstacle is the way and spouting more Stoicism double-talk." Isaac let out a long sigh, and shook his head.

"How far is it from here to D.C. anyway?" he asked.

"About twenty-eight hundred miles," I said immediately. I surprised myself by knowing. It must have been yet another random fact that had sunk into my head during all of my studying at the Academy.

"This is all your fault for getting my hopes up, Theo. You had me convinced there would be a superhero jet."

"My mistake." I shrugged. "Wishful thinking, I guess."

Isaac shook his head again. "Becoming a Hero is not going as I anticipated. I expected glamour. The adulation of an adoring public. Maybe a groupie or two. Or twenty. I instead get latrine cleaning, memorizing so much random info that I think my brain's bleeding, working my fingers to the bone, getting blown up by a Meta assassin, and having to fly cross-country under my own power. What's next, a proctology exam from Edward Scissorhands?" He rubbed a hand over his bald head. "I once thought about being a beekeeper for a living. I should have done it."

"Why didn't you?" I asked.

"'Cause I'm afraid of bees. I've got a bad case of melissophobia. That's fear of bees for those of you not up on your bee lingo. The struggle is real." Isaac let out another long-suffering sigh. "Oh well. Like they say, there's no use in crying over spilt milk after the horse has been stolen."

"Or something like that," Neha said. She looked amused.

Isaac ignored her, saying "We might as well get started. The sooner we start, the sooner we'll get there." He started glowing as he always did when he commenced a transformation. In moments, a white pegasus stood where Isaac had been. I marveled at how quickly he was able to transform compared to how long it took him when we first met. Practice apparently did make perfect.

Neha vaulted up onto Isaac's back like a gymnast vaulting on top of a pommel horse. She patted Isaac's muscular neck by his thick white mane.

"There's a good horsey," she said. "If you continue to be such a good boy, momma will give you some sugar cubes when we get to D.C." Isaac stomped his front hooves angrily. Neha laughed.

"The best part is, he can't talk while he's in this form," Neha said to me. Her eyes danced merrily. "Maybe we can get some peace and quiet for a change." Isaac whinnied ominously.

"Come on guys, stop horsing around," I said.

Neha looked at me balefully. "How dare you. Puns are beneath you Theo." I laughed, then sobered.

"C'mon, let's get started," I said. "Like Isaac said, the sooner we start, the sooner we'll get there. Besides, you know the Old Man. He doesn't bark orders the way Athena does, but when he says to do something, he expects results."

I launched myself into the air, making the chest full of our belongings trail after me. Isaac took off as well with Neha on his back.

With Neha using the telemetry from her communicator's computer to navigate, we started the long flight to D.C.

***

The Old Man had said he expected us to arrive at his house in five days. By pushing ourselves hard, we did it in four.

I landed on the front lawn of a sprawling brick house. I set Neha and the chest full of our belongings next to me. The house was about two hundred feet in front of us. We were in Chevy Chase, a Maryland suburb about six miles outside of Washington, D.C.

Moments later, Isaac touched down next to me. Huge white wings were on his back. His naked upper body was massive, and well-muscled. A halo, glowing yellow, was around his head. His facial features were subtly different than how they normally were, changed so he was now so handsome he was more attractive than the biggest of movie stars. He was literally an angel. I had started carrying Neha during the last part of our journey because Isaac had gotten too exhausted to keep carrying her and still keep up our grueling pace.

Isaac was soaked with sweat. His chest heaved with exertion. He looked as exhausted as I felt despite the fact we had stopped a couple of times during our trip to grab some food and a few hours of sleep. Regardless of how tired I was, I was still elated by how quickly we had made it across the country. Before entering the Academy, there was no way I could have flown across the country, much less done it carrying the chest and Neha part of the way. It seemed as though with each passing day I got stronger.

Isaac shifted back into his usual form. Together, we looked at the brick house in front of us. Actually, saying it was a house understated the facts of the matter. The house was in fact a mansion. It was mostly red brick, with white brick accents, and built in a Neocolonial style. Only two stories tall, what the mansion lacked in height it made up for in length, having a square footage of around 30,000 feet unless I missed my guess. The front of the mansion was symmetrical. There was an accented front door in the middle of it, and huge, evenly spaced windows all along the front. I had gotten a good look at the property the mansion sat on before I had landed, and it appeared the property was about five or six acres. The grounds were as green as a well-maintained golf course, and the grass looked like it had been carefully cut by someone armed with a jeweler's loupe, a pair of scissors, and a level. The tall shrubs surrounding the house were cut into various images and shapes. Clearly a group of skilled topiarists had worked their magic on the greenery.

The three of us looked at each other. Isaac's mouth was open in disbelief.

"Are you sure this is the right place?" I asked Neha dubiously. This place was a far cry from the spartan living conditions at Camp Avatar.

"Positive," she said. "This is the address the Old Man gave us."

Isaac rubbed his hands together in satisfaction. He looked suddenly energized despite the rigors of our trip. He said, "Now this is more like it. We didn't get a superhero jet, but we do get a dope mansion to live in. I'll take that. Guys, we're moving on up in life. I feel like George Jefferson."

"I think you mean George Washington," Neha said. "Since we're right outside the city named after him, you should get his name right."

"Maybe he means Thomas Jefferson," I suggested. "Jefferson was President just a few years after Washington. It's an easy mistake to make."

"I don't mean either George Washington or Thomas Jefferson," Isaac said in exasperation. "You think I'm stupid? I meant George Jefferson."

Neha and I looked at each other blankly.

"From *The Jeffersons*?" Isaac said impatiently.

Neha and I shrugged in ignorance.

"The classic TV show from the seventies and eighties?" Isaac sounded increasingly indignant.

"Never heard of it," I said.

"Me neither," Neha added.

Isaac looked at us with disbelief. "You two know-it-alls can lecture me on the best way to disable a man with a clothespin and dryer lint, and tell me so much about Hannibal crossing the Alps that I feel like I personally saw it happen, but you don't know about *The Jeffersons*?" He shook his head in dismay. "I've fallen into the clutches of cultural illiterates." Muttering to himself, Isaac stalked off towards the front door of the mansion. Neha and I hung back.

"You know about *The Jeffersons*, I assume?" she asked.

"Yeah. We didn't have cable or satellite TV when I grew up. Too expensive. The only thing we had was broadcast TV. One of the five channels we got aired classic shows, including *The Jeffersons*. I used to watch it all the time. You?"

"Of course I've heard of *The Jeffersons*." She grinned. "It sure is fun to get Isaac all riled up, isn't it?"

"It's better than television," I agreed.

We hastened after Isaac so we could find the Old Man together.

CHAPTER TWENTY-SIX

The dream began as it always did, and ended with the same inevitable fiery conclusion.

I abruptly sat up in the bed with visions of flames dancing in my head and the smell of cooked human flesh in my nostrils. My eyes burned, my cheeks were wet, my body was damp with sweat, and my chest heaved. After a few seconds of sickened confusion, I realized I was not holding my Dad's charred body. I was in my room in the Old Man's mansion.

It was not the first time I had had that dream. I knew it was not going to be the last time. The dream seemed to occur more and more frequently these days. It was as if the universe was taunting me about things I could not change and about tasks that were still left undone.

The mansion was still and quiet in the way it was only in the wee hours of the morning. I looked at the glowing clock on my nightstand. It was 2:34 a.m. I grimaced. I had to be up at 4:30 a.m. for strength and conditioning work before the first tutor of the day showed up for class. Going back to sleep until then was out of the question. I was very much wide awake. I knew from bitter experience from being awakened by that dream many times before that there was no way I was going back to sleep.

I threw my covers off. I got up, and flicked the lights of my bedroom on. I squinted against their brightness. I peeling off my damp tee shirt. I used it to wipe my face and the sweat off of my torso. I then threw it into my laundry basket. I put on a fresh shirt, all while thinking about the past, what was, what could have been, and what one day would be.

Thinking that it would do me no good to sit in my room and mope, I opened the door and left, intending to go downstairs and make myself a sandwich. With us Apprentices training as hard and as often as we did, I was constantly hungry. Though I have always had a big appetite, ever since starting Hero training my body had kicked it up a few notches. My stomach was an all-consuming fire that was always in need of refueling. I frowned. I really wished I had not thought of that fire metaphor.

It was surprising even to me how much food I was capable of putting away. I had joked to Neha once that maybe I had tapeworms. She had said she could come up with a gas that would kill any tapeworms my body was carrying around. She had added there was only a ten percent chance the gas would kill me too, which were pretty good odds. I was pretty sure she had just been joking. I was not positive though. You never could be quite sure with her.

Neha, Isaac, and I had been Amazing Man's Apprentices for over four months now. If we had thought training like Olympians and swallowing books like we were English majors minoring in Everything Else would end upon graduation from the Academy, we were sorely mistaken. The main difference between the mansion and the Academy was we Apprentices did not have to run from task to task like our hair was on fire. Otherwise, we still maintained a grueling schedule.

Among other things, the Old Man's mansion housed a gym that would have put a commercial one to shame, an armory containing so many explosives and weapons it looked like it had been stocked by Athena, and a holographic combat training room. The mansion and the grounds it sat on had so many secret security measures in place, it was like living in a fortress. Our lives at the Old Man's mansion over the past few months had settled into an endless routine of working out, sparring with each other and holographic opponents, studying both on our own and with the assistance of private tutors, going on patrol with the Old Man, and training with both our powers and with weapons. Thanks to the Old Man and a retired FBI bomb technician the Old Man had retained, I now knew so much about explosives I could have hired myself out as a one-man wrecking crew. When I had asked the Old Man why we were learning so much about explosives, he had said, "Because you never know when you'll need to defuse a bomb. We live near D.C., a prime terrorist target. Besides," he had added with a grin, "it's fun to blow stuff up."

The patrols with the Old Man were my favorite part of the Apprenticeship so far. Sometimes he took us out on patrol individually, other times as a group. On those patrols, we had captured street criminals, helped so many people I was starting to lose track, and had even fought a few Rogues. I was learning so much from the Old Man. Sometimes it felt like he had forgotten more about being a Hero than I would ever learn.

I padded down the stairs in my bare feet. As I approached the kitchen, I saw that the light was on. I thought I would find Isaac or Neha also trying to squeeze in a quick pre-workout meal. I was surprised to instead find the Old Man sitting at the marble island in the middle of the kitchen. He was drinking a beer. At least a dozen empty beer bottles sat on the island in front of him.

The Old Man only had on black shorts and a white short-sleeved tee shirt. It was quite a difference from the chrome blue and silver costume I had grown so used to seeing him in before I became his Apprentice. The Old Man's tee shirt strained against his massive muscles. Silver hair covered his thick forearms. The Old Man was also not wearing a mask. He never did when the four of us were alone at home. After all, he did not need to hide his true identity from us. He had told us his real name the day we showed up to begin our Apprenticeships. His name was Raymond Ajax. He was a wealthy retired industrialist and still active philanthropist. We Apprentices never called him by his birth name, of course, not even in the privacy of the mansion. It would have been like calling the Pope by his first name.

"Good morning!" the Old Man said cheerily once he spotted me. His cheerfulness was almost obnoxious for such an early hour. Despite the time and the amount of beer he had apparently drunk, the Old Man looked as sharp and focused as he always did. His steel-grey eyes were bright and shiny. He was even freshly clean-shaven, which was more than I could say.

The Old Man saw my eyes linger on the empty beer bottles. He grinned, taking another long swig of the beer in his hand. He finished it off.

"One of the benefits of having a heightened metabolism is it is impossible for me to get intoxicated," he said. He wiped his mouth with the back of his hand. "I haven't been so much as tipsy since my powers first manifested when I was eighteen. It's a mixed blessing. Sometimes a man feels the need to get rip-roaring drunk. I still like the taste of beer, though I might as well be drinking water for all the effect it has on me."

He reached for an unopened bottle and twisted off the top with his bare hand. "Want one?" he offered.

I was tempted, but since I took my training regime very seriously, I was careful with my diet. Plus, unlike the Old

Man, my metabolism was not heightened. Being tipsy while you used your superpowers was not a good idea.

"No thanks," I said, going to the refrigerator to instead get a bottle of water. I sat on a stool at the island across from the Old Man. "Besides, the drinking age in Maryland is twenty-one."

"You're an Omega-level Metahuman and a graduate of the Hero Academy. You've fought supervillains and have seen, done, and been through things most people can't even imagine. If that doesn't make you an adult, I don't know what does. If you want a beer, have one."

"I'm good with water."

"Suit yourself. Salud," he said, raising the fresh bottle of beer. I raised my bottle of water in turn. We each took long pulls. A companionable silence stretched out between the two of us. I found myself thinking again of Dad and the night that changed everything.

"Still having the dream?" the Old Man suddenly asked, jarring me out of my reverie.

I nodded. I had told him before about my recurring dream. But, how did he know I had it again? I smiled ruefully. "Are you sure telepathy isn't one of your powers?"

"It doesn't take a mind-reader to decipher the look on your face. Plus, why else would you be up at this ungodly hour?" His face was uncharacteristically serious. The half-smile that normally adorned it was missing. It was as if the Old Man went through life not taking it completely seriously.

"Feel like talking about it?" he asked me.

"No," I said, taking another drink of my water. Then I realized that I was wrong—I did want to talk about it. "He's still out there."

"'He' being Iceburn, I assume."

"Yeah. I kind of thought that after I became a licensed Hero—if I become a Hero—I would track him down." I surprised myself by saying that aloud. This was the first time I had shared that with anyone but Isaac and Neha. I did not tell the Old Man the whole truth, though. I did not intend to wait until I was licensed before I found Iceburn. I would hunt him down as soon as I could do it without the Old Man, Neha, and Isaac interfering. Despite my earlier promise to Neha and Isaac, I had come to realize I had to confront Iceburn on my own. Neha and Isaac had almost gotten killed the last time they helped me go up against Iceburn. I would not put them in harm's way again. My problem with Iceburn was precisely that: mine. I would handle him alone. Dad deserved as much. Plus, I did not want anyone around when I killed Iceburn. They might try to stop me. Or, the authorities might think they were in cahoots with me when I murdered him. That was what I planned: murder. No need to mince words about it. Might as well call a spade a spade. I would not be able to live with myself if Neha and Isaac went to jail or lost the chance to become a Hero because they helped me.

Between graduating Hero Academy and the months I had spent under the Old Man's direct tutelage, I was no longer the weak boy Iceburn had first encountered. And, I was even stronger and more adept in the use of my powers now than when I crossed swords with him the second time. I felt like I was now finally ready to tackle Iceburn and take him down. Or, die trying. Maybe that was why I was having the dream about Dad's death with increased frequency lately. Perhaps my subconscious was anxious to get on with the task at hand.

If I managed to track Iceburn down—no, when I tracked him down—I would make him pay for the night he killed Dad. Every second of it. I found my eyes welling up with tears again at the thought of it. I blinked them back, embarrassed. Grown men did not cry. I had seen Dad cry exactly once in my life, namely at Mom's funeral. What would the Old Man think if he saw me cry?

If he saw me struggling to contain my emotions, he had the good grace to not show it.

"Do you have any thoughts as to how you're going to find Iceburn?" he asked. "A guy like that is not going to be easy to find if he does not want to be found."

I nodded. "I know. Frankly, I have no idea how I'm going to track him down," I said. I was lying through my teeth. I had devoted a lot of time to thinking about how I would find Iceburn. I had settled on a plan I would execute as soon as I saw an opportunity. I felt guilty about lying to the Old Man, but I did not want to tip him off as to what I planned on doing. "I'll find him, though. Even if it takes me the rest of my life, I'll find him."

"And then what Theo?" the Old Man said quietly. He looked at me intently. "There's no statute of limitations on murder. Will you turn Iceburn over to the authorities and let the system do its job? Or, will you take matters into your own hands?"

I met his gaze. I should have just lied again and told him I would turn Iceburn over to the authorities like a good little Hero-to-be. However, I could not bring myself to outright lie again to the man who had taught me so much and whom I admired.

"I don't know what I'll do," I answered. "I'll cross that bridge when I get to it." *Burn that bridge is more like it*, I thought. In my mind's eye, I had killed Iceburn more times and in more ways than I could count. In one scenario, I had ripped his legs off with my powers, grabbed one of them in my hands, and used it to bludgeon him to death. In another, I ripped Iceburn's heart out of his chest with my powers, gleefully watching the expression on his face as I did so. I held his heart up in front of him, letting him watch as his heart beat weakly before coming to a stop forever. I often wondered which would stop working first—his eyes, or his heart.

The Old Man studied me for a few moments, and then nodded. I was glad he could not actually read my mind. Silence filled the room again as we sipped our drinks. I finished the water, and put the empty bottle down. Staying seated, I opened the refrigerator with my powers. I floated a beer out, removed its cap, tossed the cap into the trash, and moved the beer through the air into my hand. I took a long pull. One beer would not kill me or derail my training. The Old Man watched me with an amused look.

"Well, if this whole Hero thing doesn't work out, you have a bright future ahead of you as a bartender," he said.

I did not respond. I polished the beer off with several quick swallows. I put the empty bottle down. I floated another beer out of the fridge and put it down in front of me. I would stop at two. The beer sat in front of me for a bit as I thought long thoughts.

The Old Man was the first to break the silence again.

"Did I ever tell you that some of my family were murdered, too?" he asked. Surprised, I shook my head in the negative. The Old Man rarely spoke of his personal life.

"I was in grad school when it happened, studying towards my first PhD," the Old Man said. "My powers had manifested years before then, but going through the process of becoming a Hero was the furthest thing from my mind at the time. I had followed the law and had dutifully registered as a Metahuman when my powers first appeared, but had no intention of or interest in actually using them. I was content with living a normal life, going to school, dreaming of making a boatload of money, chasing girls, hanging out with my friends, the usual."

He sat his beer down. He looked off into the distance as if he was replaying events in his mind's eye.

"And then one day I woke up with a feeling of dread. It was as if something somewhere was wrong. I went on with my day, but I could not shake the feeling. I went to lunch with a couple of my fellow grad students, and I remember telling them about my feeling. They were scientists, and they laughed at me. 'Maybe you're psychic,' one of them teased me. 'You should go buy a lottery ticket,' the other said.

"When we got back to the university lab, there was a message waiting for me. My sister Simone had called. She was four years older than I. We were completely different from each other. Like night and day. We had nothing in common other than swimming in the same gene pool. Perhaps because of that, we weren't even the slightest bit close. The only time we saw each other or spoke was during holiday gatherings. So, her calling me was unusual to say the least. With the feeling of dread I had been carrying around all day, my first thought when I saw she had called was that one of our parents had died and Simone was called to tell me.

"I immediately called her back and asked her if everything was okay. I could hear her husband Dale shouting in the background and their daughter Sybil crying. Simone said everything was fine. I asked her why she had called me then, and she just told me never mind and hung up. I just shrugged and went on with my day."

The Old Man picked up his half-empty beer bottle. He held it up to the light. He peered at the amber liquid like it held the secrets to the Universe.

"Dale shot and killed Simone within an hour of her getting off the phone with me," he finally said in a soft voice. "He then shot Sybil. Killed her too. Simone was twenty-six. Sybil was two." The Old Man shook his head. "One spouse killing another is not uncommon. Not that this justifies anything, but Simone had a way of finding and tap dancing on your last nerve. So Dale getting mad enough to want to kill her I can at least wrap my brain around. Though I can't excuse it, I can understand it. But shooting a two-year-old? Your own daughter? What kind of animal does that?"

If it was not a rhetorical question, I did not have the answer. I said nothing. What was there to say?

We were both silent for a long time.

"I often think about how things could have been different if I had done something," the Old Man finally said. "I knew something was wrong. I had powers. I could have flown over to Simone's house. I could have stopped Dale. I could have taken the bullets instead of Simone and Sybil. Although my powers weren't fully developed, I was mostly invulnerable even then. The bullets would not have hurt me, at least not much. Simone and Sybil weren't so fortunate.

"Simone and Sybil dying are what made me become a Hero. After their deaths, trying to live a normal life seemed silly. Frivolous. I had been gifted these powers, this ability to change things, whether for good or ill. I did not help Simone and Sybil, but I could help other people. You know what's strange, though? With all the people I've helped over the years, all the lives I've saved, it still doesn't make me feel better about Simone and Sybil. When I started out as a Hero, I thought it would." He shook his head ruefully. "I was wrong."

I thought about that for a bit. "What happened to Dale?" I asked.

"Dale wound up pleading guilty to two counts of first degree murder. His lawyer initially had made some noise about pleading insanity, but they gave up on that idea in exchange for the prosecutor agreeing to not seek the death penalty. This all happened in Alabama, where they're looking for an excuse to stick a needle in your veins and kill you. They don't coddle violent criminals down there the way they sometimes do up here. Dale's currently serving life in prison with no possibility of parole. He's been there for many decades now. Periodically I check to make sure. One of the dirty little secrets of the criminal justice system is that life in prison does not actually always mean life in prison, even in Alabama. Laws can be changed, palms can be greased, sentences can be commuted, pardons can be issued. Especially when enough time passes and people forget exactly how heinous someone's crime was." He paused. "I for one will never forget. Dale will never see the light of day outside of that prison again. I'll make sure of it."

I thought of Iceburn. "Did you ever think of, uh, taking matters in your own hands?"

The Old Man looked at me frankly.

"Every damn day," he said. "I know the prison they are keeping Dale at. It's a prison for non-Metas. There's security, of course, but it's not Meta-proof security. It's not like MetaHold, the federal facility that's designed to keep Meta criminals in and also keep them out. It would be child's play to go into that Alabama prison and get to Dale. I could open that place up like a tin can. No one would be able to stop me."

"But you don't."

"But I don't," he agreed. "I'm a Hero. It's not what we do. There are rules. There are limits. If people like us don't follow them, who will? We are supposed to set an example for the rest of society, even when we don't want to. Especially when we don't want to. Never forget what we taught you at the Academy: Society before self. Those aren't just words. They are a way of life."

That thought marinated in the room for a while. The Old Man finally spoke again.

"Look Theo, nothing you can do will bring your father back, just as nothing I do will bring my sister and niece back. All we can do is try to make sure what happened to us and our families doesn't happen to anyone else. That's impossible, of course. There's a big world out there full of some mighty scary people, and there are only so many Heroes to go around. We can't save everybody." The Old Man smiled grimly. "But we can try."

I thought about that for a bit. In light of what the Old Man said, I felt guilty about my plans for Iceburn. Only a little, but some. The guilt would not stop me, though.

I then raised my still undrunk second beer. "To trying," I said.

"To trying," the Old Man repeated, clinking his bottle against mine in a toast. We both drank. The Old Man put his now empty bottle down. He wiped a bit of foam off his mouth with his hand.

"I think I'll suit up and fly around the city a little. Clear my head." The Old Man smiled grimly. "If I run across a Rogue, so much the better. They can help me work off some steam."

"You want some company?"

"No offense, but no. Sometimes a man needs to be alone with his thoughts. Besides, you've got a full day of training and tutoring ahead of you."

"Ugh," I said, already regretting having to work out with a bellyful of beer. "Don't remind me."

The Old Man stood.

"Hey, no complaining." He grinned down at me. "Being a Hero is a tough job, but somebody's got to do it."

CHAPTER TWENTY-SEVEN

"I have some bad news, and some good news," the Old Man said. He sat in an armchair in front of me, Isaac, and Neha. The three of us were all clustered on a large curved couch. At the Old Man's request, we three had skipped our morning workouts and we were instead assembled in the mansion's great room.

"Let me guess," Isaac said. "The good news is that I'm the best Hero Apprentice you've ever seen." He grinned. "The bad news is that these other two are the worst."

"Apparently, in your bizarro world, best means worst and worst means best," I said to him.

"Does the sun only shine at night in your fantasy world too?" Neha added.

"I'll jump in with a question before you three come to blows," the Old Man said. He smiled. "Though if that happens, my money is on Neha. She's meaner than you two. Fights dirty too. Since we're talking about things in reverse, here's a question for you Isaac: what mythological creature has backwards feet?" With the Old Man, everything was a teachable moment.

Isaac's face was blank. He shrugged.

215

"The Abarimon," Neha interjected when it was clear Isaac did not know. "Despite their feet being on backwards, they were said to be able to run at incredible speeds."

"Nobody likes a show-off. Or a know-it-all," Isaac said. Neha stuck her tongue out at him. The Old Man laughed.

"Neha is exactly right," he said. "Since your powers are myth-based, you really should have known Isaac. Two weeks from today, I want you to research the Abarimon, write a fifteen page paper about them, and be able to successfully transform into one of them. And don't double-space the lines and give them overly large margins this time. You're not fooling anybody. I mastered every formatting trick known to man before any of you were born. Assuming you don't go, that is." Isaac groaned before stopping himself.

"Go? Go where?" he asked.

"That's what I was going to tell you all before you got me sidetracked. The Heroes' Guild needs me and a few other Heroes to go into space for a secret mission. The good news is I pulled some strings, and my Apprentices are allowed to accompany me." The three of us perked up. We were going to go into space? What self-respecting Hero's Apprentice would not want to go on a mission into space? "The bad news is that only two of you can go as there's limited room. One of you will have to stay behind."

The three of us looked at each other.

"Wait, back up," I said. "Two of us are going into space? How will we get there? And what's the mission?"

"The answer to the first question involves a transporter. Beyond that, I'm not allowed to discuss it with all three of you since one of you is not going. As for the mission, that too I cannot discuss with someone who is not going. It is a secret mission, after all. The two who go with me will also have to keep our mission under wraps. I know you three are tight, but the one who stays behind cannot be told of our mission. All I can say is that we'll be gone for at least a week and probably longer."

"So who's going to stay behind?" Neha asked. "Isaac or Theo?"

"Us?" Isaac said indignantly. "What about you? I've seen every episode of *Star Trek* and every *Star Wars* movie. Even the three bad ones. I'm practically an astronaut."

"And definitely a nerd," she said.

The Old Man stood. "I'll leave it to you three to decide who stays and who goes. I don't care how you decide as long as it doesn't involve murdering one of you. Let me know by the end of the day what you decide. Whoever stays behind won't be able to use his or her powers while I'm gone as I won't be around to supervise. I'll need to brief the two who are going and we'll need to make preparations. We will leave in two days."

The Old Man left the room. The three of us looked at each other questioningly.

"Does anyone want to volunteer to stay behind?" Neha asked. A long pause. No one said anything. "I'll take that as a 'no,'" she said. "I didn't think anyone wanted to voluntarily stay behind, but it was worth asking."

"We can decide who stays using rock, paper, scissors," Isaac suggested. The three of us decided a lot of things we could not agree on that way. I was about to protest when Neha jumped in before I did.

"That's not fair," Neha said.

"How's roshambo not fair? It's random," Isaac said.

"It's not random. You go for paper first fifty-seven percent of the time. Theo, you go for rock first sixty-one percent of the time. I know it, and now you two know it. I also know what your second choice usually is. I have a competitive advantage because I know your tendencies. I think it's awfully sporting of me to share that with you. You're welcome."

Isaac and I looked at Neha incredulously, though we should have been used to how she was by now.

"How do you even know this kind of stuff?" I asked.

She shrugged. "I pay attention."

"Roshambo is out then. We'll draw straws," I said definitively before someone could suggest something else. With my powers, I opened the closet on the other side of the room and pulled out the straw broom that was inside. I ripped out three straws of uneven length. I floated them over to the table in front of us so the other two could see them. "Short straw stays behind."

Neha stood, grabbed the straws, and put her hands behind her back.

"Wait," Isaac said, "before we choose, let's agree this will be a completely honest contest. No tipping the scales by using powers."

"Agreed," Neha said.

"Agreed. I won't use my powers to win," I promised.

Neha thrust her left hand out. The three straws poked out from her closed fist, arranged so their tips lined up evenly and Isaac and I could not tell which was the shortest. I hastened out of my seat to pick first. As I reached for Neha's hand, I exerted my powers, reaching out with my mind to feel the straws and determine their length. I made my selection accordingly, pulling the straw free from Neha's hand. Then Isaac pulled a straw out. Neha then opened her hand, and the three of us compared our straws. Neha's was the longest, followed by Isaac's, and then mine.

Isaac and Neha looked at me sympathetically. "That sucks dude," Isaac said. Neha patted me on the shoulder.

I shrugged. "Win some, lose some," I said, trying to act more disappointed than I actually was. I had not lied to them before. Choosing my words carefully, I had promised to not use my powers to win. I had not promised to not use my powers to lose. I would have simply volunteered to stay behind, but then Neha and Isaac would have suspected something was amiss.

I did not want to go to space. No, scratch that. I did want to go to space. What self-respecting person with an ounce of adventure in him, much less a Hero's Apprentice, would not want to go to space? So yes, I did want to go. But, I wanted to confront Iceburn more. The Old Man, Neha, and Isaac being gone would allow me to put the plan I had formed to find him into motion without them stopping me.

I did not want to be stopped. I did intend to stop Iceburn though.

Permanently.

CHAPTER TWENTY-EIGHT

I t was the woman's screams that alerted me. Their shrillness pierced the night air like a fire alarm.

I was flying in northeast D.C., not too far from Union Station. It was after midnight. I swooped out of the sky towards the screams like a dive-bombing eagle. My cape flapped loudly in the rushing wind as I descended. I assessed the situation before I even touched down: four men surrounded a woman in an alley. Her back was against the alley wall. She struggled against the men as they held and groped her, trying to pull her skirt up. Despite the men trying to cover her mouth, she twisted her head around, wailing in fear and anguish.

I landed behind the men. Three black, one Hispanic. Now that I was closer, I could see they were young. Closer to boys than men. Nonetheless, they towered over the struggling woman. I stretched my hands out. With my powers, I yanked the two young men closest to me off the woman and backwards, off their feet. They yelped in sudden surprise. I sent them sailing through the air past me, towards the opposite alley wall. Their shouts stopped like they had been turned off with a switch when the men slammed hard against the wall. I released them, letting them fall into the heaping piles of garbage below them. Though I did not turn to look, I used my powers to make sure they were no longer threats. One of them was still. The other rolled weakly in the filth a bit.

Cursing, one of the two remaining men rushed at me. I stepped in towards his attack, creating a force field around my fists to avoid injuring them. I hit him with a left jab that was made all the more powerful thanks to the man's forward momentum. The punch rocked him back. I followed up with a right cross that landed on the underside of his chin with a thud. The man's head was flung to the side. He collapsed heavily on the ground like a felled tree.

I turned my full attention to the sole remaining man. He frantically reached into the waistband of his jeans. He pulled out a pistol. He pointed it at me. The silver-plated gun glinted a bit in the moonlight. The gun shook a little in the man's hand. Adrenaline, fear, or both? Regardless, the look on the man's face clearly said he thought he had the drop on me.

He said, "I'm gonna pop a cap in your ass you freak motherfu—" The man's bravado was interrupted by my powers. His gun hand flew up towards his face, like he was puppet with his strings suddenly and violently jerked up. I of course was the puppeteer. The gun hit the guy square in the nose with a sickening crunch. Blood sprayed out. The man screamed. The sound was somewhat muffled by his now ruined nose. He dropped the gun, bending over and pressing his hands to his bleeding face. The gun clattered on the ground. I sent it skittering away from the man with my powers. I didn't think he even noticed. He was too busy clutching his face, shrieking like a little girl. It was hard to look like a tough guy when you were wailing like a spanked baby.

I spread my left hand open into a claw, visualizing choking the bleeding man. The man's screams abruptly stopped. He suddenly straightened as my power exerted itself around his neck. He was lifted onto the tips of his toes as I choked him with my powers. I pressed hard into the sides of his neck, cutting off the flow of blood to his brain through his carotid arteries. Gasping, his eyes bulging, the man clutched at his throat, trying to free himself from hands that were not there.

The man's struggling and twitching got weaker and weaker. In just a few seconds, it stopped all together. His eyes fluttered closed. His arms dropped limply to his sides. I released my hold on him. I just wanted to knock him out, not give him brain damage or kill him. He fell heavily to the ground. He did not move. I could had lowered him gently, but I was not inclined to be gentle with someone who attacked a woman and pulled a gun on me.

The whole fight lasted no longer than a minute, and probably not even close to one. Other than the moaning, barely conscious guy I had flung against the wall, the alley was now quiet other than the loud gasping of the woman.

Wide-eyed at my sudden appearance and what she had just witnessed, the woman pressed herself against the alley wall as if she was trying to merge into it and disappear. She stared at me like I was a strange dog who might turn on her. Her chest heaved. It was the first time I got a good look at her as I was too busy dealing with her attackers before. She was white, maybe in her mid-twenties, with shoulder length brown hair. She had pale skin, though her face was blotched with red spots as she gasped for air. Red lipstick was smeared wildly around her mouth, making her look a little clownish. She was pretty even in her panicked state, and a little on the heavy side. Neha, never one to mince words, would have said she was overweight; the Old Man would have said she was voluptuous; Isaac would have said with appreciation that she was thicker than a bowl of oatmeal. Her clothes looked expensive and stylish. One of her high-heeled shoes was off, gone who knew where. Her black skirt was scrunched up high on her bare shapely legs. Her maroon blouse was ripped open, exposing a white bra and deep milky cleavage. I realized I was staring at her chest. I tore my gaze away, forcing myself to look her in the eye.

"Are you all right?" I asked her. She did not respond. Her eyes frantically scanned me from head to toe. In addition to my red cape, I had my mask on and my Academy uniform, over which I had thrown a blue hoodie. The hood was up over my head because I had thought it made me look older and more intimidating.

"I'm a Hero. I'm not going to hurt you. Are you all right?" I repeated. The woman's eyes lingered on my cape for a moment. She looked at the four guys on the ground. Finally, she nodded. Fat tears started to roll down her cheeks. Her body lost a little of its rigidity. She took a step away from the wall and towards me. She looked down, realizing how exposed she was. She tugged her skirt back down. She pulled her ripped blouse closed and held the fabric together in one hand.

"I was on my way home from a bar. I walked past those guys, and they pulled me in here. I don't know what they would have done to me if you hadn't saved me," she said. Her voice shook a little. It was higher than I would have expected. She sounded younger than she was. She managed to muster a slight smile. "Thank you."

"You're welcome." The Old Man's orders to not use my powers and stay at the mansion while he was gone still rang in my ears. Though I felt guilty about disobeying the Old Man, I still felt pretty good. It was only the first night after the Old Man, Neha, and Isaac had left for their secret space mission, and I had already managed to help someone.

"I'll stay here with you until the police arrive," I said to the woman. Using my communicator wristband, I called 911. I quickly described the situation to the dispatcher, and gave her our location. Meanwhile, the woman looked around and spotted her purse, which lay just a few feet away. Apparently the men who had attacked her were more interested in her than they had been in it. She hobbled over to it in her single shoe. She rifled through it. Since her hands were busy, her ripped blouse fell open. With an effort, I averted my gaze from her chest again, embarrassed. This woman was a victim, not someone I should be ogling. In my defense, she was the first female I had interacted with in a while. Well, there was Neha, as well as the female Academy trainees I had spent so much time with. And there was Athena, of course. But, those women were Metas. Comrades. This woman was a *girl*. Being around an attractive woman, even in this context, made me nervous. The Academy and the Old Man had taught me how to act as a Hero, not how to act around girls. Especially not one built as generously and as well as this one was.

The woman looked up from her purse. Her eyes were blue. She had stopped crying. She seemed calmer now. She held up a wallet she had pulled from her purse. "Can I give you some money? You know, as a reward."

"No thanks. I did not help because I'm looking for money."

She stuck her wallet back into her purse. "I didn't think you had. It just seemed like I should do something other than simply thank you." She pulled a smartphone out of her purse. "If I can't give you something, can I take something? A photo with you. I've never met a real-life Hero before." She suddenly seemed shy.

I was looking for publicity. Besides, she was cute. "Sure, why not?" I said. I walked over to stand next to her. She pressed up close against me. If she was aware her blouse was open, she did not seem to care anymore. I felt the softness of her breast against my arm. She smelled faintly of perfume. Something floral. My heart beat faster than it had when I had disposed of her attackers. The woman stretched her arm out and took a photo of us together.

I blinked away the brightness of the camera's flash in time to see hear the wail of approaching sirens. Soon the flash of police lights appeared at the mouth of the alley. Since I was not actually a licensed Hero and was breaking the law by using my powers, I had no interest in sticking around to talk to the cops. It was time to go. Besides, I had just picked up in my earbud which was tuned to the police band a new alert. There was an armed robbery in progress in the southeastern part of the city.

I rose into the air. The woman craned her neck to look up at me. Her blouse was still open. I am not ashamed to admit I got a good bird's-eye view of her considerable assets. I did not look away this time. I might be an Omega-level Meta, but I was still an eighteen-year-old guy. I was not made of stone.

"I don't even know your name," the woman cried up to me.

"The name is Kinetic. Yours?"

"Amanda."

"Tell the police about me, Amanda. Tell your friends too," I said. Amanda's scent lingered in my nostrils. The side of my body she had pressed up against felt warm. *Say something cool, say something cool,* I urged myself.

"Have a good night citizen," I said instead. *Ugh!* I winced as soon as the words were out of my mouth. I streaked off into the night sky towards the southeast before Amanda could see me flush with embarrassment.

Why didn't you go full dork and say "Up, up, and away!"? I thought sarcastically as I zoomed towards the armed robbery call.

I really needed to work on a good catchphrase.

***

Four grueling days later, I sat in the Information Room of the mansion in front of its bank of large monitors. It was a couple of hours before midnight. I would go out on patrol yet again in a few hours. Despite the fact I had not gotten much sleep over the past few days, I was wired. My crime fighting spree in Washington, D.C. and the surrounding area was bearing fruit.

The bank of monitors bathed me in light and sound. They were tuned to various news channels and to social media sites. I had wanted to attract the media's attention, and had succeeded in doing so. I had already gotten the attention of local media a couple of days ago, but it was the fire at Georgetown University in D.C. I had helped fight yesterday that had finally gotten me national attention. Though I had not known it at the time, Dwight Gomez, one of the students I had saved from being burned alive, was the son of a United States Senator. That Senator was also the front-runner for the Democratic nomination for the Presidency. Focusing on Dwight, the news only made passing mention of the other twenty-six students I had saved from the fire. Yes, all men were created equal, but being the son of a prominent Senator made you even more equal than others.

I was also trending on Twitter and Facebook. Well, not me Theodore Conley. Kinetic was. A thread about Kinetic had also made it to the front page of Reddit. Then I noticed a segment about me entitled "Hero or Rogue?" was about to air on CNN. I muted the other monitors so I could hear it:

"Over the past week, a new Metahuman has made his presence felt in Washington, D.C. and the surrounding suburbs," came the voice of a male reporter. A picture of me in my mask and cape filled the screen. I realized it was the picture I had taken with Amanda. I saw something in the picture. I leaned closer to the screen and squinted at it. Could it be? Yes, it not only could be, it was. I had a giant zit on my chin in the picture. Sheesh. Of course I did. I did not know how in the world I had not noticed it the night I had taken the picture with Amanda. The zit looked like Mount Vesuvius about to erupt.

"This new Metahuman goes by the name Kinetic," the reporter intoned. His voice snapped me out of beating myself up for not taking better care of my skin. In my defense, I had a lot on my mind. Slathering myself with Clearasil was not exactly high on my to-do list. "Since this image was first taken of him last Tuesday night, Kinetic has foiled a multitude of assaults, burglaries, robberies, and carjackings. He has also saved many lives, including that of Dwight Gomez from a fire at the dorms of Georgetown University in D.C. last night. Mr. Gomez is the son of Michael Gomez, the U.S. Senator representing the state of New Mexico. Here is some footage of Kinetic's activities at that fire, filmed by a student with her cell phone." The footage showed me rocketing through a window of the burning dormitory. I flew out a few seconds later with a sooty and coughing Dwight floating in front of me. I had not known I was being filmed at the time it happened. I was satisfied to see the footage was a nice clear depiction of me and my powers in operation. My vanity told me I looked positively heroic with my mask on and my cape flapping majestically behind me. Best yet, the footage did not get a close enough look at my face to pick up any blemishes. I did not think of myself as particularly vain, but what person in his right mind wanted to look a hot mess on television?

"No one we have contacted for comment in the Hero community has ever heard of Kinetic, which begs the question of whether he is a properly licensed Hero or is a Rogue using his powers illegally. We reached out to the Heroes' Guild to ask if Kinetic is licensed. Ghost, the Guild's chief investigator, refused to either confirm or deny Kinetic's licensing status. He said that, and I quote, 'Commenting publicly about a Metahuman's license status is against the regulations of the Heroes' Guild.' The D.C. Metropolitan Police has informed me they are on the look-out for Kinetic so they can question him regarding whether or not he is properly licensed. Regardless of whether Kinetic is in compliance with the Hero Act of 1945, some members of the D.C. community do not seem to care in light of Kinetic's recent flurry of activity." The screen cut away from a replay of the footage of me at the Georgetown University fire. The tall form of Senator Gomez walking down the halls of the U.S. Capitol now filled the screen. He was surrounded by reporters.

"As a Senator sworn to uphold the law, I know I am supposed to withhold judgment on Kinetic until it is determined whether or not he is licensed in compliance with the Hero Act," Senator Gomez said to the reporters as he walked. He stopped, and looked directly into the camera. "But, speaking as a father, I don't care if Kinetic is technically a Hero or a Rogue. All I know is that he saved my boy's life, plus the lives of many other parents' sons and daughters. That makes Kinetic a hero in my book."

I had seen and heard enough. I hit a button that shut all the monitors off. I stood up, yawned, and stretched. Sitting and watching the monitors had taken some of the edge off of me being wired. I was suddenly exhausted. I had not gotten a full night's rest in days. I had been too busy rushing around thwarting every crime I could find and saving every person I could. Frankly, I did not feel like going out on patrol again tonight. I would go anyway. "A man does what he has to do, whether he feels like it or not," came the words of Dad floating to the top of my mind. Another Jamesism. I had gotten heartily sick of all of his sayings when he had been alive. What I would have given to hear him tell me more of them. I would have hung on his every word like a groupie hangs on the words of a rock star.

I was engaged in this flurry of crime-fighting for Dad. Sure I enjoyed the fact I was helping people. But to be honest, that was not my primary purpose. My primary purpose was to make as big of a splash as possible so I would attract Iceburn's attention. I did not know where he was, and had no idea how to go about finding him. But, if I drew enough attention to myself in the media, he would be able to see where I was. Maybe he would find me. He had done it twice before. I hoped to lure him into making a move against me again.

This time, I was ready for him. Or, so I hoped.

Bait was on the hook, and my line was in the water. Now, I just waited for my fish to come along and take a bite.

CHAPTER TWENTY-NINE

I looked at my handiwork with satisfaction. It had been a bit of a struggle at first, but I had pulled it off. It was a job well done.

I got up out of my crouch and stood up straight. My cape rustled as I did so. My hands were filthy. I clapped them together in a vain attempt to clean them off some. My back felt tight from me being bent over for so long. I resisted the urge to stretch it out. There were people across the street, filming and taking pictures of me with their phones. They were memorializing a hero in action. Stretching did not look heroic.

I stepped up onto the sidewalk. "Looks like you're all set," I said to the woman I had come to the aid of. Her name was Mrs. Wilson. She looked like what would come up on your computer if you did a Google search for "little old lady."

"I don't know what I would have done without you," Mrs. Wilson said with gratitude. Despite her age, her voice was clear and strong. Her thin white hair was up in a bun, and her shoulders were slightly stooped. Her blue eyes were huge, magnified by her thick glasses. "You're a lifesaver."

"I'm just glad I was here to help."

Mrs. Wilson glanced at the people across the street filming the incident. She shook her head in disgust.

"All these people, and not a single one of them lifted a finger to help an old woman change her tire," she said. "They're more than happy to gawk when a superhero stops to do it, though. Other than people like you, are there no gentlemen left?"

"What is the world coming to?" I asked in agreement.

We were in Adams Morgan, a neighborhood in the northwest quadrant of Washington, D.C. It was dusk. In a little while the streets would be much busier than they were now as Adams Morgan had a thriving nightlife. I had been flying by on patrol when I had spotted Mrs. Wilson down below, struggling to change her own flat tire. I had landed and asked her if I could help. Thanks to the conspicuousness of my mask and cape and my newfound fame, a bit of a crowd had gathered as I changed the tire.

Once I had loosened the frozen lug nuts, changing the tire had been a snap. I knew all about changing tires. Not because of the Academy. There were no automotive maintenance classes there. Dad had taught me how to change a tire before he even taught me how to drive. Thanks to him, I also knew how to change oil and do routine car repairs. If I got a car, I would not need a mechanic. If I ever bought a Kineticmobile, I was ready.

Kineticmobile? Huh. I could work on the car itself, but the name still needed work.

"In my day, things were different," Mrs. Wilson was saying. "Back then, men would go out of their way to help someone. Now they won't spit on you if you're on fire. And the women were women. Now they're part woman, part man, and half monster. It's shameful."

"Kids these days," I said, growing uncomfortable. My mind groped for a non-rude way to fly away from Mrs. Wilson before she had a chance to tell me more about the Garden of Eden society allegedly used to be. I need not have bothered. Something hit me on my right side so hard, I was knocked off my feet. I gasped in surprise, swallowing water. It roared in my ears.

Before I could react, I was slammed against the glass storefront of a neighboring business. The glass shattered. It felt like I was jabbed by a thousand needles. I was flung inside the business, surrounded by water, spinning wildly in the air. I hit something hard. I caromed off of it like a cue ball. An instant later I hit something else, something big and solid that stopped me from flying through the air further. I saw stars. The air whooshed out of my lungs. I fell. I crumpled to the ground.

Darkness closed in on the edges of my vision. I fought to stay conscious. I felt water dripping off of me. I coughed up water. My lungs and throat burned.

It was touch-and-go for a few moments. But finally, my vision started to clear, like I was slowly walking out of a dark tunnel. I groaned. I staggered to my feet, feeling as old as Mrs. Wilson had looked. My face was on fire. I reached up to my face, feeling something hard and jagged there. I tugged on it. I pulled out a long piece of glass from my cheek. It was covered with my blood. My blood mingled with the water I was soaked with, dripping onto the carpet.

I was inside a large office containing several desks. Right behind me was the wall I must have slammed into. Directly ahead of me was the broken glass facade I had apparently been thrown through. Based on the partially destroyed lettering etched on the outside of the glass, I was inside an insurance agency. In between where I now was against the wall and the glass facade was an overturned desk. I guessed I had hitting that desk to thank for at least some of the aches in my body. Wet paperwork was everywhere, like the sprinklers in a paper factory had been activated right after a bomb had gone off.

I was not alone. There were maybe half a dozen people in the office. Some sat, some stood, all were open-mouthed with surprise and alarm as they stared at me. It reminded me of the way cows looked at you when you approached them. I might have laughed if my throat—not to mention everything else—did not hurt so much.

"Is everyone all right?" I asked. My throat was raw, my voice strained. A couple of people nodded. Everyone else just stared at me like I was Bigfoot.

"You're the one who's bleeding," a heavyset black woman said to me. "We should be asking you if you are all right."

Wetness dripped into my eye, obscuring my vision. I wiped my brow with the back of my hand. It came away red. My tongue probed at the inside of my mouth. A tooth was loose. I felt like I had been in a hurricane and then hit by a truck. Being thrown through glass was not a walk through the park the way it seemed in movies. Regardless, I remembered my Academy training. A Hero was supposed to always appear in control of things, especially when he was not. "Never let them see you sweat," Athena had said time and time again. It was bad enough these folks were seeing me bleed.

"Never better," I said. "Sorry about the mess." My words were a little slurred. My tongue felt thick, like it had been partially anesthetized. With more effort than it usually took, I formed a force field around myself. I zoomed out of the hole in the glass storefront like I had been shot out of a cannon. Once outside, I saw who I expected to see:

Iceburn.

He stood on the sidewalk, about a hundred feet away from me. I landed on the sidewalk, facing him. I still had my personal shield up. Around us, people shouted and ran. I was only faintly aware of them. I only had eyes for Iceburn.

"Howdy kid," Iceburn called out. "Did you miss me?"

"Desperately. I wondered how long it would take you to find me." Iceburn was in the same head-to-toe black costume I had always encountered him in. As always, the surface of the costume looked cracked. Lines of energy glowed in the cracks.

"Once you became a one-man anti-crime spree, it wasn't hard to find you," Iceburn said. "You became D.C.'s resident caped crusader to attract my attention, I assume."

I nodded. Iceburn was a killer, but he was not stupid.

"Well, congratulations—here I am," he said. "It's time for me to finish the job I was hired to do. I'm a professional. I've been paid a lot of money to take you out. Fortunately, my employees have now authorized me to dispose of you even if there are witnesses. The fact I haven't managed to kill a snot-nosed kid yet is making people start to wonder if I'm slipping. It's bad for business." He had the gall to sound faintly offended, as if I was being unreasonable by not having the good grace to roll over and die.

Iceburn hesitated for a moment. "This is where you're supposed to tell me to give myself up and turn myself over to the authorities to be punished for my heinous crimes. That's how the script normally goes. You Hero types are so predictable."

I shook my head in the negative.

"I don't want you to give yourself up. I'm not turning you over to the authorities."

Silence.

"I see," Iceburn finally said. He sounding surprised. "So it's like that, is it?"

"It's how it has to be. You've killed a lot of people. My father." My voice caught. I swallowed hard. "Those people caught in the wildfire. God knows who else. An eye for an eye, a tooth for a tooth."

"An eye for an eye?" Iceburn repeated. He barked out a laugh. "That's the spirit! You know what kid? I like you. You're starting to remind me of me."

"Now you're just being offensive."

"I've just started being offensive." Iceburn raised his arms towards me. His left palm glowed blue; his right one glowed reddish-orange. "I would say 'see you around,' but I don't suppose that I will. If you see him, say hello to your daddy for me." A blue beam shot out of Iceburn's left hand. Simultaneously, an orange-red one shot out of his right. The beams combined, forming a massive stream of water that raged towards me like river rapids.

Unlike a few minutes ago, this time I was ready. The water hit my shield, splashing around me harmlessly. Even so, the force of the water was so immense that I took a couple of steps back. I braced myself harder, pushing against the back of my body with my powers to counteract the tremendous water pressure. The water roared in my ears. It sounded like I was standing under Niagara Falls.

I couldn't see further than a half inch in front of me thanks to the rushing water. I needed eyes on Iceburn. I strained against the water pressure, flying up into the air, out of the torrential stream of water. I could see again. There Iceburn was. With my powers, I flung at him the three heavy metal manhole covers I had lifted from the street while I had been trying to distract him by talking to him. They rocketed towards him like deadly discuses. I would lop his head off like it had been guillotined.

Iceburn must have spotted one of them out of the corner of his eye. He turned his head towards one of them. The spray of water abruptly stopped. His body glowed white hot. Even as far from him as I was, I felt the searing heat emanating from him. He became blindingly bright. I squinted, but dared not look away. I needed to aim the manhole covers.

Unfortunately, thanks to the intense heat Iceburn emitted, the manhole covers literally melted in mid-air as they got close to him. With my powers, I felt them become mere droplets of molten metal before they impacted him. They got so small I could no longer control them.

The paint jobs of several nearby cars bubbled. A green awning behind Iceburn burst into flames due to the intense heat he gave off. Several people screamed. The street was now even more of a madhouse. I cursed myself for my stupidity and tunnel-vision. I had been so focused on Iceburn, I had lost sight of the fact there was a decent number of people around. Someone might get hurt. It was time for a different battleground.

I rose higher into the air. I went more slowly than I was capable of going. I did not want Iceburn to lose me. I hoped he would follow. He took the bait. He dimmed down to his usual black form. He leapt up into the air after me. I darted off towards the east. I looked back. Iceburn was in hot pursuit. Literally. A jet of fire speared out from his hand, engulfing me in flames. Even with my personal shield up, it felt like I had been plunged into a bed of hot coals. I could not contain a shriek of pain.

I dove down, out of the flames. I moved quickly back up, to the left, to the right, constantly randomly zigzagging so Iceburn could not get a bead on me. Jets of flame danced in the air around me. Target practice was not much fun when you were the target.

Despite my evasive maneuvers, I still made sure to head east. Soon, I spotted familiar buildings down below. I quickly dropped down out of the sky at a steep angle like a missile rocketing towards its target. The wind screamed around me. In moments, I was flying amid some abandoned buildings I had scouted out before in my earlier patrols. Iceburn followed, still taking potshots at me. I dodged most of them. Some I could not. The ones I could not dodge made me feel like I was being cooked like a rotisserie chicken. I could not take much more of this.

I weaved in and out of gaps between the buildings. I could not shake Iceburn. Rather, he got closer and closer, which made his blasts of fire at me more and more accurate. We were flying low to the now-blurred ground since D.C.'s buildings were relatively short. Unlike many other big cities, D.C. was not a city of skyscrapers. By law, no building could rival the height of the Washington Monument. At 555 feet tall, the monument was the tallest structure in Washington other than a radio tower. It's strange the random facts that flit through your mind when you were fleeing for your life, trying to keep your goose from literally being cooked.

I approached two old, abandoned structures built close to one another. High fences were around them to keep loiterers out. No one had been inside them when I had checked days before. There was a narrow gap between them. I glanced at one of my wristbands. It told me my airspeed. I looked back at where Iceburn trailed me. I made a rough estimation of how far he was behind me. I did a quick calculation in my head. I would have to time this just right.

Right as I was about to enter the gap between the two abandoned buildings, I hit a button on my communicator. An invisible electronic signal went out to the explosives I had set in the old buildings days before. I had taken the explosives from the Old Man's armory. I had set different booby traps all throughout the city. This was but one of them. As Sun-tzu wrote in *The Art of War*, "Don't depend on the enemy not coming; depend rather on being ready for him."

I felt the explosions before I saw them. The force of the powerful shock waves from them knocked me to the side, into the building on the left. My shield was still up. Thanks to my forward momentum, I bounced off the side of the building and out of the gap between the buildings like a tennis ball rebounding off a wall. Even with my protective force field, the impact made my insides rattle.

Though shaken like a martini, I managed to turn in midair once I cleared the buildings. I watched Iceburn and the now collapsing buildings. Just as I had planned, they were collapsing towards one another, into the gap between them. Iceburn tried to veer out of the way, but my timing had been right. It was too late for him to change course sufficiently. His forward momentum carried him right into the falling debris. Pieces of the building pelted him. I helped by grabbing all the pieces of falling debris I could with my powers. I slammed Iceburn with them. He dropped towards the ground, surrounded by roaring debris and dust. Soon he was lost from view.

Iceburn had dropped a building on my friends and me before. Turnabout was fair play.

The buildings' collapse took less than a minute, though it took longer for everything to settle. When it was over, the scene was as still as a grave in contrast to how loud it had been when the buildings were falling. Dust and particles from the collapsed buildings hung in the air like fog. The building on my right had completely imploded. With the one on my left, perhaps a fourth of the structure still stood. The surrounding buildings were untouched by the explosion. Not bad for a first-time controlled demolition. Maybe, after the authorities eventually let me out of prison for murder, I could go into demolition work. I certainly could not be a Hero.

A huge pile of rubble stood where the gap between the buildings once was. It was over. I would dig through the rubble to find Iceburn's body to make sure, but it was over. I was sure of it. Nobody could have survived that. Well, the Old Man could, and Avatar certainly could have before he had been murdered. But those Heroes were invulnerable. I had no reason to believe Iceburn was.

I hovered in the air, surveying the destruction. As I did so, I took stock of how I felt. I felt like crap physically, of course. My body felt like someone had shoved me into a bag and then pelted me with rocks. My Academy uniform had protected my body from getting all cut up when Iceburn had shoved me through that glass, but I could not say the same about my face. It still bled and felt like it had been slashed in countless places. I was exhausted and in a lot of pain. I looked down at my hands. Some of the skin was bubbled up. I was burned pretty badly. I shuddered to think of what I might look like now naked. Thanks to Iceburn's blasts of fire, I was like a half-boiled lobster. But, I'd live. That was more than I could say for Iceburn.

What I felt emotionally surprised me. I expected to be happy. I expected to feel triumphant. Jubilant. I had dreamt of this moment ever since experiencing the nightmare of holding Dad's smoldering body in my arms. I had worked for this, planned for this, hungered for this.

Why, then, did I feel so terrible?

I was trying to pin down why when the top of the rubble shifted a bit, like a disturbed anthill right before the ants come pouring out. A hole opened at the top of the rubble. Iceburn, his costume torn and coated with dust and blood, crawled out of the hole. He got up on one knee. Shaking, he struggled to get on his feet.

Seriously?

I was on the move before I consciously even thought about it. With my personal shield up, I shot towards Iceburn like a stone out of a slingshot. I rammed him like a linebacker sacking a quarterback, wrapping my arms around his waist. I flew him off the tall pile of rubble. I felt him getting hot in my grasp. The heat burned my skin more than it already was. I instantly made my shield impermeable to air. It kept Iceburn from burning me further. It also kept me from getting fresh oxygen. But, I would not need to hold my breath for long.

I arched up into the sky to gain more altitude. Then, I flipped around in midair, holding Iceburn in front of me like a nail about to be hammered. Flying as fast as I could, I rocketed straight down towards the ground. Everything around me became a blur as the ground rushed up to greet us.

We hit the ground like a ton of dropped bricks. It sounded and felt like a bomb going off. Incredibly, even through my shield, I felt some of the force of it. If it had not been for that shield, I no doubt would have been smashed like a bug hitting the windshield of a speeding car.

Instead, I was thrown clear of the point of impact. I sailed backwards through the air almost parallel to the ground, barely conscious, my cape fluttering behind me. I hit the ground back-first. Everything in my body exploded with pain. It felt like fireworks were going off in my brain right behind my eyes. I skidding for several feet before slowing to a painful stop. It felt like someone had ripped the flesh off my back like it was old wallpaper. The pain from it made me realize I must have dropped my shield in my semi-conscious state after hitting the ground with Iceburn.

All I wanted to do was to close my eyes and go to sleep. Or, more likely, pass out. The temptation was almost irresistible, like a siren song. No! There would be time for that later. I forced my eyes open. I struggled to my feet. I collapsed a couple of times. Finally, I managed to stay standing. It reminded me of what some really old people looked like when they tried to stand up. My legs were like jello. Everything hurt. If this was what getting old felt like, I would happily take a pass on becoming elderly.

I looked for Iceburn. Though I did not see him, there was a hole in the ground near the rubble from the buildings I had blown up. I slowly and cautiously staggered over to it. I was in no condition to fight more, but I would do what I had to do.

Iceburn lay in the bottom of the shallow hole. It was more of a crater, really. It was about two feet deep. Iceburn, his costume in tatters, was face-up. One of his legs was folded under him and bent at a weird angle. The whiteness of his femur was exposed through his skin. His mask was mostly gone, exposing white skin, sandy blonde hair, and his eyes. His eyes were open. He did not move. I thought he was dead until his eyes shifted to look at me. He blinked a couple of times, focusing on me with obvious effort.

"I think my back's broken, kid," he whispered hoarsely through split and bloody lips. "Can't move. Can't feel my legs and arms at all."

I did not trust Iceburn any more than I would trust a rattlesnake. While keeping an eye on Iceburn, I quickly glanced around. I picked up a nearby fist-sized rock with my powers. It tapered to a point, like a knife a caveman might have fashioned back in the Stone Age. I brought it over so that it hovered over Iceburn. I forcefully dropped it, pushing it through the skin and flesh of Iceburn's unbroken leg. Blood spurted out like a geyser. Iceburn did not move or otherwise react. He did not even cry out. He apparently had been telling me the truth. Would wonders never cease?

Iceburn watched all this like he was watching it happen to someone else.

"Trust but verify, huh kid?" he croaked.

"I'd sooner trust the Devil," I said.

I floated a piece of the buildings' rubble over, this one about the length of a loaf of bread and maybe three times as wide. I stepped down into the crater. My legs screamed at me in protest. I knelt down, straddling Iceburn's broken body. I lifted my arms overhead. With my powers, I lowered the piece of rubble into my hands. I released my power's hold. I almost dropped the piece of rubble. I was exhausted and it was heavy. More than heavy enough to do the job.

I wanted to smash Iceburn's head in like it was an eggshell. No, I did not just want to do it. I ached to do it. I needed to do it.

And yet, I hesitated.

I wanted to kill him. I wanted to kill him two or three times, savoring each time. I wanted to squeeze the life out of him like juicing an orange. I wanted to take his body apart piece by piece and spread the bloody bits so far and wide that the police would have to pick him up with tweezers. I wanted to erase him from the face of the Earth so thoroughly that God Himself would have a hard time locating his soul, assuming he even had one.

And yet, I hesitated.

It hit me like a thunderbolt from heaven. I suddenly realized why I had felt so terribly when I had thought I had killed Iceburn by collapsing those buildings on him. If I killed him, I would never become a Hero. And, I desperately wanted to be one. Because of my training, I had met and become a part of a new family. Amazing Man, Myth, and Smoke were but its immediate members. My extended family included all the other graduates from the Academy, plus all the licensed Heroes who existed, both famous and not famous. If I killed Iceburn, I would never become one of them. Nor should I be allowed to become one. Heroes had too much power to be allowed to use it unchecked and without limits. The Heroes at the Academy had told me that over and over. They were right.

Killing Iceburn would make me feel better. It would certainly make the world better. Of that I had no doubt. But would killing him make me *be* better? "Vengeance is when you seek revenge on someone by stabbing yourself in the soul." Dad used to say that. Another of his Jamesisms. I guess I paid a lot more attention to them than I had thought.

Iceburn had said when we were in Adams Morgan that I was starting to remind him of himself. I didn't like that. I didn't want to be like him. I wanted to be like the Old Man. He did not kill his sister's and niece's murderer even though he could have. I especially wanted to be like my old man, my father. He had been a good Christian man. A lot of people called themselves Christians. Their every word was God, God, God, yet all their deeds were foul, foul, foul. Unlike those so-called Christians, Dad had always walked the walk instead of just talking the talk. He worked hard, loved his neighbor as he did himself, and said what he meant and meant what he said. He also turned the other cheek. I had seen him do it countless times. He had counseled me to do the same to the Three Horsemen, and to John Shockey when he had betrayed me by lying about me.

Dad had not had powers. That did not make him any less of a hero. He was my hero. Always had been. What would he do in this situation?

Iceburn saw my hesitation. His eyes looked puzzled.

"What the hell are you waiting for, kid? End it. To the victor belong the spoils. If I were you, I'd have bashed my skull in already."

His words removed all doubt about what I needed to do.

With an effort, I threw the piece of rubble away from me. I slowly stood up.

Iceburn's stared at me like he could not believe his eyes.

"You've got me at your mercy and you don't have the cojones to finish the job? You really are a prize idiot, aren't you?" he said. His tone was contemptuous.

I shrugged. The movement hurt.

"Probably," I said. "But I'm also a Hero. Or at least I'd like to be."

I used my communicator to call the police. I did it quickly, before I could change my mind.

CHAPTER THIRTY

To say the Old Man was pissed at me would be an understatement. If I was a famous and respected Hero who returned from a mission in space to find one of my Apprentices languishing in a Washington, D.C. jail, I guess I would be pissed too.

The police took Iceburn into custody once they arrived at the scene of my battle with him. They took me into custody too. The United States Attorney's Office for the District of Columbia charged me with multiple counts of unauthorized use of Metahuman abilities, plus several counts of destruction of property. I cooled my heels in city lockup until Amazing Man got back from space and retained a lawyer to get me out. While I waited in jail, I ran across some guys who were there thanks to me and my crime-busting spree in D.C. By "ran across," I mean they tried to punch my lights out. One guy even tried to stab me in the stomach with a shiv. Fun times. After the first few fights—which I won without using my powers as I was in enough trouble as it was—the D.C. Department of Corrections moved me to solitary confinement. I did not mind solitary. It gave me plenty of quiet time to think.

Besides, it was nice to go to sleep without having to keep one eye open out of fear of getting jumped.

Mr. Sawyer, the lawyer the Old Man hired, eventually got me released on my own recognizance pending my trial in light of the fact I did not have a criminal record. Mr. Sawyer told me he was pretty sure I would not wind up going to trial at all. He thought the U.S. Attorney would eventually drop most of the charges, if not all of them. I had apparently made quite an impression on the public in my attempt to lure Iceburn out into the open. The U.S. Attorney was eyeing running for D.C. mayor, and Mr. Sawyer told me it was unlikely she would want to incur the voting public's wrath by prosecuting someone as popular as I apparently now was. Plus, Senator Gomez himself got into touch with my lawyer and offered to lean on the U.S. Attorney to get her to drop the charges. I guess what they said was true: It was nice to have friends in high places. Not too long ago, I hardly had any friends at all in either high or low places. A lot had changed since then.

Speaking of friends, the first thing Isaac asked when I got out of jail was whether I had gone "gay for the stay." I answered him by walking up to Neha, grabbing her by the shoulders, and kissing her right on the mouth. She melted into me and kissed me back. I would never forget how good it felt to have her body pressed against mine again. I would never forget the look on Isaac's face, either.

I had missed both of them during their space mission. However, I had not missed Isaac enough to kiss him on the mouth.

The authorities identified Iceburn by running his prints through several criminal databases. His real name was Jason Sydney. They threw the book at him for the deaths of my father and the people who died in the Oregon wildfire. He was a person of interest in several other murders and crimes as well. Despite prosecutors offering to go a little easier on him if he would disclose who had hired him to kill me, he was not talking.

As it turned out, I had broken Iceburn's back and paralyzed him from the neck down. The doctors said he would never walk again. If I said I was sorry about that, I would be lying.

Iceburn was just the triggerman. Whoever had hired him to come after me was just as responsible for killing Dad as Iceburn was. They were still very much at large. And, if what Neha had told me was right, they were almost certainly big-time Rogues. That meant whatever I had gotten caught up in was not completely over. But, unlike my earlier plans for Iceburn, I would take down the people who had hired him the right way. The Heroic way. Dealing with them was a mountain I would have to climb later.

I would have to climb it later because I was temporarily barred from using my powers as a condition of my release from jail. Since, as the Old Man put it, "a superhero without powers is like a bird without wings," he put my Apprenticeship on hold. He told me to take some time off to recuperate from my injuries and to clear my head. Honestly, I had feared he would end my Apprenticeship altogether in light of what I had done while he was off-planet.

"If you think I'm going to unleash on the world a half-trained Omega-level Metahuman who apparently thinks he's the second coming of Gary Cooper in *High Noon*, you've got another thing coming," he had said. "You're staying my Apprentice if for no other reason than so I can keep an eye on you." I had been so relieved, I did not have the heart to tell him I did not know what *High Noon* was. Maybe it was a Cheech and Chong movie. Them I had heard of.

My Apprenticeship being on hold was why, early one morning, I found myself on Interstate 95 in a car the Old Man had lent me. I had just begun a nine-hour drive south. Though I wore jeans and a long-sleeved tee shirt, I felt naked without having my Academy uniform and mask on. At the Old Man's insistence, a stack of history and physics books rode shotgun in the car. Apparently my Apprenticeship being put on hold did not mean I was free from having to hit the books.

And the car the Old Man had lent me? It was a mint condition 1970 Ford Mustang Boss 302, dark red with black stripes. As far as I knew it had not been specially modified so it could fly, but it looked and felt like it could. People stared at it as I drove by. It was not a superhero jet, but it was still pretty freakin' cool.

I was heading home. Or, what used to be home.

***

The first thing I did when I got back to South Carolina was I stopped at the cemetery where I had buried Dad. It was just a few miles from the farm I had grown up on. Mom was buried here, too. Mom and Dad had decided many years ago they wanted to be buried here and not in the cemetery of their church much further down the road. I think Dad wanted to lie in rest as close to the farm he loved as possible. If it had not been against the law, I would have buried him on the farm itself. His body could have nourished the soil he spent most of his life toiling on. I think he would have liked that. He would not have liked being separated from Mom, though. He had told me more than once she was the only woman he had ever loved. I hoped to one day find someone who looked at me the way my parents had always looked at each other. Neha, maybe. Who knew what the future would bring?

After pulling up the weeds that had sprouted up on their adjoining plots, I stood facing Dad's headstone. Other than his name and the dates of his birth and death, the headstone simply read "Husband, father, farmer."

"I hope I did the right thing Dad," I said aloud to him. "I hope you're proud of me. You too, Mom." There was no answer. I had come to realize there rarely was.

I stayed there a little longer in silent contemplation. I did not linger for too long though. "Life is for the living," Dad had said to me over and over again after Mom had died when he found me depressed and moping. Yet another Jamesism. Now I suspected he had been reminding himself of that as much as he had been teaching me.

I got back into the Old Man's car. It was not until then that I realized I had made the drive from Maryland to South Carolina completely comfortably, without a second thought about it. Just making the short hour's drive from here to Columbia used to make me nervous. A lot had changed since then.

I sat in the car for a bit. Visiting Mom and Dad was the main reason I had come back to South Carolina. Now I did not know what to do or where to go. I supposed I could have gone to see Uncle Charles, but I did not think of him as family anymore. The only family I had that mattered was nine hours away.

Itching to see a familiar face, I make the short drive to the University of South Carolina at Aiken. I went into the coffee shop that was attached to the Student Activities Center. I lingered there for hours over a cup of coffee. I spent part of the time reading a novel I had brought along with me. It was the first piece of recreational fiction I had read since entering Hero Academy. It was a science fiction action adventure with lots of improbable twists and turns. It seemed silly in comparison to what I had just been through. The truth really was stranger than fiction.

Other than reading, I spent the other part of my time at the coffee shop people-watching. Most of the people who flowed in and out of the busy shop were strangers to me. A few people I recognized, though. Nobody spoke to me. That was not terribly surprising. It was not as though I had been Mr. Popularity when I had been a student here. Even so, some of the people I recognized seemed to recognize me too, turning to whisper to each other after I saw a flash of recognition in their eyes.

My coffee did to my body what it always does, and eventually I got up to go to the bathroom. As I used the urinal, I realized it was the same bathroom my powers had first manifested themselves in. I had come full circle. That incident with the Three Horsemen here seemed like it happened an eternity ago. It also seemed as if it had happened to a completely different person. Maybe it had.

I washed my hands. The scars from where they had been burned in my fight with Iceburn were almost gone. While I dried them, the door to the bathroom opened. Donovan Byrd, one of the Three Horsemen, walked in. He saw me and stopped in front of the door. Other than us, no one else was in the room.

"People told me they saw you back here, but I didn't believe it," Donovan said. He shook his bald head. "I didn't think you'd have the stones to show your face around here again." Donovan was just as I remembered him: a tall, muscular, light-skinned black guy with a shaved head.

Donovan very deliberately looked me up and down.

"You're bigger than when I last saw you," he said. "Still not big enough."

"I've been eating my Wheaties."

"Is that supposed to be some kind of joke?"

"Yes."

"And what the fuck happened to your face?"

"Got into a fight with an electric razor," I said. "The razor won. They're mean little suckers." Iceburn's water spout shoving me through the insurance agency's glass had cut my face up pretty badly. With all the stitches that were now in my face, I looked a little like Frankenstein's monster.

My hands now dry, I dropped my used paper towels into the trash. I stepped towards the door. Donovan barred my path. There was no way around him.

"Excuse me," I said.

"You're not leaving here until after I kick your pasty ass," Donovan said. "I'm going to fuck you up good. You caused me a lot of trouble with that magic shit you did to me the last time. I couldn't play football for a whole season. Lost my prime chance for the pro scouts to see me."

"It's not magic. Regardless, sorry about that," I said. I was not. "There's nothing I can do about it now. Move out of the way."

"No."

I stepped closer to him, stopping just outside of his reach. Though I had grown since I had last seen Donovan, he was still taller and heavier than I. Regardless, I looked at him with a steady, level gaze.

"Move," I said, "or be moved."

I don't know what it was. Maybe Donovan sensed I was not afraid of him anymore. Maybe he was only as fearless as I remembered him being when he had his friends around to back him up. Or, maybe he saw in my eyes the hardness that was now inside of me. I had changed. I knew it, and maybe he saw it. Regardless of why, he blinked a couple of times. He then looked away. He stepped aside.

I walked past him towards the door. I halfway expected to be sucker-punched as soon as my back was to him. It did not matter. I was ready for him. To my surprise, Donovan did not take a swing at me.

I had my hand on the bathroom door and was about to pull it open when Donovan spoke again.

"Just so you know," he said to my back, "you're nothing but a piece of poor white trash. You were born white trash, and you'll die white trash. Just like your father. The apple doesn't fall far from the rotten tree."

I jerked my hand from the door handle like it was a hot stove. I breathed in deeply, filling my lungs. It hurt a little as I was not completely healed up from my fight with

Iceburn. I let the air out slowly in a long, calming breath. I turned around to face Donovan.

"You want to fight? All right, let's fight," I said. Despite the fact I felt a little hot, my voice sounded as cold as ice.

"Okay," Donovan said. He looked and sounded less sure of himself than before. He clenched his fists and lifted them a bit. He looked like someone badly impersonating a boxer in a movie. Athena would have yelled at and belittled him for the way he held himself. "And fight fair. None of that magic stuff."

"Agreed. I won't use my powers." I strode towards him.

I knew I would not need them.

The End

In **Trials**, *Book Two of the Omega Superhero, Theo's powers become stronger, as does the resolve of his unknown enemies. He must undergo the rigors of the Hero Trials all while combating the shadowy forces that are conspiring against him for their own nefarious reasons.* **Trials** *is available for purchase through Amazon.*

If you enjoyed this book, please leave a review on Amazon. Even a simple two word review such as "Loved it" helps so much. Reviews are a big aid in helping readers like you find books they might like.

ABOUT THE AUTHOR

Darius Brasher has a lifelong fascination with superheroes and a love of fantasy and science fiction. He has a Bachelor of Arts degree in English, a Juris Doctor degree in law, and a PhD from the School of Hard Knocks. He lives in South Carolina.

If you would like to drop him a note, he can be reached at darius@dbrasher.com.

Other books by Mr. Brasher available on Amazon.com:

Omega Superhero Series
Trials
Sentinels

Superhero Detective Series
Superhero Detective For Hire
The Missing Exploding Girl
Killshot
Hunted

37888859R10154

Made in the USA
Middletown, DE
03 March 2019